Mad About The Boy

I take my handbag from the floor by the bed and pull out a pile of notes. They feel scrunchy and a little warm in my fist. There's something sexy about money. Not sexy like I want to roll around and have sex in it. Or even that I'm particularly materialistic – not by today's standards anyway – but there's something about money in this situation, just the holding of it, that does it for me. It's the power I suppose. He wants it. I've got it. And that means I can have what I want from him in return. That's even prettier than the way his sharp hipbones jut out from under his pale skin.

I climb up on the bed and kneel next to his helpless body. Gently, I brush the notes against his cheek, before putting them down on the bedside table. I shiver a little as I do this. I love it when I use real hard cash. When I bring the very literal money I am paying up close to the very literal man I am paying for. To me that really cements what I am doing. Paying for sex. Paying for power. Paying for him.

I leave the money where I'll be able to see it all the time. And I let myself shiver a bit _____ it's my birthday.

By the same author

Peep Show

Mad About The Boy
Mathilde Madden

BLACK LACE

Black Lace books contain sexual fantasies.
In real life, always practise safe sex.

First published in 2005 by
Black Lace
Thames Wharf Studios
Rainville Road
London W6 9HA

Design by Smith & Gilmour, London
Printed and bound by Mackays of Chatham PLC

ISBN 0 352 34001 0

1

The engine is purring, and so am I, as I cruise down Brighton seafront past endless empty souvenir shops and tacky little out of season emporia.

I'm clocking all the dark and dirty side streets that lead away from the sea. They all look deliciously shadow-shady this late in the afternoon, which is nice, because deliciously shadow-shady is roughly the theme I'm going for right now. And it's not just the street planning that's in tandem with my mood, even the elements are playing ball.

The sky has been the colour of milk all day, but that's leeching away now. Everything's losing its high contrast edge as the dark begins to roll in. (Mind you, at this time of year sometimes it starts to get dark at lunchtime.) The day is starting to slide over the horizon, and it looks like the world has gone from pure, high-contrast black and white to a million shades of grey.

As I pass one of the taller buildings on the seafront, The Palace Hotel suddenly looms into view, sort of ghostly in the late afternoon wash, looking rather like a very mysterious (and very gigantic) wedding cake. Just before I reach it I take a left, nipping down the little side street that leads to The Palace's underground car park, mirror-signal-manoeuvring with all the Highway-Codeesque precision I can muster, and I begin to prepare myself for something special.

I have to grip the steering wheel extra tightly to

stop my hands from shaking as I guide the swanky hire car into the subterranean darkness and find myself a space. But somehow, despite my rather preoccupied state, I park quite neatly, without hashing it up.

Moments later I am positioned in the hotel lobby, scanning it for my quarry. And it doesn't take long to spot him. Because I'm dressed as a business woman and he's dressed like he's doing business.

He's alone. Perhaps not quite lurking under a lamp-post, but at least leaning up against the bar in a pose that might as well be a 'for sale' sign flashing above his head. He's all tight jeans, tight top, tighter arse. It's all on show and he can't hide what he is.

Because today he's for sale. Today he's a whore. Today's my birthday and he's practically gift-wrapped.

He looks so out of place – although I know this really is his territory – whereas I blend in perfectly. So, I don't approach him straight away. I give myself plenty of looking-time.

He catches me looking and seems pleased about it, acknowledging my attention with an amazing smile. Teeth so much whiter than they ought to be in the inadequate halogens of the hotel lobby; reddish lips that seem swollen – sore – from pouting. It's clear he's displaying himself, showing off his wares and trying to make a sale, and I take my time as I peruse them, staring at his slightly over-long, red hair, his skimpy mesh top that hides nothing, and his denim-clad crotch. His jeans are so tight. It actually looks like he has an erection. Maybe he does. It is his job after all. Maybe he can just get one, if he needs to. And it turns me on to think that he is hard as I look at him right now. As I inspect him.

I let myself dwell, for as long as I want to, on the

fact that I can have him. I can pay him and I can have him. Right now. And at this moment, that thought turns me on more than anything.

Then, after an ice age, I finally glide over to him and take up a new position, floating on the bar stool at his hip. When I speak to him he lolls against the bar for a moment, not replying, sucking his tongue and continuing his posing in his incredibly tight jeans and fishnet T-shirt. He's so stunning I don't even feel annoyed about the time he's taking to answer. I simply wait, with a single raised quizzical eyebrow for punctuation, and enjoy the sight. I could easily stay here all day. I have such a great view; it isn't warm in here, the big glass entrance doors opening and closing create enough whippy cold air in the lobby that I can clearly see the effect the cold is having on his tightly erect little nipples. And I want to know whether he'll moan with arousal or cry out in pain when I bite them – I really don't know which I'd prefer.

Eventually, though, he answers my question – the only possible question, with a, 'Yeah, alright.'

As I stand up he links his arm into mine. I inhale sharply and hope to every God there ever was, through my current heady daze, that I can still remember how to put one foot in front of another – at least for long enough to get me to the lift.

One or two people turn to give us odd looks as we cross the lobby – we do make a notable couple I suppose – although we'd probably have got away with it without any kind of mortifying embarrassment if my companion hadn't chosen to lean out of the lift as the doors slid closed and shout, 'What, haven't you ever seen *Pretty Woman*?' Which I have to confess is funny, but only in a totally mortifying way.

As we ascend, floor after floor, I try to think of something to say. It takes me a worryingly long time to come up with, 'What's your name?'

'What would you like it to be, lady?' is the reply, topped with a wink and a flirtatious grin.

Which makes me cringe a bit, so I just respond with a sigh. A sigh and then a smile though, because, hey, he's still pretty.

He shrugs, noting my lack of interest in this particular game and changes tack. 'Rex,' he says. 'It's Rex.'

'I'm Sophie, Sophie Taylor,' I reply. And then, with introductions over, I have to force myself to stop stealing glimpses at his long body – languid and sprawling against the lift's carpeted wall – for the last part of the short journey.

After six floors of heart palpitations and furtive glances at my most recent purchase, the doors whisper open and we leave the lift.

In the corridor I find I'm still watching him – so blatantly. He pauses and leans against the flock wallpaper, posing quickly under a brass uplighter – giving me a freebie, just a taster of what I'm about to receive. I look at him forever.

The corridor seems so quiet. There's no sign of life and every surface seems to be covered with some kind of sound-sucking plush material, be it deep carpet or lustrous wallpaper. The deafening hush makes me feel a bit like I'm in church, the thought of which makes everything seem even naughtier. I suppress the urge to sample my purchase right here in the hallway – scolding myself that I've paid good money for a room.

When we reach my door, I fumble briefly with the entry card and, with only minimal under-breath swearing, manage to get the door open.

'Well this is nice,' Rex drawls, as he saunters past

me, heading straight for the bed and draping himself across it with an air of someone who knows exactly how to drape themselves across furniture for maximum effect. I find myself staring again at his outfit: the tight jeans and the semi-transparent top. God, he looks so unbelievably, edibly good. I still can't get over the fact he's all mine. That, right now at least, I own him. I can feel myself getting wetter at the sight of him.

'So what do you want me to do? What do you want?' he says, after a few moments, pulling himself into a slouchy half-sitting position and propping himself on an elbow.

I freeze for a sec. Mouth suddenly bone-dry with arousal.

He flickers a tongue over his top lip. 'I'll do anything you want, Sophie. I'm all yours and you can have me. You can do anything you want to me. Things you can't do with anyone else. Perhaps there are things you would like me to do to you. Some powerful women like to lose control, would you like that? Would you like me to control you, Sophie?'

And that makes me smile, because he's so near and yet so far.

With a couple of quick movements, I pick up my oversized handbag and then empty its contents onto the bed next to Rex. A whole heap of black and silver hardware spills out. 'Actually,' I say, as Rex's features contort a little, registering the fact I've just tipped the contents of an Ann Summers back-room onto the duvet. 'I was thinking more the exact opposite.'

He looks at me, then looks at my little collection on the bed a while longer. His expression is strange. I can only guess that he is trying to weigh up whether I am a mad murderer or someone he can trust not to go too far while he is utterly vulnerable. I try my best to look sane – kinky, but sane.

'Okay,' he says, after a while, 'you're the boss. Tying me up'll cost you extra though.'

'Fine,' I say, having to squeeze out the word because that little pronouncement he just made about tying him up costing extra, has turned me on so much, so fast, I can feel my knees start to shake.

But what's even better than that though, even more limb liquefying, is his reaction. He actually almost hid it. Almost, but I can tell from the tiniest flicker behind his eyes that just the thought of being restrained is really turning him on. He likes it; and I love it when they like it.

The first thing I ask him to do is strip. I don't really want to – his super seedy whore clothes turn me on so much – but they'd only get in the way later. He slides off the bed and stands right in front of me, not more than a foot away.

'Why don't you take my clothes off for me?' he says, his voice sounding darker and huskier than it did before.

I shake my head. (He needs to know who's in charge here.) 'I said, "strip",' I whisper, feeling the blood pounding so hard through my whole body, as I assert my authority over him, that I can barely hear myself think.

He shrugs and pulls the flimsy fishnet thing over his head. His chest is small, but just defined enough, and a pretty little criss-cross of sandy-coloured hair shades and emphasises his musculature – accentuating the positive.

I reach out and touch his chest, gently. And then I can't stop myself, I grab one taut rosy nipple in each hand, pull him towards me, and kiss him, hard.

He gasps into my mouth, squirming and moaning as I twist his nipples viciously. I like the way he struggles: not enough to break away from me, but enough to let me know that I'm making him uncomfortable.

It feels indescribably good to kiss a whore – it always does – my brain keeps on telling me that I own him, that I can do anything I want to him. And I love this. I really love this. This is as good as it gets!

After a long and very satisfying kiss, I finally release him, very reluctantly, so he can take off his trousers and underwear. I stand and watch him, looking at his body hyper-possessively, like it's my property – which it is. He has very long, newborn-Bambi, legs. They seem kind of pale and vulnerable. Pretty. Picture perfect.

And when he's finally naked, he doesn't even need to be told to get on the bed and spread himself for me.

I follow quickly and fasten him down. I wrap his wrists and ankles each in a neat black leather cuff and then rope them to the bedposts. I can't resist pulling the ropes very tight, to show off his long limbs and tight hard body. And when I'm finally done I look at him and sigh for what seems like the hundredth time since I picked him up. Even prettier now.

'Well,' I say, taking a step back to get the full effect, 'shall I sort out payment now? It'll make things easier later.'

He turns his head to see me better, the ropes are so tight he can barely lift it off the pillows. 'Huh?' he says, 'OK.'

I notice then that he's hard. I'm not sure exactly when he got hard, probably when I tied him down. I remember back in the lobby where I picked him up, and thinking he had an erection then and wondering how 'real' it was. Again, I can't help wondering how much is genuine arousal and how much is all part of the service. Either way, the fact he's hard right now is pretty hot.

I take my handbag from the floor by the bed and pull out a pile of notes. They feel scrunchy and a little warm in my fist. There's something sexy about money. Not sexy like I want to roll around and have sex in it. Or even that I'm particularly materialistic – not by today's standards anyway – but there's something about money in this situation, just the holding of it, that does it for me. It's the power I suppose. He wants it. I've got it. And that means I can have what I want from him in return. That's even prettier than the way his sharp hipbones jut out from under his translucent whey-pale skin.

I climb up on the bed and kneel next to his helpless body. Gently, I brush the notes against his cheek, before putting them down on the bedside table. I shiver a little as I do this. I love it when I use real hard cash. When I bring the very literal money I am paying up close to the very literal man I am paying for. To me that really cements what I am doing. Paying for sex. Paying for power. Paying for him.

I leave the money where I'll be able to see it all the time. And I let myself shiver a bit with excitement, because it's my birthday.

Lifting up my handbag again – which is starting to seem a bit Mary-Poppinsesque in its resourcefulness – I rummage in the depths of its torn lining for a minute and find a last little item, one that I didn't tip out in the confetti swirl of glittering bondage gear earlier: little silver chain – little crocodile teeth. Nipple clamps – they haven't been far from my mind since I glimpsed his tightly straining buds through the mesh of his shirt back down in the bar.

Some mouths are just made to be kissed, some arses are just made to be spanked, and some nipples . . . well.

His eyes go a little wide when he sees them, but not too wide. He doesn't patronise me. I know he's seen it all before. I slide them up his downy chest once or twice, before I snap both sets of teeth home together, harsh, almost brutal. I feel myself flood with warmth as my sadistic side takes hold. And then it feels like I'm overheating as I hear his cry of pain turn to a moan of outright pleasure. Wow-wee. Boiling point.

He likes the pain. Did I mention that I love it so much when they like the pain?

I slide down his body slightly, until I am straddling his hard cock. I rub against it a little and feel it move with me. So perfect. Then I move a little further down his body.

I can see his erection close up now. It's such a pretty, pretty thing. His pubic hair is sandy coloured and soft, and such a contrast to the hard, red-tipped erection that juts out from it, taut against his firm abdomen.

I lower my head and take his cock in my mouth.

He tastes amazing. He makes me think of sour cherries. I swirl him with my tongue and let the pretty blushing head pop in and out of my wet, greedy mouth. I take him and suck him over and over: sometimes so full and deep that my world fills with pheromones and tickly hair; and sometimes soft and light and teasing, so he keens with frustration and strains in his bondage.

I could do this forever.

Well, almost.

I reach up under my long brown skirt and fiddle my knickers off, trying to be elegant, failing, and distracting him from my lack of strip-tease skills with some more languorous cock sucking. Once I'm naked beneath my skirt, I let his cock slide out of my mouth, then scoot up his body a little, and slide myself down.

Now I move slowly. I know he's on the edge from my merciless blow job, and I don't want this to end too soon. I lean down and press my mouth to his. My lips are dirty with his arousal and I want him to taste it too.

And he likes that too. He sucks the taste of himself from my lips like he's starving for it.

I start to move a little faster. He gasps. And that gasp is what finally does it. I'm close now. Close enough that I can break into a sprint for the finish.

I lean close into him again, missing his mouth this time to press my lips against his ear. 'Whore,' I say softly, liking the way the word feels on my breath.

And I don't even know which of us starts to come first.

About ten minutes, and a complete reversal of fortune later, Rex smiles, and I reach up to unfasten one of his wrists. As I lean across him he strains up to lick my shoulder, where my T-shirt has slid down off it, and whispers, 'Happy Birthday, baby.'

I smile down at him.

'So, what's been your favourite present so far?' he twinkles, with a haven't-I-been-a-good-boyfriend smirk.

I climb off the bed to untie his ankles and then take the cuffs and ropes and stuff them back in my handbag. I retrieve the pile of cash from the bedside table too and slip that carefully into the little zip pocket in my bag that it came from.

And then I look at him. He still looks beautiful. 'Sweetie,' I say, softly, 'you always give me the best birthday presents.' (Which is, of course, one of the main things one looks for in a boyfriend.)

Now untied and free to squirm, Rex repositions himself, lounging back against the pillows. If he still smoked he'd be smoking now, but as he doesn't anymore he settles for looking ridiculously smug and sated.

And I just can't help smiling like an idiot as I snuggle even closer. 'How can I ever repay you?' I murmur.

Rex shrugs. 'Move in with me.'

I groan at this, actually groan and lift a finger, placing it on his lips. 'Oh, Rex. I would have left you tied up and added a big ball gag if I'd known you were going to start.'

'You asked!' says Rex, indignantly.

'Baby,' I roll over so I'm facing him, propped up on my arms. 'You're so sexy, and that was fantastic. I love you, but I just don't want to live with you – you would drive me crazy. And can we please not discuss this on my birthday.'

Rex makes a face, but he doesn't say anything.

And I huff to myself that I could think of one or two better ways we could have ended our little perv-o-rama session, but I don't complain.

Half an hour later, I'm staring at myself in the bathroom mirror. My face is still all post sex puffy and I really can't decide if this is a good look for me or not. I pout at my reflection.

Over my shoulder, in the mirror, I can see through into the bedroom, and Rex still lying on the bed. He looks like he might have fallen asleep.

'Babe,' I yell at the reflected image of crumpled sheets and peek-a-boo arse, 'table's booked for eight.'

He groans, but there appears to be some movement. I look back at my face in the mirror. 'Thirty-one,' I mouth at my reflection. Which isn't so bad. Not really. Not when I say it right.

Thirty-one.

Thirty. One.

2

Oregano's, which just happens to be my favourite restaurant, five people, 8p.m. Okay, so it's now five past eight and only Rex and I are actually here, but that's okay. It's cool. At least it's okay and cool with me.

'Fuck! Where the fuck are they?' Rex says, so loud I want to slide under the tablecloth away from the stares of the other diners.

'Will you calm down,' I say, setting down my glass. 'This is my birthday party, not yours. Anyone'd think it was you that was being stood up.'

Rex shoots me the withering pity and then goes back to his rant. 'I too am being stood up. Pete is standing me up.' He's so loud now it makes me glance nervously around the restaurant – but nobody is looking at us.

'How do you figure that?'

'Because Pete is my friend, ergo, it's me he's standing up. Birthday girl or no birthday girl.'

'Hang on,' I say, picking up my glass and then putting it down again without drinking anything. 'Pete is my friend too. In fact he's more my friend than he is your friend.'

'He so isn't.'

'Yes he is, come on, old university chum beats work colleague any day.'

Rex thinks for a sec. 'He's not just my work colleague, he's my partner,' he says, deliberately. 'My right hand. The yin to my yang. And besides, I see him every day, you don't.'

'So what? You see that bossy girl with funny hair every day and I don't notice you calling her your best bloody mate and your ying-yang.'

Rex looks decidedly cross. 'Well,' he says, in the voice of a petulant child, 'when Pete gets here we'll just have to ask him who he likes the best won't we. If he actually does ever get here.'

I sigh. Why is Rex being such an arse? Is he just joking around, or is he still pissed off with me over the bloody moving in thing?

'He'll get here,' I say, 'He texted – and you might like to note here that he texted me, not you – to say his bus was stuck in traffic on the seafront. He'll be here, they'll all be here. And Kate and her new bloke won't be long either. Kate's always fifteen minutes late because that's part of her reason for existing.'

'New bloke? Who's she bringing this time?' Rex says, rolling his eyes. And well he might, because Kate, being almost a whole year older than me, has recently decided that her singledom-without-being-pitiful meter is running out and has taken to bringing random men to every social occasion we invite her to, in the vague hope that love might blossom, or something.

'Yes,' I say, 'it's someone off the internet.'

'I suppose we should just be grateful it's not some-one from the bus stop,' Rex bitches, pouring us both refills even though my glass is still two-thirds full. 'Honestly, Sophie, I'm surprised she hasn't asked me out.'

'Well, you know Rex, she has got the entire male population of Brighton to get through before she needs to resort to that.'

And I laugh.

And I'm still laughing a few moments later when Pete suddenly appears behind me. Which means he says, 'What's so funny?' And I try, to explain my not-so-clever joke, but the moment has so gone – if it were ever there in the first place.

Pete dismisses my ramblings quickly and instead turns his attention to air kissing his way round the table – well, there are only two of us to kiss, but it's still quite a performance. And before he even hits his seat Rex starts to question him about whether he is mostly my friend or mostly Rex's.

Pete frowns. 'Can't I be friends with both of you?'

'Well, not if we split up,' I point out, 'then you'd have to choose between us.'

Pete pulls a face. 'Oh God, you two are never going to split up. Six years and you're still screwing each other's arses off. Forget it. You've got the life sentence – you might as well be married.'

'We did split up – last August, remember?' I attempt, but no one takes me seriously, or even really listens, probably because the break up I am alluding to lasted less than twelve hours.

Finally, after three attempts by waiters to remove the extra place settings and/or move us to a smaller table, Kate arrives, giving us the usual 'sorry' speech. All flustered yet elegant.

But I'm not even pretending to listen to her latest woeful tale of Reasons to be Tardy, and not just because I've heard this speech a million-billion times before, I'm not listening because of what she has brought with her.

Just behind Kate is the kind of man who is so

beautiful it makes me have to actually check my mouth isn't hanging open (with my tongue hanging out and drool pooling on the table).

My God, but he is so beautiful.

He's gorgeous ... let me count the ways. He's tall, but not too tall, not, like, freak tall. And he's got all the usual facial features, but perfectly arranged so that each one seems to enhance the beauty of another. For example, his eyebrows seem to be positioned perfectly to draw attention to his indigo-denim-coloured eyes. His slightly curly, slightly too long hair seems to just scream about how perfect his cheekbones are. And his smile, which he cracks as he slides into a vacant chair next to Kate's, is so hypnotic I'm surprised Paul McKenna hasn't bought the rights to it. I manage to surreptitiously glance at his backside before it hits the velveteen and, my God, if there isn't something in the Bible about coveting your neighbour's arse, then there bloody well ought to be.

Rex stands up to kiss Kate hello and then says loudly, 'Oh God, Kate, I was going to get her a really good-looking, really sexy man. I suppose I'll just have to take mine back to a shop.'

'Rex!' says Kate, sounding unnecessarily shocked. (Kate is so easy to wind up.) 'He isn't from a shop. Everyone, this is Mark. A friend.'

As he settles back down, Rex says, 'And with friends like that, who needs porn?' I think he meant that to be an aside to me, but he's already drunk and everyone hears him perfectly clearly. Which is embarrassing.

I sigh into my glass. Happy Birthday to me.

The evening wears its way on through a variety of peaks and troughs like that. While Rex and Pete talk shop – apparently they have big contracts to bid for (yawn) – and Mark is off powdering his beautiful nose (a sight I wouldn't mind being a fly on the wall for), a sozzled Kate almost falls off her chair while telling me how much she loves me and how glad she is that I've got Rex.

I've had a few glasses of wine myself, by this point, which means I am feeling rather soppy towards Rex now. So I'm about to agree gushingly when Mark suddenly returns, sliding into his seat in a sort of boneless flowing way that makes me (yet again) have to check my tongue is still in my mouth.

But before I embarrass myself too much with the blatant staring, Kate and I both notice that Pete has opened up a new topic. And the conversation suddenly becomes very slurred and very filthy in the way that Pete conversations can get. Pete is telling a tale of how he picked up a policeman at a club and then went back to his and found an exciting new use for truncheons. And as this news permeates, the entire table, understandably, tune in.

'Okay, so I didn't know – obviously – because, he doesn't wear his uniform in a night club. Well, maybe he should, but he doesn't. So I just pick him up, cute enough guy and it's not until I'm in his flat, well, in his bed actually.' Short pause, breath for effect, 'But not actually inside him.' Coy smile. 'That I find out. I ask him what he does, and he says, "I'm a cop," just like that. And I'm so turned on so fast I almost go blind.'

We all laugh encouragingly.

'Because I've always had this thing about policemen. The handcuffs, the uniform, the sarcasm. So – long story short – after a little bit of persuasion I'm bent over the bed wearing nothing but his special silver bracelets and he's talking to me like I'm some half-cut whore he's picked up on the prom for dangerous good looks and being sexy without due care and attention. It was fabulous. And what he did to me with his truncheon wasn't bad either.'

I squirm a little in my seat, and Pete winks at me. I've known Pete longer than anyone else at this table; I can't help wondering how much of that little story is actually true.

Kate, who has always loved Pete's sordid tales, says, 'Do they still have truncheons? I thought they had all gone over to those funny bent sticks?'

Pete doesn't really answer her question, though, because he's going elsewhere with this story and he says, 'Trouble is, a policeman had always been my number one fantasy. Now I've actually gone and done it, what am I going to aim for?'

And I say (and this is when I know I'm properly birthday drunk), 'How about some kind of extreme, extra twisted version of your ultimate fantasy?'

And then I realise I'm going to have to say more than that. Everyone is looking at me, I appear to have inadvertently made myself centre of attention during Let's Talk About Sex hour.

A glassy-eyed Kate looms towards me. 'So, Sophie, what's your ultimate fantasy?'

'And more to the point,' adds Pete, 'what's this one you've already fulfilled and had to upgrade to an extra twisted version?'

Shit. Did I really just give that much away?

I bite my lip and look around the table. Actually, I don't really mind admitting to this. Well, not all that much. Maybe. Pete kind of knows, Kate might have guessed and Rex, well Rex helped write the damn thing. Okay, saying it out loud is a newie, but it's too late for fumbling now. So, figuring I have no choice, I say, very fast, 'I always thought it would be hot to pay a man for sex. That's all.'

And, before I even properly finish speaking, Pete yells, 'Still! You're still dreaming about that. Shit, baby, you've got to just get that one out of your . . .' And he stops, and I can actually see it dawning on him. 'Hang on, didn't you say you had fulfilled your fantasy and now had a new twisted version?'

'Uh, yeah,' I say, sheepishly. And I can't help sort of smiling.

'Who?' says Pete, who clearly can't believe he has anything left to know about my sex life, which makes me heh-heh to myself because it's about time Pete found out that not everyone is a total kiss-and-tell merchant.

Pete is still exploding. 'What is going on? Who did you pay for sex? I demand to be told immediately.' And he actually bangs his fist on the table.

And Rex says, 'Me.'

And I say, 'Oh God.' But that's not the end of it – not that (I'm willing to bet) I'm ever actually going to hear the end of it.

Because Pete then says, 'So, you'd always wanted to pay a man for sex, and then you paid Rex for sex, which not only rhymes but is also a story we have so got to hear, but we mustn't forget to enquire – what's the new extra sordid twist on the classic?'

'No,' say Kate, 'first the paying-Rex-for-sex story. Since Rex is actually your boyfriend. I think it needs some in-depth explanation in its own right.'

'Well,' I say, 'that's sort of a long story, but well . . .' I'm stumbling over my words because this is far, far harder than I thought it would be. 'Well, sometimes, when Rex and I are together, we kind of pretend that he's a, well, a male prostitute or something.'

And I screw up my face with the embarrassment. But everyone is still looking at me, frighteningly expectant. 'What,' I say, indignant, 'do you want me to go into explicit details, or something?'

Pete says, 'Yes.' But at the same time Kate says, 'No.' Rex reaches across the table and gives Pete a pretend smack. I take another drink. I don't look at Mark, because I'm pretending he isn't there.

'Hang on, hang on,' says Pete, who is still flapping his arms around, endangering all the drinks on the table as he fends off Rex, 'OK, I don't want details about your revolting heterosexual couplings, obviously, but what I do want to know is what is this extra twisted twist you've put on the fantasy to give you something to daydream about now Rex is your personal whore?'

'Oh,' I say. And oh, indeed. Because I had kind of forgotten, in the weird drunken embarrassment of making true confessions about my sex life with Rex, that I had even alluded to this – a far darker secret.

But I can't actually see a way out, because I'm surrounded by glowing little upturned faces, expectant children at Christmas, every one of them (well, apart from Mark, who I've cunningly edited out of my mental picture of the current situation, because la-la-la incredibly sexy man I don't really know is so not sitting at the table right now).

'Well,' I say, because that's always a good start, 'well, acting stuff out with Rex is all very well, but it's not real is it – just pretend. So when I want to, um, think about something really exciting I just imagine paying for it for real. Not with Rex. With the genuine article. A real, you know, prostitute. That kind of gets me really hot.' I gulp and then pick up my nearly full wine glass and swallow the contents.

And Kate says, 'Ew! T.M.I. Too much information.'

Pete gives her a withering look. 'Oh my God, Sophie, that isn't a new fantasy, that's the same fantasy. And if that's your ultimate fantasy, then, at your age, you should so do it.'

I think I ought to respond to this, but I don't appear to have any say in the matter, because Kate immediately counters with, 'No she shouldn't!'

'Why not,' says Pete.

'Because, I don't know, it's not safe.'

'Oh, don't be so silly and bourgeois.'

And then Rex, who has been being uncharacteristically quiet, says, 'Um, Pete, I am still here you know.'

By this time, my cheeks have got to be burning cherry red – and I mean nasty artificial glacé cherries, not nice burgundy posh ones – and so I excuse myself to the loo.

3

Now, here's the slightly weird thing: despite the horror of the true confession session, on another level, talking about this stuff has made me feel really quite turned on. So I'm rather glad when, as I'm making my rickety way down the steep steps that lead to the underground dungeon where Oregano's choose to keep their toilets, Rex appears at my elbow. Without a word, he guides me into the Men's loo. We cross the sticky floor as quickly as we can and make straight for the lone cubicle, locking the door and rushing headlong into a crazy snog.

His mouth seems softer than usual. Candy floss and marshmallow delicious as he glides it over mine. I open up a little bit wider and he slips his tongue between my lips. I love kissing him. We don't seem to have grown out of it. I've read in a million and one magazines that it's supposed to be one of the things that couples who are in it for the long haul stop doing – but Rex and I don't seem to have lost the glow yet.

I nibble at his tongue a tiny bit and get rewarded by a soft little pleasure noise, which is so delightfully cute. I find I'm laughing into his mouth and that's when we stop kissing and Rex uses his mouth to paint me the most wonderful pictures instead.

He pulls off his shirt, right over his head without unbuttoning it and then says, 'I want to do something really special for your birthday.'

'We did, earlier remember? That whole picking you

up in the bar of The Palace, *Pretty Woman*, role-play thing.'

'Yeah, I know, but something else.' Rex licks my cheek and I can hear his breath in my ear – molten and cracking with arousal. 'Maybe we could print up a card, you know like in phone boxes. Pictures of me posing as a whore for you – wanton and sluttish.'

He's unbuttoning his jeans now and they snake down his little hips onto the toilet floor. 'And we need to find somewhere really seedy to do it too. The posh hotel was good, but what about a really nasty hotel or, maybe, do you think we could find an actual brothel and see if they'd hire us the room but not the prostitute?'

He stumbles out of his underwear and shoes until he's naked and drops to his knees on the floor in front of me. I really, really love it when he's naked and I'm still dressed. And he knows it. He's so good at hitting all of my buttons, sometimes I think he must take notes when I'm not looking.

Of course, I've figured out exactly what he's up to. I know what this is all about. He's trying to find ways of pinning down that elusive – I want it for real – that I was talking about. Of course he's onto a loser – I'm sorry to say – because it can't be real with Rex. The bottom line is: I'll always know he's really an Advertising Copywriter, and I know he doesn't need the cash I pretend to give him. In fact I know that he'll give me the cash back when we're done and I'll put it back into my current account where it came from. And the actually wanting the cash thing, that's the whole point about the 'for real' fantasy.

Rex lifts my skirt, whispering something about how he wants me to throw the cash on the floor as I leave the room so he has to crawl about to pick it up, and he presses his mouth into the soft angles between my thighs as he says it. His breath is warm and slightly damp on my super-sensitised skin. I'm rubbing myself gently against him. He nudges my knickers aside and presses his tongue against my bare skin.

And it's so intense. I might know that Rex is on a hopeless quest if he wants to fulfil my real pay-for-play fantasy, but he's still unbelievably hot. He glides the tip of his tongue over my clit twice, then teases further down, twisting and arching until I'm scrabbling wildly at the glass-smooth tiled wall for a hand hold.

I find a way to balance, somehow, and I look down at him, kneeling naked on the nasty floor. The dirty bitch – getting on his knees in a toilet. He looks so hot I think I could actually come just from the sight of him, even if he wasn't twirling his tongue expertly against my clit – looping the loop like one of those magnificent men. I grab hold of his hair, feeling a sudden nasty urge come over me, and force him hard against me, twisty and cruel.

I hear a muffled moan and match it with my own, trying hopelessly not to be too loud, as I come messily, fuzzily, stumblingly but, oh, so sweetly, into his open mouth.

As I reach out to open the cubicle door, Rex takes my hand and pulls me back. At first I assume he wants payback for the orgasm he has just given me, which makes me a bit miffed because it's my birthday and I should get freebies. But when I see his face I realise it's not quite that. He's stopped because there are noises coming from outside the stall.

A man and a woman. (Much more of this sort of thing and Oregano's is going to have to get a special licence.) And then I listen more, and that's when I realise why Rex is smirking quite so much, it's not just any man and woman: it's Kate and, I assume, Mark.

I give a little shudder when I realise that Mr-amazingly-sexy-man-who-I-hardly-know has now not just heard my deepest, darkest sex fantasy confessions, but also may have just heard me come. However, when I tune in to what they are actually saying, they don't seem to have heard anything.

He is saying, 'Are you sure? You don't want to find yourself home alone later really regretting it.'

'I'm sure,' she says, 'I'm just not really up for that.'

'I really like you, that's why I'm pushing it. I'd really like to spend the night.'

'Thanks. But really, no.'

My jaw drops. Sexy man is offering Kate, well I don't know exactly what, but I doubt I'd be barking up completely the wrong tree if I assumed it was sex, and she's saying no.

Kate! Of all people! Saying no! To sexy man!

I glance at Rex, who shrugs, clearly as baffled as me.

Then we hear the door go. So someone has left (or come in). And there's no more talking. Rex slips his clothes back on. We wait a few moments longer and then emerge into a room empty apart from some lonely urinals.

As we head back to the restaurant proper I realise I didn't actually get to have the wee I had intended, and nip into the Ladies' while Rex makes for the restaurant.

When I come out of the cubicle there's someone standing by the sinks. I do a double take. It's sexy man. The same sexy man who knows my deepest and darkest fantasies, and yet probably doesn't even know my last name.

I try to casually square up to him, wondering if acting cool is a good option for disguising how knee-weakening I find him, which means I am, almost certainly, still a bit tipsy. 'So, Mark Valentine,' I say to him, drawling out his dubious name, 'what sort of a name is that anyway?'

'An invented one,' Mark says, with a knowing smile.

'I thought as much. You internet blokes are all the same.'

Mark looks at me, coolly. 'I'm not from the internet.'

In fact coolly isn't even the half of it, his gaze is so Arctic-ice he is making me feel decidedly hot and flustered. I swallow and hope I'm not blushing. And hope that if I am he'll realise that it's just the amount of wine I've drunk and not his alarmingly charismatic presence. 'Well I know that,' I say, petulantly, 'no one really is from the internet.'

'No, I mean Kate didn't meet me on the internet. Well she did, but not a dating site like she told you.'

'Oh, well, I mean I can't say I'm surprised, she's been bringing men from all over. Did she meet you at a bus stop, because that would be such a coincidence because Rex said . . .'

He cuts me off, mid-drunken babble. 'Sophie, no, she did not meet me at a bus stop. Actually, Sophie, she ordered me. She bought me.'

I frown at him. It would be putting it mildly to say that this is not exactly going the way I would have expected.

'She hired me. Do you see? I'm exactly what you were talking about in there just now. I'm a male escort.'

I swallow hard. He can't be saying what I think he's saying. Can he?

I'm confused, I'm too drunk, I'm babbling, 'What, like, really? But you don't actually do the sex and stuff, do you? You just go to places with women. Like those women who want to have a partner for important dos, wedding and that sort of thing. I've seen that in films.' What I don't say is that I've probably seen every film ever made with that as the subject matter – even the slapstick comedy cringe-a-thon ones.

'That's where you're wrong Sophie. Okay, I do do the odd wedding gig – that's actually quite unusual – but I also really do "the sex and stuff" for money, with whoever pays me. Women, men, occasional undecideds.'

I clap my hand to my mouth in shock and surprise, and then find myself having to speak round it. 'God, you mean Kate is paying you to have sex with her.' But even as I'm saying that I realise that what I overheard was Kate turning down a bit of pay-for sex.

'No, Kate is just paying me to come here,' Mark says, 'but you could, pay me that is, to have sex with you.'

I swallow hard. It's difficult to really know what to say. I'm pretty sure I made it pretty clear that the whole paying-for-play-for-real fantasy was something I wanted to keep a fantasy – for now, at least. But the fact is, when I said all that, I didn't expect to be met with an unbelievably sexy male prostitute soliciting me in the Ladies' of my favourite restaurant.

If only Mark wasn't so sexy. I know I'm staring and I know I can't help it. I keep noticing tiny details about him, like the way his dark curls reflect the light so prettily, or the way his lips are still a tiny bit pillowy and pouty even when he's not actually pouting. Oh, I know he's turning it on for me; I know he's trying to make a sale, just like Rex in the hotel bar, except that, and God this makes me so wet, he's really trying to sell, not just faking it. This is for real. So, not like Rex at all. And I'm tipsy, and it's my birthday – this isn't fair.

'This isn't fair,' I say out loud.

And Mark reaches forward and catches my chin in his hand, stroking along my lower lip with his thumb as he speaks. 'Oh no, Sophie, it's very fair. It's the fairest thing you can imagine. The fairest of them all. You can pay me, and you can have me. Hire me. Own me. For real. The real thing. And then you can do anything you want to me, because I'll be your property. You can have anything you want from me. I know that's what you want. That power.'

His tongue flicks out his mouth and caresses the corner of his top lip. And I know I'm melting. I can't help it.

But then I hear a voice call my name. 'Sophie!' And it's Kate's voice. 'Sophie, where are you!' and the spell breaks, shattering like glass.

'Sophie, come on.' A tousled blonde head appears round the door of the Ladies' loo. 'There's cake. I didn't want to have to tell you there was cake, because it's Rex's big surprise, but you'll find out in a minute anyway. And it's not like cake on your birthday is such a big surprise, anyway. So, come on! Cake!'

So I follow Kate out. She doesn't give anything away, but I know she saw the way Mark was holding my chin and I know she knew what he was going to ask. But I don't say anything and nor does she. And bare seconds later all is suddenly forgotten in a sea of candles and tuneless drunken singing and cake.

So, as intense encounters go, the Mark Valentine affair suddenly seems so many miles away as I'm sat back next to Rex and eating my fourth slice. Mark might be delicious, but even he can't compete with the five-layer Armageddon-by-chocolate that threatens to destroy us all.

I look down at the cream-festooned cakey extravaganza on my plate and grin. 'You know,' I say loudly to everyone in particular, 'I really am starting my diet tomorrow.'

'What diet?' says Kate, who loves a bit of diet talk.

'That one off Channel Four, you know, with all the seeds and shit.'

'Ooh that's a goodie,' says Kate, draining her glass of wine.

'I always liked Atkins,' says Pete, 'I wish Atkins would come back into fashion. It used to be such fun when we could talk Atkins all evening.'

'Pah,' says Kate, 'Atkins is such a boy's diet. All that steak and no chocolate. Total rubbish.'

While she's talking Rex touches my cheek. 'Babe,' he says, softly, just to me, 'you don't need to diet, you look fucking gorgeous.'

'Oh yeah, I know. I know I do. It's not a diet actually, even though I know I did say diet just then, but it's actually a thing, you know, a lifestyle.'

'Lifestyle. Right,' says Rex, blankly, turning his body so he's focused back on the main conversation.

'Oh, you know what?' Pete is saying across the table, 'there was this good thing in a magazine the other month. Sounds alright. What you have to do, right, is eat a bowl of All Bran – or that sort of thing, cereal, but not, like, Coco Pops, it has to be non-sugary stuff – before every meal and it makes you too full to eat your actual food. And the beauty of all that All Bran is you just poo it out – so you lose weight. Good, eh?'

'Huh,' I say, dismissively, 'that sounds bloody stupid. That's not a lifestyle, is it? In fact it sounds vaguely pathological.' And maybe I was a bit over harsh, because the subject is dropped then, in favour of more cake being dished out.

* * *

Mark made-up-name Valentine isn't at the table for this conversation. He appears to have decided to give the cake eating a miss, and no one except me seems to have noticed. But I can't forget about him for too long, because, once the cake has disappeared, there he is – right back at the table, and back on my mind.

I have to force myself not to look at him, as we try and keep the evening alive long after what would be considered humane under current ethical guidelines, with liqueurs and coffee and stupid drunken conversation. And every time my eyes do slide in his direction, he's always looking at me and ready to meet my gaze with a dirty look, or a wink, or a pout.

I'm almost glad when the bill arrives and we are practically ejected onto the street.

In the brisk, hand-clapping cold, we kiss our goodbyes, while we wait for a cab at the rank around the corner. Kate, Pete and Mark opt to share – even though that means something of a roundabout route. And just before we squash them into a shabby-looking Ford Escort, Mark manages to slip something into my hand. I don't even need to look at it to know what it is.

It contains everything I need to know to take me down the oh-so-tempting path of wrongness that Mark Valentine represents, and probably even a website address too.

It's his business card.

And by the time Rex and I are walking back home from the taxi rank, I can't stop thinking about Mark. Although, I'm convinced that if I had got the chance to respond to his lavatorial proposal I would have said no. At least, I think I'm convinced.

It's not that I don't like the idea. I love the idea. I'm

actually in love with the idea. But, like I keep on saying – some things are best left as fantasy.

And in the toilet cubicle Rex positively went out of his way to demonstrate that he still has some ideas for us to try out – which isn't bad going after six years.

So, even though Mark is offering the real deal. The knicker-wetting idea that he would actually be selling me his body, for real, Mark is a stranger – Stranger Danger, and all that – whereas Rex is a known quantity.

But, in some ways, that's the problem, the known-quantity-ness of Rex.

And I'm still thinking about this at home, eking out the last dregs of my birthday on the sofa. We're watching telly, too tired and drunk and sated to do much else. Well, except talk, Rex always manages to talk. So he's talking and I'm just not really listening. But I think he's talking about smoking. I tune back in just as he starts to raise his voice.

'Sophie!' he sort of yells – well, okay, taking into account how near he is to me it counts as a yell. 'For God's sake, Sophie, don't fucking pass out on me. It's your birthday, you have to stay up until midnight on your birthday for maximum birthdayness.'

'I'm awake,' I say, sort of sounding a bit like I wasn't, even though I was, just miles away.

Rex clicks his tongue at me and snuggles up closer. 'I was just saying that we should celebrate the fact that it's been a year since we gave up smoking.'

'Oh yeah.' We both gave up after my thirtieth birthday party. Because I'd always said that I'd give up when I was thirty – reasoning that that at least gave me a sporting chance of avoiding a hideous cancer-riddled death. And, of course, there was no way I was giving up and having a boyfriend who smoked. That would be too unfair and hard. So Rex had to give up too.

'Do you remember when you gave up that you said that I would have to give up too if I wanted to move in,' Rex says, a sly little note in his voice as he brings up the subject he promised not to mention on my birthday.

'Well, yeah, I did say that. And I meant it metaphorically.'

'You so didn't,' Rex almost shrieks. 'You so did mean it for real, you bloody liar.'

'Hang on.' I jab a finger at the winking green of the digital clock on the video. 11.59. 'You can't talk about this for another minute.'

And then we both sit there in silence, waiting for the clock to flick and finish my birthday reprieve forever.

'Ha!' says Rex as soon as we hit midnight. 'You can't fight the laws of physics, baby – birthdays always end. Anyway as I was saying . . .'

But I interrupt him, because I'm so good at evading this topic, and say, 'Oh, look, my birthday is over. Which means I can go to bed. Ha!'

And I all but sprint out of the room, clattering across the floorboards to the eternal annoyance of my downstairs neighbour, and burying myself under my floral duvet. When Rex comes in a few seconds later I fake sleep – quite badly because my 'snores' sound like pig grunts and my shoed feet are sticking out the end of the bed.

'Okay, okay,' he says – addressing a lump of duvet and some cute red kitten heels, 'I'll drop it. But if we can't talk about me moving in, can I at least stay tonight?'

And I lift up the edge of the duvet, still keeping my eyes tight shut, and let him crawl inside.

Even I think it's possibly a bridge too far when Rex slides into bed behind me and presses his warm bony body against my back. I can feel his erection somewhere near my kidneys and, flattering as it is, I find myself saying, 'Rex,' in a chastising kind of way.

'What?' says Rex. 'Come on, Sophie, it's your birthday.'

''Tisn't. We watched the clock, remember.'

I'm answered by a wet mouth on the back of my neck and a very persuasive grind.

'Rex!' I say again, in that same Down-Boy tone of voice. 'I can't. I'm spent. I've come twice today. And I've got work.'

'Nah-ah,' says Rex, a triumphant little note creeping into his voice. 'We watched the clock, remember. It's Friday now, which means you haven't had a single orgasm yet today.'

'But I'm tired.'

'Well that doesn't matter, does it. It's not like you • have to do anything.'

So I give in. I let Rex drag me over onto my back with a gentle tug of my shoulder. I let my knees drift apart and my eyes close in super slo-mo. The last thing I see before the shutters come down completely is Rex's tousled ginger mop disappearing over my horizon, heading for base camp.

I guess I'm still quite wet from the frisky fun at Oregano's, or the major session at The Palace Hotel, I don't really know which, but I do as soon as Rex's tongue finds its way inside me when I suddenly rise to the occasion, going from edge-of-sleep bleariness to being as turned on as I've been all day.

But this isn't a good idea, because my too-damn-tired mind wants to make this quick, wants to get this done asap so sleep can retake its position as number one priority. Which, I think, is why, as Rex's tongue glides over me, as Rex's lips press close, close and soft, I find myself imagining Mark Valentine's tongue and lips are working between my legs. And that's not good.

My brain runs a quick and totally unauthorised fantasy scenario where I call up Mark (using the number on the oh-so-handy card he gave me) one quiet afternoon and, when he arrives, I simply indicate with a nod that I want him to go down between my legs. Mark drops to his knees and, nudging my knickers aside, teases and coaxes me to loud orgasmic bucks and swirls with all the ease of a seasoned professional. And then, before I've even come down, he leaves, grabbing his money from my bedside table. In minutes he's back out in the street without a word. With his lips still swollen. Still breathing me.

And so, as Rex takes me there himself, in the dark bedroom, I'm picturing Mark Valentine, out in the street with his dirty mouth and dirty money. Dirty whore.

4

After the excesses and confusions of my birthday on Thursday, Friday at work was pretty vile, even with the kind of understanding bosses I have – i.e. those who at least acknowledge the fact that the day after one's birthday one is hardly going to be on top graphic designing form.

The place I work – The Fantastic Design Company – is pretty tiny, just my three bosses (all business partners) and me. When I started working here, six years ago, one of them put up a poster next to my desk from the lame eighties film *Three Men and a Baby*, which I still think is kind of funny, even though the poster is tatty and fading now, and it continues to cause a lot of bemusement among visitors to the office. It gets a lot of frowns, a lot of double takes, a few questions. I guess most people decide not to ask, for fear of finding out that it is actually my favourite film, or something.

My bosses are called Dave, Steve and Ed, but I like to call them all Dave-Steve-Ed, because that's kind of how I think of them – both collectively and individually – as one strange three-headed Ray Harryhausen-type claymation monster. Albeit a reasonably benevolent one.

It's a pretty relaxed place to work – Dave-Steve-Ed are all pretty cool, typical Brightonite geeky organic types, although they do still like to have their hierarchy in place. So, while no one really tells me what to do very much, and I don't have to fill out elaborate time sheets, or petty cash requests, or any of those things that I hear happen in other jobs (personally, I have no real experience of such other jobs, myself, this is the first 'proper' place – i.e. non-retail – I've ever worked), they are still the bosses and I am still the employee. Essentially this means that I'm the one who makes the tea and answers the phone. I hated being the one who answered the phone when I started this job at twenty-five – but answering the phone at the age of just-turned-thirty-one is really quite buttock clenching. Although not as buttock clenching as the thought of actually doing anything about the situation.

Ah, the dangers of the comfort zone! The best and worst thing about my job is that it is easy. And low pressure. And local – so very local – I can get away with getting out of bed at nine fifteen and still have five busy-looking windows open on my thrumming computer, before even one of my bosses has managed to find a parking space for his mid-life crisis soft-top. So phone answering and tea making has to be swallowed, along with my pride, on the third ring of the ever demanding telephone.

This particular post-birthday, hung-over Friday, I manage to spend almost the entire day fiddling with one boring page of one boring catalogue which, considering the rack of deadlines I have (and the amount of emails in my inbox marked 'high priority'), is a pretty dire state of affairs, even for a post-birthday girl in a delicate state. But needs must and today my needs involve an awful lot of staring out of the window and thinking about Mark.

Oh, I don't really mean to. I mean, I know it's stupid to obsess about someone I vaguely know. (Oh, okay, let's be accurate, someone I don't know at all.) After all,

I'm a grown up woman of thirty-one. I know obsessions are kind of teenage. I know full well that I know nothing about Mark. That everything I've suddenly decided is so Goddamn perfect about him is just my own projection onto his deliciously man-shaped blank canvas. But even so – I do it. How can I resist? I'm sitting here with a big window next to my desk, complete with howling wind and lashing rain, counterpointing how warm and cosy I am in my smoked-glass work station. More computers than we could ever need are humming in freakish harmony with some awful, awful jazz-type music (a soundtrack which means that even the severely visually impaired would know right away they were in a graphic design office.) And these are all factors which just scream – stare out of the window, Sophie! Stare out of the window and have unconvincing, but strangely satisfying fantasies about Mark 'made-up-name' Valentine.

I am so weak.

But at least it has to stop at in-my-head fantasies, because one of the most irritating of the many irritating things about my office is the fact it is far too open plan for, say, looking up the website which is given on Mark's business card.

Now, when I say my office is 'far too open plan', I don't mean just plain old everyday open plan – which is more or less a given everywhere these days, I mean very open plan. See, in normal style open plan there's still some chance of a bit of privacy, especially if you take a bit of care with desk allocation and get lucky with a corner desk or some of those partition things. But not here.

The key factor here, the key to privacy and peace of mind and looking up dubious websites, is can other people in the room see your monitor screen? And the unfortunate answer, where I work, is a great big 'Oh', followed by an even bigger 'Yes'.

There is no chance of any stealth cloaking here, no matter how wise one might be to the truth about key desk selection. We don't even have the most basic of cubicles. It's just one big room with all the four workstations facing the walls. One quick swivel in my chair and I can check out what everyone else has on their screen at any particular moment. And so can Dave-Steve-Ed. It's totally exposed. We're all totally exposed. What is possibly even worse is that I'm right by the super swingy well-oiled main door, even if I were alone in the office I couldn't be certain that my privacy wasn't about to evaporate any second.

So the simple fact is, everyone can see everyone else's computer from almost any point in the room, which is why I'm stuck with my memories and window staring. There is absolutely no way I can take things further by slipping Mark's card out of my wallet, firing up Mozilla and perusing his website – I might as well whip out a porn mag and start reading it at my desk!

It might be pretty laid back here at Fantastic – but there's laid back, and there's taking the piss. So I just stare blank-eyed at the dull-looking layout on my monitor and let my mind wander. I hatch an exotic Mark Valentine fantasy where I hire him to play the role of kidnap victim for me and we enact a scenario where I snatch him off the street – roughing him up gleefully with no qualms about taking it too far or overstepping the mark. Not when I'm paying for the privilege. I really like the delicious twistedness of paying him and then 'kidnapping' him. I'm enjoying myself so much I practically dream the whole day away.

Back at home that evening things are rather more relaxed after my day of fevered imaginings. I kill some time stooging about, eating some pasta, watching some telly, etc. It crosses my mind to look at Mark's site but, of course, now I'm at home and can do so with impunity, I find the idea just isn't so attractive. I actually find myself wondering what the hell I'm thinking, mooning over Mark Valentine to such an embarrassing extent. But, despite my new-found cool abstinence I don't need to worry that my evening will be completely deviance free, because Rex has his own ideas.

Rex's train from Victoria usually gets in to Brighton station at about half seven. Which means that, so long as there aren't any crazed deadlines looming or post-work drinkies on offer (which there are about fifty per cent of the time), he tends to crash through my door at about quarter to eight on a week night. This has been the state of affairs for at least three years, despite the fact that Rex has a home of his own. Or claims to. I really don't know why he wants to 'move in', considering he spends almost every night at my house and has stuffed my wardrobe with his whiter-than-white shirts, one of which he tortures on an ironing board every morning at daybreak, dressed in just his pants, while I lie in bed whining at him to turn off the light/close the curtains/turn the telly off.

Anyway, it's deviance ahoy, because this evening he parades into my sitting room, right on time, carrying a huge stack of dirty magazines.

'I have presents,' he says, answering my yet-to-be-asked-question, 'sleazy presents.' And the magazines drop from his arms onto my stripped floorboards, sliding over each other glossily, like a sort of naked-man-slick.

I pick up the nearest one. It's called *Boy Time* and it looks like a gay porno. 'Rex,' I say, brightly, turning the shiny prettiness over and over in my hands, 'do you have something to tell me?'

Rex laughs, shaking his head cheerily. 'Sadly not – I was still heterosexual last time I checked. But you know, if I had turned to the dark-side in the last twenty-four hours, I so would tell you by throwing a pile of gay porn across your front room.'

'So what is all this? Some light reading?'

'It's for you,' Rex says and smiles a different sort of smile. Not the cheeky-monkey beam he had on a minute ago when he was joking with me. But a different one. An I've-been-a-good-boy-now-give-me-my-treat sort of smile. I'm confused.

I open up *Boy Time* and flick through it. Actually it's not much of a porno, not like I first thought. It's mostly gossip and listings, kind of like *Heat* or something. The only porny bit is the pin-up in the centre pages. I crinkle up my forehead. 'I give up, Rex. Why?'

'Have a look at the back pages.'

I flick past the telly guide to the last section. It's all classified ads. Oh. Gotcha.

The two pages inside the back cover are a veritable directory of men for sale. (Admittedly they are men for sale to other men – I guess that is the main market after all.) But still, blimey, it's like being caught in some kind of naked torso blizzard.

Of course, I can't actually pretend to have never seen these sorts of classifieds before. I've been Pete's best friend for over ten years and he gets all these magazines – 'for the fashion'. I have 'borrowed' (read stolen, because I never actually asked or gave them back) more of these magazines from Pete than I dare to think about. But this is kind of different. Because stealing his magazines, or what I like to think of as the Pete-Friendship-Dividend, was only ever about me having a bit of downtime fun dreaming about ordering up one of these men as if he were a deep pan with extra cheese. Because this whole buying a man thing was/is – and people round here seem to have a lot of trouble with this concept – only ever meant to be a fantasy!

But Rex, oh God, Rex has bigger ideas. These magazines aren't even the be all and end all of my promised 'presents' – they are merely the menu.

I stare at the pages. It's funny how quickly pictures of backs and chests and arses and cocks become, well, meaningless really. The more I look the more I feel like I'm just staring at some kind of weird abstract picture. It's a bit like those posters that are everywhere now – in the window of every tat shop – where it looks like a big picture of Gandalf, but when you get closer it is actually lots of tiny pictures from *The Lord of the Rings*. Anyway this endless parade of tiny pics and mobile numbers is like that, except the big overall picture is just a weird sort of boxy pattern and the mini pictures are as pornographic as the magazine's distributor will allow.

Other than trying to construct these bizarre thoughts into a witty comment that Rex will appreciate (he has pretty high standards on the witty comment front) I don't actually know what to say. So I don't say anything. I stare at the pages of ads until my non-speaking has become a huge oppressive force in the room. Until it becomes clear that one of us is going to have to say something soon or we may be sitting here until the end of time.

At last Rex breaks the silence. He's always such a gentleman. 'You don't like them, do you?'

I screw up my face. 'It's not really that, it's just, well, I don't really understand them.' And that's true. I understand the parts of the ads which consist of a photo of a naked man with his face all blurred. And I understand the mobile phone numbers that adorn each and every one. But the rest is all weird jargon. Things like in/out, versatile, uncut. Okay, I know what uncut means, but it still seems bizarre and jargony in this context.

'What's to understand?' says Rex, confused. 'They are men for sale. You know, free market, modern capitalism and all that. Pick one you like, or pick one at random, and we'll call him up and see what happens.'

I swallow hard, surprised that Rex thinks doing something like that would be so easy. 'We can't.'

'Sure we can. That's the whole point.'

'Well, apart from anything else, these are gay magazines, these are all gay men. They won't want me.'

'Oh don't be so daft. They don't do the wanting part. If you've got the cash they won't give a monkey's. Anyway I thought of that. See this, here.' Rex points to the letters SBM, in one of the ads. 'That stands for single bi male. And that.' He points to the letters SGM in another ad. 'That stands for single gay male. So, basically, you just need to pick one of the Bs.'

'You've done your homework,' I say, before I realise something that almost paralyses me with embarrassment. 'Oh God, you've talked this over with Pete, haven't you?'

'Uh . . .' says Rex, which is all he can say really. Because it's bleeding obvious. Of course he has.

This, really, mortifies me. 'Oh my God, you have haven't you. The two of you have been sitting there in your big shiny penis-shaped office and instead of thinking up some great new concept in the world of soap powder advertising that will rock the modern world to its foundations you have been discussing my sexual hang ups.'

'They're not hang ups . . .' Rex tries to say, but I keep talking right over him.

'I don't care. They're private. It's my private stuff – just fantasy. I don't mind talking to you about them. In fact I quite like talking to you about them. Or I used to. But you are not discussing them with your colleagues at work.'

'Pete isn't "my colleagues". Pete's known you longer than I have! Pete's known about this longer than I have! You were only telling me at your party how Pete is more your friend than he is mine.'

But, even though a part of me knows that that is a good a point, I'm far too far gone to reign back now. 'Just go, Rex, please. I don't want to talk about this anymore.'

So – go me – that's my evening ruined.

5

Something I could never explain to Rex is that one of the reasons I couldn't enjoy the magazines is because of my new-found Mark obsession – which is still exerting an alarmingly strong hold on me despite my valiant (and soon to prove short-lived) not-looking-at-his-website earlier on this evening.

Oh, I would never have agreed to actually call any of the guys up, but less than a week ago I would have enjoyed flicking through them with Rex and then retiring to the bedroom for some of our signature role-play sex. Not now though. God, it sounds awful to admit this, even to myself, but I don't just want any old male escort in my fantasy now. I don't even want one played by Rex, anymore. My man-for-sale fantasies are exclusively about one man now, and that man is Mark made-up-name Valentine.

The very same Mark Valentine whose card has been tucked into the back of my wallet ever since he slipped it to me at the end of my birthday meal.

It has a phone number on it. And even though I know that calling Mark up would be a very, very wrong thing to do, I sort of know I'm going to. Why not? I've driven my boyfriend away on a Friday night. I'm getting obsessional about a man I don't know. I can't exactly make things any worse (which, I do realise is exactly the kind of train of thought people usually have before they make things a hell of a lot worse).

I actually consider calling him on my mobile. Kind of like my landline would be too risky. Even though I am the only person who lives here and uses this line. Even though I am the person who pays the phone bill. Even if my concern was that someone might see my itemised BT bill lying around and somehow do a Poirot and work out I had called Mark from it, then that's stupid because even if that were possible it could happen with my mobile bill too.

But despite this sudden info dump from Captain Logic, it doesn't seem right to make a call like this on a landline. Even though I know, from films, that landlines are actually more secure than mobiles, because if you are a drug dealer, or something, in a film you use call boxes to make your ultrasensitive calls. And when I think that, I do, for a moment, consider going out into the street and using the nearest pay phone, before I have to mentally slap myself around the face, repeatedly, for being such a dithering ninny pants.

I pick up my phone. My normal phone. I dial 141 and then the number on Mark's card. And hyperventilate for three rings.

'Hello.' Mark's telephone answering voice is low and slow – instantly seductive. I guess he doesn't give this number to his friends and family. I guess he wouldn't answer the phone like that if it might be his mum calling. But I don't go too far down that road because I don't actually want to think of Mark as having a mum. What I actually want to think is that Mark was bred in a test tube in some despot's secret sex stud laboratory. (And now I've totally lost track of when my Mark fantasies went completely out of control.)

'Er, hi,' I reply, trying to think of a way to introduce myself that sounds interesting and flirty and cool. Strangely I really want to impress him, even though I know I don't actually need to and that the fact I don't need to make any effort is the whole point.

'Don't be shy, sweetie. I'm Mark. What's your name?' And although I know that tone and turn of phrase would be patronising on anyone else, because it's him and because it's now, it kind of works. I guess because I'm so nervous a little bit of hand holding is kind of nice. And I guess he knows that. I guess that jumpy, nervy, about-to-slam-the-phone-down-at-any-second clients are what he gets ninety per cent of the time.

'It's Sophie. Sophie Taylor. We met at my birthday dinner last night.'

'Sophie!' I can hear the smile. And I fall for it instantly, the clever little artifice he constructs with that one word – my name – that he has been waiting by the phone for me all this time. 'I'm so glad I gave you my card now. I wasn't sure if you were going to call me.'

It's a bit like that thing that sometimes happens with tradesmen, when they are so charming and so good at making you feel relaxed that even though it's kind of obvious that they are charging over the odds for fixing the toilet – or whatever it is – it kind of feels okay to let them. Mark's like that. I know he's turning it on for me. I know it's all totally insincere. And I kind of like it.

'Well, I have, uh, called you that is.' And this is the moment where I realise it might have been a good idea to at least think for a couple of seconds about what I was going to say to him. Perhaps even actually decide why I was calling. That might have been more useful, on balance, than headless-chickening around worrying about phone bills and call boxes.

'And what can I do for you?' Mark says. I hope he

hasn't twigged that I really have no idea what I'm doing making this call.

'Um...'

I'd really love to have an out-of-body experience right now. Suddenly start drifting off towards the ceiling and look down to watch myself slowly drowning in a sea of indecisiveness and mortification. Because, not only would that be rather more interesting to watch than to experience, it would mean that I wouldn't have to consider what on earth to do next. Slamming down the phone and hiding under the duvet is suddenly looking rather attractive.

But, of course, I am reckoning without Mark and the fact he has done this a million-billion times before.

'Hey, it's OK,' he coos, in a voice like a massage. 'Don't worry, you don't have to do anything. We can just talk if you want. No strings. I don't expect you to just trot out your address and credit card number and leave the front door on the latch you know.' Meaningful pause. 'Unless that's what you want.'

I sigh with relief. Quite loudly. He can probably hear me. But he doesn't comment.

'You don't need to explain,' he goes on, his voice now so melting and hot-fudge-sundae I'm surprised it doesn't actually start oozing out of the earpiece. 'You explained it all last night. It made perfect sense. You want to pay a man for sex. You like having that power and you know that the more real the power is the more you are going to get off on it. I'm a man who you can pay and have that power. All we need to do is find a way to convince you that what you want to do is OK. Because that's the only problem isn't it?'

'Maybe,' I say. On the one hand, he sounds so convincing – but on the other, it also sounds like this is some kind of prepared speech. 'But I'm really not sure I actually want to do it for real. With a real prostitute, or escort, or gigolo, or whatever it is I'm meant to call you. God, do you see? It's my ultimate fantasy and I don't even know the word for it.'

Mark laughs. A refined little laugh. You could play his laugh on a violin. 'You're right,' he says, 'there isn't a decent word for what I do.'

And then I laugh. It's just nerves, of course, but I do.

And when Mark speaks again, the tone is totally different. 'So maybe you should just refer to me as a whore. Some of my clients like to do that. The ones like you that is. The ones who really get off on the power trip of it all. I've had one or two who liked to push me around a little, pull my hair or slap my face while they called me a "fucking whore". Would you like that? Would you like to see that I get so very hard so very fast when a woman like you does that to me?'

And I've never stopped laughing so fast in all my life. 'Huh?' I say, although it sort of sounds more like a gulp or perhaps just confused and sudden arousal.

'You would like that wouldn't you?' His voice has dropped until it is so low and gravely it is somewhere between mesmeric and downright ought-to-be-illegal. 'Why don't you say it right now – call me a whore. Say something like, "Mark, I hear you're a whore".'

My mouth is so dry I'm not sure I can say anything, or, at least, I'm not sure how it will come out, but I can't resist. I say it slowly. 'Mark, you are such a whore.'

And that, just that, is possibly the most erotic thing I've ever done in my life.

Mark says, 'Would you like me to be your whore?'

I can still hardly speak. But not answering a question like that is not exactly an option. I swallow and say, 'Maybe, it depends what you mean.'

'What I mean, Sophie, is would you like to get your cheque book out, write a few lines, perform a simple financial transaction and then own me, own my body, for whatever use you chose to put it to. And then use me. Tie me down if you like. And I know you would like. Tie me down and hurt me. I'd love for you to hurt me. Write "whore" across my body and hold up a mirror to show me what I really am.'

I swallow. Hard. Now I really can't reply. This is so not like role-playing with Rex. This is a whole different planet of erotic.

'Do you like my body?' he asks, after a few seconds of dead air.

'Well,' I manage, 'what I've seen of it seems pretty, uh, pretty interesting.'

'Have you looked at my website? You have my card, right?'

'Yeah,' I say, although it sounds weird, more like yuh-uh. 'I mean, yes. I mean, yes I have the card. I haven't looked at the site yet.'

'Well take a look. You might find a few things on there that'll help you decide whether you want me or not.'

After that Mark says he has to go. It's kind of sudden, considering how atmospheric everything was getting, but apparently he has a client. I manage a respectable good-bye though, and then sprint for the kitchen in need of sugar.

Sadly my kitchen is a bit bereft. All I seem to possess on the sugar-containing front is a packet of weird wafer and marshmallow things that appear to contain absolutely nothing of any kind of nutritional value. Not very healthy-eating-plan-not-diet. I must have bought them when I was pre-menstrual, before I decided I was going to try and do the diet from *You Are What You Eat*. I come over all virtuous and take an apple from my groaning fruit bowl instead.

And then after a short hiatus for crunching and staring out of the kitchen window, I head back into the sitting room, because really, all this apple-eating has all just been so much time-killage before I do the thing I really wanted to do as soon as I hung up the phone.

I wander over to my not-at-all-swanky work station, which is a complete contrast to the huge monitor and thrumming tower that I have at work, and a long, long way from the slinky state-of-the-art machine I really want so I can follow my pathetically non-realised dreams about designing freelance.

But, although my crummy computer might not be a designer's dream, the internet connection works OK. Which means I am gawping at a whole screen full of images of Mark in just a few slow-downloading seconds.

Or, sort of. Actually the site is a bit of a mess. The design of the site is a bit, well, amateur. I hate to sound snobby, but it's got a super naff background pattern and the font looks so weird I think it might have corrupted. I can't help betting it would look horrid in alternative web browsers too. But I do manage to find the pics page. And once I do, I shoot out of work-mode pretty damn quick.

Mmm, and suddenly my desires for an extra large monitor increase about tenfold.

Staring at the images filling my screen right now, I realise I didn't really look at Mark properly last night. Oh, I looked enough to be dazzled by his divine beauty.

But that's exactly it – I was dazzled. Too rabbit-in-headlights to really see him properly. To get a good look at Mark one would have to stare at him continuously for quite a while, long enough to let one's brain adjust to the brightness. And it can be a bit hard to do that kind of blatant staring when faced with a real life person. Not to mention when one's sort of boyfriend is sat, like, right there too. But now I have pictures, not living breathing flesh to gawp at, and I'm blissfully alone. I stare hard at Mark's website images and in less than five minutes I know his body at least as well as that of anyone I have ever dated.

My very favourite of the very many website images are, in no particular order (because, really, there are some things in this world that it would be disrespectful – sacrilegious, almost – to put into a top five or something like that. Oh, who am I kidding, I have my top five worked out, right clicked and saved to my hard drive before the site has finished loading up properly).

Anyway, so, at number five, Mark in a pair of leather trousers. Yeah, that could be kind of cliché and boring, but it is saved by two strokes of genius – Mark's chest, which I can only describe – and pretty inadequately at that – as ripped, and Mark's expression, which is somewhere in the vicinity of coy, but with a very definite nod towards knowing. Kind of like, I know this is such a cheap shot – but I really do look fucking great don't I? That sort of expression. It works.

But, although I could dwell on that one shot all evening, I need to move on if I am ever going to get this list sorted out in my mind. I turn my attention to my number four. It's Mark in white underpants. Like a Calvin Klein pack shot. In fact so like a Calvin Klein pack shot it's probably a deliberate thing. Mark's face is cut off somewhere mid chin, so all that is in the shot is a pair of snowy white underpants, a pair of lean thighs, two pecs that look like two deliciously firm premium pillows – the type I wish I could afford (pillows that is, not pecs) – and a set of abs that look every bit as delicious as the six squares of Dairy Milk that they resemble. Mmm. Sugar cravings or not I think Mark's abs would just about squeeze out the chocolate in a what-I-would-most-like-to-lick-right-now competition.

At number three is the cock shot. Which had to be there, I guess, and is kind of nice. Certainly as nice as any artily lit black and white snap of a penis is going to be. It's a nice shape and a nice size and, although I really prefer the pics that include some face and some personality, it's in my top five because it's nice just to feel I've seen it, at this stage in our relationship.

At number two, well, this is when things start to get really interesting, because the last few shots I've chosen aren't just photographs, they tell whole stories. In this shot Mark is wearing his leather trousers and bare chest combo again, but instead of showing off his physique, he's sitting in a designer swivel chair (a bit like the one I sit in nine to five) and showing off a huge pair of big black motorbike boots. He's not showing them off to me, the viewer, or the camera, though, he's showing them to another man. The other man is crouched at his feet in a pair of jeans, and very clearly pressing his tongue against the leather. It's beautiful. It tells a better and more enthralling story than most of the films I have seen. And it's so fucking sexy.

And then I'm at number one. In a perverse way it's almost a relief to reach the end, like when you struggle through one of those interminable marathon count-down programmes on Channel Four. But I have to cheat. Because I still have two pictures than I simply want to marry.

In one of them he's on his knees, and, frankly, that would be enough, but there's so much more than that. To limit a description to just the barest facts – he's handcuffed and he's sucking another man's cock. I can't really say anything else about that picture – it wouldn't come out coherent if I tried.

The other image in the tiebreak for number one is every bit as stunning. He's tied to a bed, naked. Actually it's not really a bed, sort of a bed frame. All wrought iron – black and gothic. And he's lashed to it with the snowiest, whitest ropes. So the contrast is gorgeous. Even if the photo wasn't so unbelievably hot it would still be a pretty, pretty shot. But this way it's got everything. It's damn near perfect.

There's one more shot I save to my hard drive, the whole top five thing having now gone completely off the rails. It's the one from his home page. Just a close-up of his smiling face. Nice, simple, and probably my real favourite of them all. In fact, it's the only one I actually print off. And, although my scrappy printer – which wouldn't have enough toner if it were made entirely out of toner and thus usually turns out mottled patchy looking versions of my document – is handling the job, it prints this piece of black and white eye-candy perfectly.

I shove the pic in the back of my wallet, along with Mark's card.

Once I've shut my computer down and paced about the flat a bit, I realise I am going to need a bit of a release now if I'm going to go to sleep. It's lateish, I was on that website for a really long time, but I decide to take a really rather naughty way out of the tricky little situation I have created for myself.

I call Rex's mobile.

I can tell before he even speaks that Rex is in the pub. I can practically hear the smoke and old booze clinging to his denim jacket.

'Hey,' he says, 'you OK?'

'Come home, baby.' My voice is so husky. It sounds like it used to the morning after a hard night on the nicotine.

'Home?'

'My home.'

'Why?'

'Can't you tell?' Because surely it is obvious in my voice that I am practically rubbing myself against the furniture as I'm talking.

'Well,' I can actually see the naughty smile that is dancing across his lips in my mind's eye. 'Either you want me to pick you up a huge bar of Galaxy.' Long dramatic pause. 'Or you want me to come over and slide my tongue inside you.'

I'm a puddle on the floor, but I still manage to say, 'Bring the chocolate anyway, for afterwards.'

So poor old Rex ends up being a Mark Valentine substitute for the second night running. Or, twice in one day, using his own strange logic.

Later, as we sit up in bed, with him still wearing the black leather bondage cuffs round his wrists, and I put two squares of the chocolate into my mouth, I feel bad. In fact, I feel so guilty I almost tell Rex what I was thinking about while he was tied down underneath me and I was teasing his cock until he was incoherent. But when I look at him I know the blissed-out look on his face isn't just because his mouth is also full of chocolate.

So I say nothing.

6

It's nearly a week later. Bleeding Wednesday, in fact. Can't yawn and blame the start of the week any more, but not yet on the home straight. And never ever anything good on telly. Wednesdays are my least favourite weekdays.

At least they used to be before I started working here. Because here at The Fantastic Design Company Wednesdays are salvaged from the midweek gloom, by the fact that Dave-Steve-Ed has a weekly whole-after-noon-long Team Meeting. I don't go to it – there's no Sophie in team – because someone has to hold the fort, i.e. answer the phone. But I'm not at all precious about that, oh no, because it means that on Wednesdays I have perfect peace and perfect privacy, alone in the office. Just my outsized monitor and me. It's also the only time I get to choose what goes on the CD player, so my relaxing afternoon is made even more perfect for being scored by George Michael (with some almost imperceptible assistance from Andrew Ridgeley).

And things are cool with Rex. Actually, Rex has been a star. When I woke on Saturday morning the maga-zines were gone. Fantasies have not been mentioned once, except in the context of my bedroom – where it was strictly just him and me and our usual fun and games. So I can't complain. Well, if I were really trying to find complaints I could say that I wish we still had the magazines. Just in case I fancied looking at them some time in the future – when I've got over my stupid

Mark obsession, of course – which I haven't at the moment.

In fact my level of obsession is still high enough that I even found a few Rex-free hours over the weekend to re-visit Mark's website. Not to view the pics. No need with the shiniest examples safe on my hard drive (and backed up on CD, because I'm a bit anal like that – I'm neurotic enough to back up). No, I went back to Mark's site to look at the design faults. Because, as I'm a designer, when it comes to Mark's rather flawed website, I can rebuild it.

Of course I have questioned my motives in doing this. The part of my brain that had the audacity to claim that I was only doing this because I'm a professional and I have the skills and it would be a good challenge (and because someone as pretty as Mark should have a pretty website), has been forced to sit in a dark room with an anglepoise shining in its face until it collapsed sobbing to the floor and admitted the truth. I'm doing it because I think Mark might be impressed.

So, right now at my desk, on a miserable Wednesday (it feels like it's been raining for about a fortnight), I'm tinkering with Mark's website. Not with any of the dirty parts, obviously, not in my office, but with a few graphics and a layout that I worked on over the weekend and then emailed to myself.

It's the first time I've actually tinkered with Mark's website during working hours. Not actually through virtuousness, but simply because for most of this week I've just had too much on to fiddle about with anything extra-curricular. I've been working hard, hard enough that by the time the Wednesday afternoon freedom arrives I get to play. And even if a Dave-Steve-Ed comes back from his meeting suddenly and catches a glimpse of what I'm doing – no problem. Because what I'm doing looks almost indistinguishable from real work. It's the perfect crime.

I've made the site grey. It was black before. And black is so over for websites. Really, only porn sites are black these days, and even they are beginning to realise how crappy it is to look like a porn website – even if you actually are a porn website. In fact, Mark's site wasn't just black – it was black with a horrible sort of lacy ice-blue pattern all over it, which served only to make the site look like it had been designed by someone who's web design capabilities extended no further than using the Fill Effects button in Microsoft Word (which is probably the case). And, as if that weren't reason enough to jettison the vile background, it was also making most of the text headache-inducingly hard to read. The illegible look – also, so over for websites.

And Mark deserved better.

So, anyway, I've gone with a grey. Grey with khaki – for machismo – and a bit of pink – for that softer side. I'm really pleased with it.

I've also found the right font in our library. With me the right font is like the right shoes, it makes everything else fall into place. So all I need to do now is knit the whole thing together – make sure all the links work – and then add the finishing touches.

Mmm, the finishing touches. My favourite part. All the hard work done and just the flourishes and serif curls to add. In this case, the finishing touches are some very pretty graphics I've made using the images from the old site. I've taken the dirtiest pictures, but I've cropped and tinkered and tinted them so it's impossible to tell what they are, exactly. But there is a kind of erotic suggestion in each one. Just a hint. Which is kind of the mood I'm going for with the whole site. Utter filth, but only suggested. I'm having such a great time. I could work on this forever.

'Mark Valentine? Who's that?' Dave-Steve-Ed is standing right behind me. I don't know how he crept in without me noticing – perhaps he has been having secret SAS training, or perhaps I was so wrapped up in my work adjusting the colour balance on an extreme close-up thumbnail of Mark's jaw line to notice.

'Oh,' I say, my mind whirring to think of a quick cover up. 'Yeah. It's a new client.'

'Right,' says Dave-Steve-Ed, quite vacantly. It seems he has other things on his mind. 'Actually, Sophie, would you mind coming down to the boardroom. We'd like to have a chat with you.'

And, I suppose it's because I feel guilty about the fact I was skiving off, but I am suddenly filled with dread. It can't help but sound ominous can it? 'We'd like to have a chat with you.' I'm scared.

But, as running out of the door feels like a bad idea, I follow Dave-Steve-Ed down the stairs into the basement, where the meeting room is. It's nice down here. All pristine and white to impress clients. I take a seat at the big beige laminate table and smile nervously at the three over-familiar faces. I wish I knew what the hell this was about.

'Hi Sophie,' says Dave, which sounds weird. He talking like he hasn't seen me for days, when in fact we were chatting about a new DL leaflet only an hour ago.

'Hi,' I say. And then the other two greet me as well. So far, so bloody weird. Okay, most people wouldn't call this formal, but for us, this is pretty damn formal.

This can't be to do with Mark's website, can it? I mean, how could they know? Unless they are using some kind of freaky über-spyware to check up on what I'm doing while they're in their meetings. But no, it can't be that. Why would they do that? They, surely, have better things to do. And, besides, we're not that kind of company. We're much more – meet your deadlines and you can do what your like. Anyway even if they did know what I'd spent the last hour doing, surely that's just a bit naughty. I mean, they couldn't sack me for it. It's hardly gross misconduct. Right?

'Sophie,' Dave goes on, 'I'm sorry to drag you down here like this. I know you're as chock-a-block as anyone.'

'Actually, I'm okay today. I got a lot of stuff wrapped up at the beginning of the week,' I say, sounding surprising breezy, under the circumstances.

'Oh good. Well, that's kind of what we wanted to talk to you about.'

'Yes,' Ed chimes in, 'Sophie, how long have you worked here?'

'Six years.'

'Right,' says Dave. 'That's what we made it too. Now, Sophie, that's a long time. Don't you ever think about developing your career? You've been doing the same job for six years. That's longer than my Guinevere's been alive.'

And yet again Dave fails to complete an entire work day without mentioning his adorable yet annoyingly-omnipresent five-year-old, and apple of his ever-doting Daddy eye, Guinevere. Who is, it must be said, absolutely button cute, but I could do without quite so much Guinevere-chat, and that's without even mentioning the numerous times the little angel calls to speak to Daddy (baby-talk ahoy!).

But I digress. I was in the meeting room. Being talked at.

And I really have no idea where this is going. So, in answer to Dave's question about developing my career I mutter, 'Um, well. No, not really.'

'You see, Sophie,' says Dave (God, why does everyone keep using my name like that? It's making this even more surreal. In fact this is starting to be a bit like a dream I once had. Except in that everyone spoke backwards. And everyone was naked). 'Sophie, you've gained so much experience and your work is excellent. But, we can't really justify having you making tea and answering the phones. We could get someone straight out of art school to do that.'

'And pay them a lot less,' Steve chips in. Steve likes to think of himself as the straight-talking one.

I frown at them all. This seems to be it. I am now expected to make a response. But, I'm not exactly sure what to. 'Um,' I say, 'um, are you making me redundant?'

'Not exactly,' says Steve, 'but that is one option. If you like we could make you redundant, with a nice little package and everything. Enough to sort yourself out.'

My stomach goes sort of icy. I'm losing my job.

'Or,' Steve is still talking, skating blithely over the ice rink where my stomach used to be, 'there is another option, where you join us as company owners. Come up to our level – as a partner – and we employ a new "you".' (He actually makes those finger quotey things.) 'To keep things going on the telephone-answering, kettle-boiling, minute-taking front.'

I really want to explain that there's more to my job than that. I swear that that is what I actually plan to say, but what comes out of my mouth is, 'I don't take minutes.'

And Ed says, 'Someone who could take minutes would be good, actually.'

Dave slides a huge pile of paperwork over the table. 'Here are the details of both options,' he says. He's using a very gentle voice, probably because I must look a bit like I've just had a good slap round the face. 'It's kind of complex – how much you need to invest, what you would actually own. You should probably take it to your accountant or solicitor and take your time over the decision.'

'Right,' I say, not looking at the papers. Not even touching them.

'So, er, let us know what you want to do.'

I don't have an accountant, or a solicitor. Why would I? But I do have a Rex. Of course Rex is working up in London, but that's not a problem for a modern girl like me. I have the technology.

(Yeah, listen to me, making out I'm a super-cutting-edge-chick just because I own a mobile phone. It's not even a great mobile phone. It doesn't do photos or anything. It doesn't even play those ring tones that sound like a tiny and tinny symphony orchestra is trapped behind the keyboard.)

So I dash down the hill to The Level – a supposed park, which is actually more like a sort of overgrown glorified traffic island with added mangy grass and tramps. After a quick scout I find a bench that isn't too wet and slump down on it, already jabbing at the tiny rubbery keys.

'Well,' says Rex, after I've given him a quick and rather frantic update, 'it sounds like they're a bit strapped for cash, doesn't it? They need you to either bail them out, or quit so they can save your wages.'

'Maybe,' I say, a bit disappointed because I wanted Rex to say that they had obviously discovered how great I was and were so enraptured that they had simply decided to give me money and/or promotion. I have to confess that since coming out of the meeting and getting outside I've started to feel a bit better about this thing. Okay, the twin prospects – leaving and getting a new job, or becoming a partner in the company – are both pretty terrifying. But, it's surely a good thing. I mean, really.

Across The Level a bloke is shuffling along. He's glugging from a dirty brown bottle and appears to be dressed in ripped-up bin bags. He weaves from side to side as he goes. It's like he's a physical re-enactment of my brain – the way it's oscillating. It's like he's acting out what my brain might look like if my brain were a drunken tramp, weebling around like something from Dickensian times – well, a sort of imaginary, Dickensian, bin-bag-wearing, times. Anyway, as analogies go, he's not bad. Not that I actually need this physical manifestation to tell me that I can't make decisions.

'Look,' says Rex into my ear, 'we can't sort this out now over the phone, and you need to think about it, and talk to the proper people – you know, those with qualifications. Why don't we go out tonight? Take your mind off things. Pete's got an idea, apparently.'

'Mmm,' I say, still looking at the tramp, who is now lying down on the wet grass, collapsing into the mud like a pile of dirty, greasy rags. 'OK.'

7

That evening, I leave the flat, not even certain where I'm going. It's not like Rex has kept it a secret exactly, I think I've just been too wrapped up in my own thoughts to ask. We're already clopping down towards the seafront – well I'm clopping, it's the shoes, Rex is just walking normally – when I think to find out.

'Where are we going?' I pant.

'One of Pete's places,' Rex answers, shouting over the wind.

'So a gay place, then?'

'Well yeah.'

And then Rex turns right, onto the wind-whipped promenade, where it is about twenty times as cold and squally as anywhere else in town. 'Ahhh,' I squeal as a particularly vicious gust of wind manages to find its way under my hem and Rex grabs me and holds me close. We can't talk at all now because the elements are making too much noise.

This is nice. Snuggled up to my boyfriend on the freezing prom. We're walking towards one of the piers – the gaudy one. It's lit up like a Christmas tree, the way it is every night of the year, its bright disco lights reflecting in the monochrome sea. I snuggle up closer to Rex. This evening out has already taken my mind off things.

We trot down the little row of gay bars that seem to have sprung up recently, making the gayest district of Brighton rather more sparkly and obvious. It's all quite different here from the way it used to be way back when I first hung out round here with Pete. Ten years ago this little strip was still the jammy centre of the Brighton gay doughnut, but it was really little more than a few seedy dives, jazzed up with two big night-clubs. Today, it's all far more fashionable and brash. Great big glass-fronted, rainbow-flagged palaces line the road, tills ringing with Pink Pounds. People spill out into the street, laughing in the freezing, breezy cold – watched by the endless space of the sea.

We don't go in to any of the big glass-fronted places though, we dive up a side street.

'Where are we going...?' I begin again, able to make my voice audible now we are out of the howling gale. But the sentence drifts away unanswered into the night because Rex steers me across a dirty and rather nasty-smelling back alley and through the door of a tiny pub. Because the tiny pubs of ten years ago are all still here, buried underneath a flashy exterior now, it doesn't take a *Time Team* special to find out what lies beneath the gloss.

As we go inside the tiny old school pub, we both get looked at. Me for being a rather unusual and exotic gender (this pub really is that old school) and Rex because people do tend to look at him – even on a low key night out like this; he has weird looks, kind of like Bambi in an orange wig and some expensive urban casual wear.

I cough in the smoke. As an ex-smoker of over a year I'm already a terrible bore on the subject of how vile smoking is, especially when faced with a lung paralys-ing atmosphere like this.

As well as being too smoky, it's also loud in here. Possibly even louder than the seafront squawl. Except

that instead of screaming wind, the sensory depriva-
tion is being provided by the shuddering bass line of
some nasty house music. I squirm in the fug.

Loud and hot with fag smoke and fag flesh, and a
tangible air of eroticised excitement. Typical Brighton
gay pub, really. 'It's a bit busy,' I complain at Rex, as
we scan the room in a hopeless search for an empty
table.

Of course there isn't one, but there is a Pete.

Pete has managed to secure half a tiny round table
and two bar stools. It's not quite enough though, so we
are left with Rex crouched on the floor. But apparently
we have a great spot because, Pete points out, 'We have
an excellent view of the stage.'

'What stage?'

Pete and Rex both laugh and look pointedly over my
shoulder. I turn my head. And ha-sarcastic-ha because
right behind me is a huge stage that appears to be
bigger than the actual pub. The stage is dressed with
black satin, covered in twinkling stars. It could be
Sunday Night at the London Palladium, if it weren't for
the huge pink sash across the entire thing that reads:
The Cum Boys. I cringe. I cringe so hard I'm not even
sure if I'm cringing at the words themselves, the nasty
misspelling, or the vile cartoon penises that adorn each
end of the banner. I pull a face at Rex and Pete, who
disappoint me by not appearing to share my pain.
Hello? Messrs professional designer and professional
copywriter – aren't you appalled by that banner on
every possible level?

But it's too loud to really start such an involved conversation in here. And anyway, I don't get the chance
to try because the ear-bleeding music fades down as
the room slides into darkness. Whoops erupt, cat calls
and bassy hollering. The stage starts to twinkle. On the

stage, incandescent brash lights flash on and off, reminiscent of the bold colours of the pier outside. More music begins, this is even more throbbing and bassy and low than the standard gay-pub conversation staller that it replaced. But this isn't some dated house sounds, this is pure sleaze-on-a-stick music.

'Ladies!' barks the PA system, suddenly enough that the whole pub seems to startle out of its skin. 'Please welcome on stage, fresh from their world tour, The Cum Boys!'

Eight young men hit the stage to whoops of delight. I have to say they're a lot cuter and smoother than I was expecting. A bit of skilful repackaging, and a better bloody name, and I'd probably be delighting in them every bit as much as the rest of the testosteroned-up crowd surrounding me are. But every erotic pump and grind is ruined slightly for me as I catch another glimpse of that cringe-inducing banner.

Eventually I can take no more. I lean across to Rex. 'The Cum Boys?' I hiss in his ear.

'What? Don't you like them?'

'It's not that. It's the name. And, I mean, cum? C. U. M.? Bleh.'

Rex reaches out and clips me round the head – in a playful way that is, it doesn't actually hurt. But it's enough to make Pete look at us. Rex gives him a comical sigh. 'It's just what you said would happen,' he says in low and-yet-somehow-audible-over-the-din voice, 'she's complaining about the name.'

Pete leans over the table to me. 'Sophie, stop being so predictable. I told Rex you'd have a moan about that. It's just a joke, honey. It's ironic, you know, taking the piss.'

'But it's so – eurgh,' I hiss.

Pete laughs at me. 'Oh you love it really, watch the show.'

I take Pete's advice, feeling a little better now he has assured me that The Cum Boys are just having a little joke with me. The stage has changed a bit from when I last looked. My stool is in a crappy position, so I have to turn right around to watch the show (but the place is so packed I don't stand a chance of moving it) anyway, though, that meant that when I was talking to Rex and Pete I had my back to The Cum Boys' antics, which means I missed the change of focus. Instead of eight reasonably attractive young men, gyrating in neat formation, there is now just one. A really rather cute Asian guy with nothing on but a black jockstrap and a neat pair of sideburns, which make him look like an exotic and underdressed Elvis. He's obviously nearly at the end of a strip-tease. Other, rather random look-ing, clothes are strewn about the stage. I stare at him. He is actually rather lovely.

Suddenly Rex's dirty lips are on my ear. 'You like him?'

I nod. I notice for the first time that I haven't thought about Mark Valentine since, well, since the work bombshell. And what's more, I haven't thought about the work bombshell since I started staring at Mr Cutie-Pants. Considering how preoccupied I have every right to be right now, Cutie-Pants's achievement is really quick remarkable.

'You know,' says Rex, sounding deliberate and husky, so it ripples on my spine, dark and burry, 'they do private lap dances here. How about I buy you one?'

I don't really listen at first. I don't really take in what he's saying. But then, as the jockstrap comes off and the crowd go wild, I twig what he's talking about.

I turn in my seat, facing back around the proper way. And frown at him.

And although I'm still totally unconvinced, I nod my head, because I know that look in his eyes, and humouring him is probably the only way out.

Rex takes my hand and we manage to pick our way discreetly through the sardine-packed crowd. And it's lucky that we're so near the front, because that means we're not far from the discreet little door that leads to the backstage area.

As Rex leads me through and into a seperate curtained-off area, he seems to know exactly where he's going, which makes me wonder exactly how much of this he choreographed with Pete while they were brainstorming new ideas for shifting tea bags.

Through the swish of the curtains, the semi-secret backstage backroom is full of dark corners and dark doings. A couple of the performers from the stage are there, recognisable in the outlandish costumes they are half wearing. Each of them is conducting some kind of performance for a seated customer, dancing and gyrating in front of them. A further, overweight and sweaty looking man seems to be directing activities.

Rex approaches this Mr Big, while I lurk in the background, feeling very odd and out of place in this room with its heavy male atmosphere. I don't really want to let on, even to myself, how erotic I'm finding what I'm looking at. The men from the stage, dancing and performing like this. For other men. For money. It's as hot as my most persistent Mark Valentine fantasy, the one where I kidnap him and take him to the deserted basement. Well, almost as hot.

While I wait for Rex, I focus my over-stimulated attention on one particular couple. The dancer is a lithe, pale blond so delicately coloured, he's almost luminous in the under-lit room. When I first saw him, as I came in through the curtain, he was wearing the familiar shirt, shades and helmet of an American Traffic Cop outfit (the type that might only exist in porn and Village People videos as far as I know, the American Highway Code not being my strong point). But it's a few moments later now and the shirt is just a screwed up blue bundle on the floor as Blondie moves like a ballerina in just the headgear and his tiny white underpants. He moves closer and closer to his punter, straddling the seated man's shaking knees and thrusting his white cotton groin right into the man's face. I lick my dry lips and swallow hard.

And watching this, watching this is beautiful, but I really couldn't imagine myself sitting there, being the client in the chair. It feels wrong. Too blatant, somehow. Too literally in your face. It's not for me. Which is a shame, because suddenly Rex has finished talking to Mr Big and is back at my shoulder. 'The Asian guy's available during the second half. Fancy it?'

'I don't know,' I say, wrinkling up my nose to make a rabbity-yuk face, because despite the hotness of PC Blond, I really do have reservations about this. Observing the hotness from a little curtained corner is one thing, but actually being the one sat on the chair – I'm just not sure. This is close to my fantasy, but it isn't actually there. It's not close enough.

'Oh go on, honey,' Rex says, 'I can tell how much you liked him. You were practically drooling.'

'I wasn't,' I say. And I know I wasn't. The guy was very cute, but it takes more than a cute guy with a couple of delicious bits of facial hair to make me lose control of my bodily fluids. It takes a man like ... and that's when Mark Valentine manages to regain control of my brain. Poor, poor old Cum Boys, they can't compete really – not long term. Their groin-pumping schlock might be good enough for this crowd of beered up gay boys (and it really does seem to be) but it's not good enough for me. It's not strippers with a little sideline in lap dances I want. It's all or nothing. The real thing. And now I've seen what the real thing could be. Mmm, Mark Valentine.

Rex slides his arm around my shoulders. 'Go on, honey. You will love it. I swear.'

I'm starting to get a bit pissed off now. I blame myself, I should have nipped this in the bud before we even got in here, but somehow, I wasn't really thinking straight. Which isn't all that surprising given the circumstances. 'Rex,' I hiss, viciously. 'I said no.' And I push his arm off me sharply and flounce out of the backroom and back through into the pub.

Rex follows me, half-shouting, 'I just don't bloody get it, Sophie. I try and sort out something really nice for you, and you just moan about it – "it's too crowded", "the dancers have a stupid name". Fuck's sake. What am I supposed to do?'

I stop flouncing and turn to face him. 'I have no idea, Rex. I have no idea why you're doing this at all.' I'm sort of semi-shouting too now, which would be fine if the floorshow was still in full swing, but, all of a sudden, it isn't. The house lights snap back on, and it seems like the entire focus of the pub has moved from the on-stage spectacle to the me-and-Rex spectacle, happening just off to stage left. Shit – not fun.

'I just want to make you happy, dammit' Rex storms back, oblivious to the fact that the music has stopped and neither of us is holding the parcel – we are fast becoming the centre of attention.

I throw a glance at Pete in the audience, who seems to be enjoying himself. Not watching Rex and me embarrass ourselves – although he would really enjoy that too – but chatting to a dirty blond crew cut, who seems to have appeared at our table out of nowhere.

I look back at Rex. 'But this isn't making me happy. Not this, not the magazines. Not any of that. I was happy as we were. Completely. Or, at least, I didn't need anyone to come along and make me happy. I don't want this. Quite frankly it's freaking me out.'

And I'm sort of bubbling over with, well, I'm not sure what with. Not exactly anger, or anything as harsh and easily defined as that, but some kind of raw all-enveloping emotion. It's not really Rex. I mean, nothing he's done has really been so bad. It's probably more to do with latent stress about work and the strange ultimatum from Dave-Steve-Ed. But I'm far too emotional now to do the rational thinking that I would need to work that stuff through. The part of my brain that is trying to work on calm rationality quickly gets drowned out by the cacophony of whatever-emotion-this-is banging around inside me.

Rex looks at me. He looks sad. Sad and confused. Poor bloody Rex. 'Maybe I should go,' he says softly.

I swallow. I don't know why but there seems to be something a bit doom-laden about what he's just said. 'Yes,' I say, listening to myself talk as if it's not actually me saying it, 'maybe you should.'

And then Rex turns, struggles through the crowd of onlookers, and walks out of the pub. I don't turn to watch him go, but I hear the street sounds and the distant roaring of the sea, as the door opens and closes. I even feel the slightest brush of cold air, cutting across the sauna-like atmosphere of the pub.

An older guy standing beside me leans down so he can whisper in my ear. He's proper Old Guard, all white handle-bar moustache and leather waistcoat. 'Trust me, sweetie, you need to go after him.'

'I know,' I say. And I don't move.

8

The lights are going down again. And I notice I'm alone at the table. Pete has fucked off too, leaving me adrift. A fag hag without a fag – just a hag then.

As the second half of the show gets going the room suddenly seems stiflingly full again. I'm stuck where I am. All alone with my suddenly fucked-up little life. Things were so much simpler when I was thirty.

I watch the rest of the show, dumbly, just letting the endless clothed and naked antics seep into my eyes. This section is kind of filthier than before, at one point they even get people out of audience and slap them on chairs while they thrust in their faces. The whole thing is kind of weird, it is sexy, but it can't really decide if it wants to be just plain sexy or sort of campy-piss-takey-sexy. I suppose that is the dilemma of The Cum Boys; are they just for titillation, or are they a campy-comedy extravaganza? Who knows? I keep on watching the show, like a kind of erotic chewing gum for the eyes, until I'm in a sort of trance state, which means I can re-run that argument with Rex enough times that (a) I realise I was a complete cow to him, and (b) I realise that I've really, really fucked up.

By the time The Cum Boys are taking their naked bows, Pete has reappeared and is lurking sheepishly over by the toilets. Bastard. He's bloody well got some action from Mr Crew Cut.

It takes a while before the crowds part enough that he can weave his way over to me. 'Hi,' he says, his face giving it all away. Super smug and sated. And then he looks around, confused. 'Where's Rex?'

I bite my lip. Now that the second half of The Cum Boys show has basically been a chance for me to meditate on what a crap girlfriend I am, I'm really not looking forward to explaining. I know full well when something is my fault. 'Er,' I say, 'he kind of left.'

Pete and I know each other so well, that all he has to do is pull a certain face, and I know just what he means – what did you do?

'I didn't do anything.'

Pete rolls his eyes at me and then pushes off to the bar. So I get a few minutes' more brooding time before he returns and shoves a frosty bottle of something unnervingly green at me. I take a quick greedy slug.

Pete does another bit of wordless communication. This time his expression says, 'Now tell, really, what did you do?'

'I didn't do anything,' I begin, but then, before I can continue protesting too much, someone slaps the music back on – the thumping nose-bleed music we were treated to when we arrived.

Pete looks up, angrily. 'Oh fuck this. Drink up, babe, come on, down in one.'

So it looks like we're leaving. I throw my drink down my neck and get to my feet – all wobbly and suddenly really wanting a fag (and I don't mean Pete).

We wrestle our way out of the pub, narrowly escaping being crushed by the scrum, that descends like several pouncing birds of prey, as we vacate our precious table.

We both know where we're going to go. Off past the pier and over the road, a few yards through town and we hit one of our favourite all-time haunts. The Pink Elephant, a pretty little cocktail bar that is dear to our hearts, partly because it looks like someone's front room, with its mismatched sofas and table lamps and ethnic rugs, and partly because it boasts the most stunning views of the floodlit pavilion – which, as always, looks like a low-rent Taj Mahal, as built by Laurence Llewelyn-Bowen out of MDF and papier-maché, but mostly we love The Pink Elephant because hardly anyone seems to know it exists.

We're out of the gay village now. The Pink Elephant lies in another part of Brighton entirely. We've crossed the Steine – the big main road that slices Brighton in two, right through its cleavage, where the two hills that make up the bulk of the city merge.

The Steine is the locus of Brighton geography. I like to think it's a bit like a river – albeit a very ugly river made of traffic – but the way it flows right through the city, nestled in a valley, gives it a river-like quality, as does the fact that crossing it seems to have a real significance. A journey to the other side. The eastern side of the Steine houses a little corner of Brighton with a character and charm all of its own – Kemp Town, the pretty little residential area where I live; and there's the gay village – all the pubs and clubs that make Brighton one of Europe's Meccas for queer lifestyle guides. And then, over on the western side of the Steine is everything else, like theatreland, home of The Pink Elephant.

The Pink Elephant is full of grey hair, cravats and velveteen. Ironically, it's a million times camper here than even the most outré of the gay bars that line the seafront.

Pete grabs some drinks at the tiny bar, and then pulls me into a sort of booth where the music is soft enough (and we are shielded enough from the braying of out-of-work actors) that we can actually talk.

'Well, I don't know what happened back there,

Sophie,' Pete begins, 'but in a way I'm glad I got you alone.'

I laugh. 'What are you on about?'

'I just mean it's nice to see you without Rex sometimes.'

'Okay. I'll make him storm off more often.'

'No, I mean because I think I need to talk to you about Rex.' Pete looks at me a little strangely. 'You know he really loves you don't you, Soph?'

'Um, yeah.' Oh shit, I feel a bit awkward. I know I'm about to get a telling off. I sip my cocktail. It's one of those chocolatey ones that tastes like a milkshake.

'And you know why he's doing this?'

'Doing what?'

'Doing what, Sophie, do I need to shake you by the hair? You do realise, don't you, that most boyfriends wouldn't exactly embrace the idea of their girlfriend going on about how much she wants to hire a male prostitute. It doesn't exactly make him look good does it?'

'I suppose not,' I say. And, God, I've been such a selfish cow. That never really occurred to me.

'But not our Rexy, oh no. He's been pulling out all the stops to find a way for you to do it. Don't you wonder why?'

'Well I do now.'

'Because he knows something is holding you back from making a commitment to him. You've been together six years. By rights you should be living together by now ...'

'Well that's what he says.'

'That's what anyone would say. Sophie, you've been living the same life since you were twenty-five.'

'And what's that got to do with anything?'

'Rex, that's what. He wants you to move on. Sort your life out. He thinks that if you got this paying-for-it thing out of your system, well, who knows where it might lead.'

I'm a bit lost. I don't really make the connection here. 'Huh?'

'Remember, I spend all day with Rex – he tells me everything. Look, Rex's theory is that you are scared to take risks. He reckons if you took this one, something like, I don't know, moving in with him, would seem small time.'

'God, Pete.' I slam my glass down hard enough to cause a small chocolately slick on the brass and glass table. 'How much time do you and Rex spend discussing me, huh? I know you talked all about getting those magazines.'

'Maybe we did a bit. But why not? After all I care about you both. I want you both to be happy. And let's face it, I know we joked about it in Oregano's, but I really would be fucked if you two did call it a day.'

'Why?'

'Well, who do I drop? I mean, really! I've known you forever, babe, but Rex is my bread and butter. So please, for Pete's sake, be nice to Rexy. He loves you so much, but if you carry on like this, well, it's not like the boy doesn't have offers.'

'Oh don't be silly.' Because, its weird, even though Rex is my boyfriend and I, personally, fancy him more than, say, chocolate or breathing, I never think of anyone else fancying Rex. Call me over-secure, but he's such a goof.

Pete gives me a Wise Old Uncle look – which is always a bit of a worry. 'I know it's hard for you to see it after all this time. But remember what Rex was like when you first saw him. Remember what effect he had on you. And me for that matter. Remember the first time you ever saw him? When you saw him for the walking sex bomb that he really is.'

9

Ten years earlier

What does any normal 22-year-old want more than party invitations? And it's always special when it's an actual invite, rather than a phone call or a passing remark. So I delight in the stiff little card that pops through my letterbox, inviting me to my University six-month reunion (in that particular self-indulgent and prematurely nostalgic way that only an ex-art student can really pull off).

It's sad really, less than a year since graduation and I'm already thrilled by the idea of a reunion. Even though it's hardly a question of 'Where Are They Now?' when most of them still drink in the student union bar, but I'm still ridiculously over-excited and I start planning my spectacular-yet-casual outfit immediately.

The party is in a tiny flat so full of cigarette smoke it's like being in a 1980s pop video.

I spend a good deal of the first couple of hours trapped in a corner with a wannabe feature film director, wearing an eye-patch (is restricted eyesight a good look for film directors?). He spends most of this time explaining to me what Film Noir is, something I didn't want to know and, in line with my wishes, still don't know, even after a good ninety minutes of hearty explanation from Long John Silver.

Luckily, my best friend, and fellow alumnus, Pete,

who has been laughing at my pain for the last half hour, dives in (eventually) and saves me, whisking me off to a corner for some urgently needed therapy – i.e. bitching about the assembled company.

With well-practised speed, we segment the room into people who are doing better than us – who are either lucky bitches or slags who have slept their way into their plum jobs – and people who aren't doing as well as us – who are, of course, idiots who we knew would never make it.

We smoke at least twenty cigarettes each as the night wears on and our eyebrows start to ache from arching them haughtily. It's getting on for 2a.m. when we see him.

It's not actually a fancy dress party, but you wouldn't know it from the way most of us are dressed – it'll probably be a good few years before we really shed our art student skins – but, despite the exotic company, he's far and away one of the most watchable people in the room.

He's skinny. That kind of taut exaggerated thinness that some people call 'painful'. I don't know about that, though. The only painful thing about him would be if you were trying to sleep on top of him – I guess then he would be a bit boney and jabbing – but in the light of a couple of fire-hazardly-scarf-draped 40 Watt bulbs, he looks gorgeous. His skin and bone look is all super-model perfect angles and deliciously clean lines. But then, I like skinny. I like hip and collarbones that jut. Always have really. I have no interest in musclemen or even men that are in any way manly. I'm so down with the beta male. I like them fragile and delicate, almost as if a high wind (or a quick shove) might topple them over.

Now, as well as being skinny, this guy is also ginger.

He has hair that is practically carrot-orange and sits like a mop on his head. This would be a weird look on almost everyone, but skele-boy somehow carries it off. Don't ask me how – he must have some kind of super powers. An orange shock of hair and the pale freckly skin that goes with it. Yet somehow, he is the sexiest, most charismatic person in the room – no mean feat in a room packed with show-offs, bitches and prima donnas. And I think that – as well as looks – it might have something to with (a) the way he is dressed and (b) the way he is dancing.

To elaborate on point (a) first, he's wearing a white singlet and a pair of gold shorts. It's like he's an extra from *Fame* or something. And, as for (b), he's dancing like, oh God, that is so much harder to describe. I've heard some people say that white blokes can't dance, and with Rex that is sort of true, except, with his ghostly pallor it's almost like he's so white he's out the other side. He's so white he's beyond white. And, similarly, his dancing is so self-consciously crappy it's brilliant. It's a brand of dancing that is partly weird retro moves, partly overly self-aware geek-boy dancing and partly pure filth. I'm entranced. And once I start staring at him I can't stop.

Pete nudges me. 'Don't waste your time, petal, he is far too good looking to be straight.' Which is actually quite an odd thing to say, because the guy we're watching isn't really that good looking – not really – he's just oiled up with sexy charisma. But it's the kind of thing Pete tends to say anytime he catches me looking.

'Huh,' I sneer back at Pete, 'don't bank on it. He's far too cool to be gay.' And Pete gives me a kind of sly look back, because we have this kind of snipey conversation a lot.

But that's kind of where it all goes arse-shaped,

because I start jousting with Pete about whether there is any sense in the statement 'far too cool to be gay', and he's pulling other people into the debate, even though I am losing badly. And I so don't care, actually, because all I really want is to talk to the gorgeous red-haired guy, or at least stare at him some more.

But, by the time I am free from *The Debating Society Redux*, the red-haired guy has gone. And when I slip out into the hallway a little later, I see he's imprisoned in a corner by the Helter-Skelter curves of a black-lipsticked brunette. Dammit. But at least I was right about his sexuality. His lips are practically vacuum-sealed with the most womanly woman I think I have ever seen.

10

The second time I see Rex is a long time later. It's at another party, about three years later. But at this party things go rather differently. Partly because this time I'm a little older and a little wiser, but mostly because it's my party – and I'll shag skinny boys if I want to.

It's my twenty-fifth birthday. And, of course, I want a party. I want far too many cigarettes, far too much drink and far, far too many people in my flat. Which is why I tell everyone I invite to 'bring people'.

Turning twenty-five is about quantity not quality, I decide. I might be gutted about having to leave my early twenties behind me (and with them my last gasp of debt-fuelled student irresponsibility), but at least I'll go out with a bang and prove positive that I'm a popular girl.

My new best friend Kate – who I met when she got addicted to Garlic Black Olives and practically had to sell her soul to the deli where I work – seems to understand the kind of hordes I'm after.

'I've just started working in a new place,' she explains. And goes on to describe the sort of biblical-epic crowds I desire in some detail.

Kate does something freelance involving charities. (Or rather the not-for-profit sector.) It's actually a bit scary. She's less than a year older than me, but somehow she manages to look and behave like a proper grown-up, i.e. she does her hair and puts on make-up every single morning, even at the weekend! Maybe that is what ten whole months of being twenty-five does to a person.

In a cute little café tucked behind the North Laine, Kate is babbling on about some charity or other where she is currently doing something or other. I tune in and out, blowing on my blackcurrant tea (I'm on a pre-birthday health kick), which is still far too hot.

(I can never remember which worthy cause Kate is raising piles of loot for, but that's OK, because often Kate can't either.) Anyway, Kate tells me that this latest place, whatever it is, is very young and happening and full of with-it twenty-somethings who are all bound to be up for a party. What's more, lots of them are very eligible. Kate is very keen on eligible – it fits in with her whole young fogey vibe – she is the kind of woman who has been trying to get herself settled down with a nice husband since 1874.

'Invite them all!' I respond, with my blackcurrant-tea-scalded tongue only slightly in my cheek. And hey, why not? Because it's my party, and I'll invite far too many people if I want to.

So my party is looking all systems a-go-go. Pete has been round all day cooking up a storm in my tiny kitchen, I'm all loved up about being the birthday girl and things are even more special right now, as I am about to reveal to my Head Chef.

'I got that job,' I tell Pete as he stirs some kind of garlicky dip, which I have already dipped half a cream cracker in and know is ridiculously yummy.

'What? The proper one?'

'Yep, the proper, graduate, relevant-to-my-degree job. No more ladling out taramasalata for me,' I say, proudly, punctuating my statement by lighting a cele-bratory ciggie.

'Babe! That's great. I'd kiss you, but you might smell the jealousy on me.' (Pete, the poor love, is still working behind the bar in a nightclub while trying to get a foot in the door at one of the big London advertising agencies.)

I laugh. 'Don't be silly. You reek of garlic. I wouldn't be able to smell a thing.'

'So, tell all, what does it entail?'

'Well, it is mostly catalogues.' I make a derisive gesture with my fag, laying out catalogues is as dull as it sounds. 'But they reckon they're going to move into more exciting stuff soon. They were really interested in the illustrations in my portfolio and hopefully they'll be something in that area too. Oh, and answering the phone. And making the tea. In fact, I think they actually might want me to take minutes. They might have mentioned that.' I shrug. Put like that, maybe my job isn't quite so great.

'Can you take minutes?'

'You know I can't,' I say, flicking some ash into an empty mug on the table.

'Well, minutes or not, it still sounds like you're doing OK. At least you've got a foothold. If I don't get on the ladder soon I'll be past it. Advertising is a young man's game. No one wants a geriatric designer – no matter how skilful I might be with my felt tips.'

I scoff. 'What? Geriatric! At twenty-four?'

'It's true, babe. Last time I dragged my Design Book up to town I was practically offered a Stannah Stairlift. You need to have your finger on the pulse – not look like you might not even have a pulse any minute.'

I pout and reiterate, 'You are twenty-four, not eighty-four.'

'Twenty-five in six months,' Pete says, theatrically maudlin. 'The beginning of the end.'

And the conversation kind of grinds to a halt then, because I can't exactly continue swanking about my great job when Pete has brought his lack of a great job into the equation. So I grab another cream cracker and help myself to more of the yummy garlicky stuff until Pete yells at me to get out of his kitchen before I get fag ash in his vol-au-vents.

By the time the clock on the wall says Party Time, my flat looks amazing. Actually my flat does do amazing pretty well, being the first floor of a beautiful regency town house, with high ceilings and a balcony and gorgeous cornices and suchlike – it has so many original features I can barely fit in any furniture. This breathtaking beauty is, of course, balanced against a few negative points, like the fact it is one of Brighton's more eccentric flat conversions, featuring a shower in the bedroom and a sitting room that can only be reached from the front door by walking through that same bedroom. But I'm still lucky to have it. I could never have normally afforded something this size on my own, what with my up-until-recently crappy job circumstances, and crippling student overdraft. But I avoided flat share hell, because I got it cheap.

The landlord dropped the price. He lives in the flat upstairs and just sort of liked me. He's an old guy, in his seventies, maybe even eighty-something, so I think he likes having people in the house who'll look out for him. It's kind of sweet really. He's even gone away to visit his equally doddery sister this weekend to make way for my party. He knows it's my birthday so I'm pretty sure he did it on purpose – bless. (Actually it probably wouldn't have mattered if I had held the party with him in residence, the dear old thing is so deaf that he probably would have slept right through it.)

As far as soundproofing the other neighbours goes, I've invited the slightly weird guy who rents the rooms on the top floor. I don't know if he'll actually come. He's hardly ever in. In fact I only remember he even lives here when I fall over his bike in the entrance hall.

But it's Irene, the woman who lives in the flat downstairs, who is the biggest problem neighbour-disturbance-wise. She's not young enough to just invite along (although I did tell her she was welcome), but she's not old enough to retire to bed with a Bournvita and snooze through every last pumping beat. When I told her about the party she said she would be out in the evening. But she'll probably be back at closing time.

When I explain all this to Pete he laughs and tells me that a party isn't a party without at least one complaint about the noise.

Pete did the design for the party. He loves doing that sort of thing, so I've let him. He has 'conceptualised' (his word) an entire party experience: music, food and décor. Although I can't really see what the concept actually is. Unless lots of dips, lots of kitsch pop and lots of fairy lights counts as a concept. It looks good, tastes good and sounds good – don't get me wrong – but I fail to see anything deeper than that.

I don't complain though. In fact, I grin when Pete turns off the main lights leaving us in twinkling pastels, and says, 'Babe, this party is going to be so you.'

And it is, insofar as it was me that invited far, far too many people – which, concept or no concept, turns out to be the most notable feature of the evening. Only an hour in, getting from room to room already involves employing a sort of wiggly weaving walk. Any sort of mission is almost inevitably curtailed by at least five people along the way who it is impossible not to stop and talk to. The crush is such that I don't see Pete for hours. I don't run into a perfectly glammed-up Kate until nearly ten, although, being Kate that may well be just after she arrived.

She flashes me a lip-glossed grin. 'Hey, birthday girl. Look, I don't know if it's a good thing or a bad thing but just about everyone from my office seems to have come. It must be a slow Saturday for parties or something.'

'Nah,' I say, 'it's great.' Although I don't honestly know whether it's great or not to be holding a party quite so floorboard-strainingly rammed, but I know I'll remember this – so that's something.

'Anyway,' says Kate, 'I ought to introduce you to people, but I'm not even sure who I brought now. Some people even brought other people so even I don't know them all.'

'Oh God. Ka-ate,' I say. Making her name into two syllables is the best way to let her know I'm about to have a moan. Not only is it great shorthand, but she can't really do it back. Occasionally she has a stab with 'So-ho-phie,' but that just sounds stupid.

And so, with Kate suitably warned, I set my voice to whiny. 'I said everyone in your office. And that was one thing. But the friends of people in your office! People you don't know!' I raise my eyebrows at her, writing a mental Post-it to thank Pete for stripping my flat of anything of any value (sentimental or monetary) and taxi-ing it over to his place for the duration.

Kate chews her lip as a kind of apology. 'Sorry, honey, the invitation just got kind of, well, kind of emailed all over everywhere to be honest.'

I roll my eyes.

And I'd say more, but Kate appears to have brought a prepared speech. 'But I'll make it up to you,' she insists. 'I'm co-ordinating some great events in July. Big ones, with proper famous people. I'm working on a pop concert in the summer and I'll definitely need backstage help with it. I'll get you in on that one – you'll get to meet Take That!'

I frown at her. 'I think you'll find Take That split up about two years ago . . .'

'Boyzone then,' she interrupts, seeming annoyed that I'm not bowled over by her offers of clammy handshakes with interchangeable boy bands.

'Oh babe, it's alright, really,' I say, with a reassuring shoulder pat. 'There were far, far too many people here before your lot even arrived.'

Kate grins. 'Well I should at least introduce you to one eligible man.' She scans the room – her eligibility detector clearly on high alert. 'Oh, hang on, what about Rex,' she says, as her antennae home in on something and she waves into the crush. And I look up. And someone turns round. And it's him.

'Sophie,' Kate says, once she has snared Rex out of the throng, 'this is Rex. He's a friend of one of the designers in the office.'

Rex squints at me and says, 'Do I know you?'

And I say, and I must be a bit pissed to even attempt this one, but I say, 'Not yet.'

This time I really don't fuck about. For example, I don't suddenly find Pete and engage in a long debate about gender politics. I link arms with Rex, promising that I'll show him where the refreshments are, and drag him into the kitchen.

I ignore the five people who try and talk to me as I weave my way across the floor, because it's my party, and I'll ignore people if I want to.

In the kitchen we kind of have room to move. The music is quieter, and we manage to fight our way to the table and Pete's elaborate dips.

'Seriously,' I say, jabbing my glowing cigarette in the direction of one bowl in particular, 'I know a dip is just a dip, really, but that is fucking amazing'. Except – because, as suspected, I really am drunk – I say 'Mamay-ay-zing.'

Rex dutifully hoists up a loaded Pringle and tries it. His expression morphs satisfyingly from intrigue to full on yum-yum. 'Fuck!' he exclaims (Pete really is a good cook.) 'That's like – oh my God – I actually don't think there is an adjective to describe it.'

I laugh.

'Seriously. I'm a professional. If I say there is no such word then there really isn't,' he says, before putting a cigarette in his own mouth and taking the one from between my fingers to light it with.

'Really, what are you? A professional dictionary?'

'I'm a copywriter. You know, I write stuff.' And he makes a scribbling movement with his now lit cigarette. 'If there's a word I don't know it basically isn't a word.'

'You sound like Humpty Dumpty: "Words mean what I choose them to mean".' I say loudly, quasi-quoting from one of my favourite books.

'Yeah kind of.' Rex grabs another Pringle and takes some more dip. 'Except not, actually,' he adds, with his mouth full. 'And anyway I'm not really a copywriter so much as a wannabe. I just graduated and I'm trying to get into advertising or something cool like that – but it's really hard.'

(I file what Rex has just said away in my head. Even though I know the right thing to do here would be to introduce Rex to Pete straight away so they can both commiserate on the difficulty of getting a super swanky, well paid, expense account job with a top London Ad Agency – but I'm so not bringing Pete into the equation at this moment. Not when I'm doing so well with Rex. Also, there's another little line I want to explore right now. I just need to clear up one little thing.)

'You've just graduated?' I ask. 'How old are you?'

'Twenty three. I started late.'

God, that's a relief. I did a quick bit of mental arithmetic after Rex told me he had just graduated and, I have to admit, I was a little concerned. In fact, I was suddenly overcome by a fear that Rex would turn out to be only twenty-one or something and then, not only would I be continually having to hide this fact from Pete, I would also have to face up to the fact that he would have only been eighteen or so when I perved on him at that party three years ago. At least his semi-mature-student status puts him close enough to my age to allay any cradle-snatching jeers.

And my relief translates into a flirty smile. 'Well don't worry. I'm twenty five and I only just got my first proper design job. And I don't even have the starting late excuse. I've been working in a bloody deli for ages.'

'Oh, are you a designer? I really need someone who is a designer to be my partner. That's how it works apparently, you sort of need to be in a team.'

(And so now the introduce-him-to-Pete-already bells in my head have become bloody claxons. Pete has been telling me for ages that he needs a copywriter that he can gel with to be his partner and help him get a job.

But, dammit, I harden my heart. And I push on with my getting-to-know-you small talk.)

'So what are you doing right now?'

'Oh God,' Rex sort of laughs, 'you don't want to know. It's such a pathetic cliché.'

Somehow, in the kitchen crush (still not as bad as the sitting room crush, or the hallway crush – but getting there), Rex and I have been manoeuvred up against the wall. Rex is the one pressed up against the horrid yellow paintwork by the cooker, and I'm the one who's getting to loom towards him, nearly igniting him with my cigarette once or twice, when someone stumbles past without due care and attention.

And I think it's the positions we are standing in that make our conversation suddenly so strangely charged. I think that's what it is, because when he says that what he does is cliché, I say, 'Oh my God, you're a gigolo.'

I say it kind of quickly. I don't really know why I even say it but, when I do, something happens between us – like a weird sort of tacit agreement that things are going to get filthy at some point later. It's just there and gone, like smoke. But, even though we carry on talking about nothing and nonsense for a good while afterwards, that smoky-sparky whatever it was still hangs around on the periphery with a special smutty promise – intangible, but unmistakably there; a sort of sex aura.

'I work for a credit card company,' Rex says, saving us from the hormonally charged silence. 'I answer the phones on the emergency hotline, you know, the one people call when they lose their card.'

I wrinkle my brow in sympathy. My crappy deli job is, well, crappy, but this sounds soul-destroying. 'Is it awful?'

'Sometimes. I work with some cool people though, we try and make it fun.'

'What do you do?'

'We muck about on the phone. We see who can say the weirdest things to the callers and get away with it.'

I kind of smile. I know a few people with awful telephone-answering-based jobs and I've heard these kind of stories before – but I know they're always funny. 'Weird things? Like what?'

'Well, some people do impressions, but I can't really do a good impression, but I do quite often answer the phone and say "Hello, Ghostbusters!"'

'What?' I boggle. 'But what did the customers say?'

'Nothing. They'd just go "What?" and then I say the proper thing ... Nobody really listens. I've never been challenged.'

I take a sip of my drink.

Rex grins and goes on, 'But there's this one guy that works there, he does such a realistic impersonation of Alan Partridge that even if the odd intelligent customer does catch on, they call other people to listen to him and ask him to say "Aha!". He was practically providing a free extra service. They ought to have put it in their adverts as a benefit, not sent round snidey circular emails talking about the professional face of the company.'

And that's when Rex sort of tails off, because the big sparky-smoky sexual chemistry thing is making its presence felt again, and suddenly neither of us are laughing any more.

'Last time I saw you,' I say, with a slow, smoky exhale – almost drawling with drunken lecherousness, 'you were wearing an obscene pair of shorts.'

So, of course, this little conversational teaser leads to me having to tell all about the six-month reunion, where, I discover, Rex was attending with his girl-friend-of-the-time – the buxom brunette, who I later saw him with. Luckily for me that relationship is long dead.

And even more luckily for me: 'I still have the shorts,' Rex says, all super teasing.

'Really? God, I'd love to see them again,' I say, quicker than thinking.

'How much?'

'How much?' I repeat, sort of querying what he has just asked. My heart is in my mouth. I feel like he has just read my mind. Unlocked a fantasy so secret even I don't really acknowledge it that much.

'Yes,' Rex says, steadier than me but still a little wobbly, 'how much do you want to see me in them?'

And then it all goes a bit now-or-never. I think he's asking me to name my price. Yeah, okay, it could just be a sort of turn of phrase: 'how much?', but he's said it twice now, and it's the way he's said it too. Plus there's the way he reacted to my off-the-wall gigolo comment. Oh, and there's the other stuff – the unspoken stuff – the stuff around me having a great new job, the him having a really not so great job. Plus the age gap, almost imperceptibly tiny, but there nonetheless. All of which probably means nothing in terms of the figures currently on our respective bank statements, but suddenly seems to mean that I'm all powerful and he's still lowly. It's there. It's not much, but its enough.

I pick up my glass, which is resting on the top of the cooker, and take a long drink of Pete's special birthday punch.

'Are you asking me to make you an offer?'

Rex cocks his head. 'Well,' he says softly, 'I need to get my car fixed and, to tell you the truth, that job I was telling you about, the phone answering one, I kind of got slightly sacked.'

'What? Because of all the arsing around?'

'Oh no,' Rex scoffs, 'I just never turned up on time.'

'Oh.'

And then, just as easily as our charged heat dissipated, Rex brings it right back again. 'Yes,' he says distinctly, 'yes I am, asking you to make me an offer, that is.'

And I say, 'Why?' Because, really, what else can I say?

And this is where the magic happens.

I can actually see Rex's mouth go dry and his green eyes turn dark – a pretty sort of mossy colour – as he says, 'Do you really want to know?'

'Yes.'

He wets his lips with a tiny and probably unconscious gesture. 'It's actually nothing to do with my car or anything, not really. It's just, I thought it would be really sexy if a woman paid for me. Like, bought me.' He shrugs. He's embarrassed. It's nice. 'And I have no idea why, but I kind of think you'd like that too.'

I feel the hairs on the backs of my arms suddenly all stand up on end as I realise that he's turned on by the idea of being paid for as I am by the idea of paying for it. And God, there's nothing like that kind of mutual compatibility: instant goose pimples.

I look down at my suddenly uninteresting glass of punch and realise I don't really want to drink it any more. In fact I don't want to dance or chat or smoke any more. I don't want to be at this party any more.

'Rex,' I say, 'let's go.'

'What?' he says, a kind of bemused confusion breaking through his obviously turned-on/drunken haze.

I look at him. He looks all fuzzy, like maybe he's gone a bit out of focus. Which might be because the bit of my brain that works focusing has been suddenly paralysed by lust.

'What would you say,' I say, with a deliberate attempt at sobriety, 'if I told you that I was as keen on that idea as you are? Possibly keener, because I really can't think of anything hotter than the idea of paying for a man, of buying him, owning him.'

'Really?' says Rex, his voice sounding sandpaper rough. 'I didn't realise you were some kind of pervert. I thought you were just some friend of Kate's who was having a birthday party.'

I smile. 'That's just my cover story.'

'Right,' he says vaguely, and I think that he might be suffering from the same lusty lack of brain function as I am. There really is only one cure for this sort of thing.

So we go. We just up and leave the party. Even though it's about the rudest thing I could possibly do. Even though there are people back in my sitting room who I have promised I will talk to – a few even got Brownie's Honour. Even though Pete will kill me.

We go, because it's my party and I'll leave and go to Rex's place and enact a bizarre sexual fantasy involving envelopes full of cash and shiny, shiny gold shorts, if I want to.

And I do want to.

11

Rex's place isn't far. It's just down from the station. It would be about twenty minutes' walk. And normally I would walk that, but we flag down a cab, partly because it is very cold and partly because I don't want to have twenty minutes of sobering fresh air to change my mind. So it's not until we're speeding away, and Rex has told the driver his address, that I realise what I am doing. It hits me, like a post-flirtation hangover.

'Oh fuck,' I say, very softly.

Rex grins and swings a long arm around my nervous shoulders.

'You've got regrets!' he laughs. 'Look on the bright side, babe. At least you're not currently having to worry about whether you can still get into a pair of shorts you haven't worn in three years.'

And I picture those long pale legs and tiny gold shorts. And I laugh.

We make a short stop at a cashpoint on the way, so by the time I arrive at Rex's house I can pay the cab driver and have a little pile of ten pound notes for the adventure to come. It's basically all my birthday money. I'm not sure what my various great aunts and second cousins would think about the way I am choosing to spend it this year – but the cards always implore me to get myself something I really want and not just put the cash towards rent and food.

Rex's flat is not as nice as mine. It's just a studio – a bed/sitting room with a little kitchen off it.

Once I've got my bearings, I start to feel a bit one-night-stand awkward. I'm on his turf and I shift from foot to foot as he quickly slips on a CD and then begins to rifle through a bashed-up looking chest of drawers. He doesn't say anything. I suppose there isn't very much to say. We both just want to rush through this bit of awkward stage setting and get to the main event.

Mercifully, it isn't long before he grabs what he is looking for – a tiny rag of gold fabric – and dashes for the bathroom.

And when he emerges he's dressed in nothing but the tiny shorts and his equally tight white vest. He looks exactly like my treasured memory of him at that party three years ago.

I've been in his kitchen while he was changing and found a couple of bottles of beer in the fridge. I offer him one, and he accepts in a slightly shaky sounding voice that makes me feel all twinkly with excitement. He seems a little shyer now, perhaps because he's so very, very underdressed, and I take up the slack, feeling a little bolder. And I like the sea change, I like it a lot.

We both drink the beer for a bit, listening to *Portishead* and our own nervous breathing. I'm semi-recumbent on the sofa and he's standing so close he's almost between my legs. I look at up him and our eyes lock for a little while.

And then it's like we both remember why we're here – why we wanted this. We both seem to relax again. In fact, Rex starts to get right into it. He moves a couple of steps away from me and with a slow hip shake, starts to dance around, milking the ridiculousness of his outfit for all it's worth, with dumb little Adonis-type poses and saucy bum wiggles. Oh, that dancing. Even to moody-ass trip-hop, it works just fine.

And, despite this pantomime silliness, I don't find the shorts ridiculous at all, well, except that I do find them ridiculously sexy, if that counts. From the back he might as well be naked, they cling to his arse so tightly – making it look rather like a Quality Street – only even more appetising.

They leave absolutely nothing to the imagination, and Rex is quite definitely erect as soon as his nerves slide away and he practically offers himself up on a plate.

He finishes his dance by sprawling over the garishly duveted single bed, propping himself on an elbow.

'What do you want me to do?' he says. His voice sounds rougher and throatier than it has all evening, and his eyes – which seem to look so much greener now he is semi-naked – are glassy and soft focus.

'Huh?' I say, because I'm not very with it, having just moved house to stare-at-Rex–ville.

'You're paying. You can have anything you want.'

When he says this I feel all fizzy inside, like sparks of energy are rushing around inside me. So, although in another time and another place I might have just said, 'I thought I just agreed to pay to see the shorts,' or something else equally flip, I don't. Instead I say, 'I know. I own you,' in a very soft, but rather husky sounding voice.

'Perhaps you ought to pay now.' He writhes back against the bedclothes, looking like he's going to be worth ten times as much as I am planning to give him.

I pull my birthday money out of my purse, wishing I really had a brown paper envelope or something equally sleaze-suggesting. He's panting so hard as I put it on his bedside table. God, I love that.

And finally, it's time to unwrap my birthday present.

* * *

It would be wrong to say our first time is great. I still have the kind of orgasm that feels like it's going to split me in two. But it isn't perfect. It isn't like something from a film or anything like that. It's clumsy and fumbling and very, very out of control.

I don't know quite why. Too much drink. Too much excitement. Too much expectation. But it is all over far too quickly. And it's all a bit of a mess.

Suddenly, I'm on top of Rex, scrambling for knee room on the tiny single bed, and he's underneath me panting and writhing, fighting his way out of the tight shorts. I reach down to help him and all but rip them off his snake hips in my frantic hand-over-hand rush.

My jeans are already off although I don't remember when that happened. Rex is pushing up my teeny-weeny *Spice Girls* T-shirt and I'm tangling his hair with my hands, pushing his face against me.

And I know because I feel it, deep down somewhere sober inside, that this is all happening too fast. That I'm not going to last an anywhere near satisfying amount of time. But it's too late, because Rex is sliding inside me and I'm already starting to see stars.

'You know what they say,' Rex whispers, just moments later, as I collapse on top of him, and we form one sweaty sticky blob on the bed.

'Huh?' I say, because, apart from anything else, I'm not really with it.

'Poor dress rehearsal – fantastic first night.'

And it's testament to how much Rex speaks my language that I understand just what he means.

A little later, a little more sober and a lot more controlled, we try again. We press against each other in the dark, moving our mouths over each other, finding new places to explore. And once I feel like I know him inside out, like every contour of his musculature is patterned on my lips and tongue, I climb out of the bed and move over to the sofa, settling down with a cigarette, so I can look at him.

There's very little light in the room, just the streetlight coming through the ill-fitting curtains. Rex lies on the bed and gazes at me, lusty and wanton. The pile of notes still sits on the bedside table. It's the perfect tableau, like a scene from a particularly atmospheric fantasy.

His naked body seems to fulfil all the promises made by his clothed one. Yeah, he's rangy and skinny, but it's the sexy kind of skinny. He has the neatly shaped shoulders I hoped for, and the delicate pelvis. His hip bones protrude lickably under pretty pale skin.

And although I can't see it right now, because he's on his back, but I just know – mainly from close observation of him while he was wearing those tighter than tight shorts – that he has one of those tiny little non-bums that all but vanishes into the tops of his legs.

'Rex,' I say, my voice strange and echoey in the sexual stillness, 'I want to tie you up.'

Rex doesn't say anything, in fact, from his expression he looks like he might not be able to say anything. But I wait for a response, hoping that his freeze-frame is due to being turned on, rather than horror. And then my patience is rewarded when he nods, gently.

Once I've regained the use of my limbs, I climb up on the bed fully clothed and straddle Rex's naked body, feeling his erect cock press against my crotch as I lean down and kiss his pretty pink mouth. I've never tied anyone up before. And, although I've fantasised about it an awful lot, I've never quite wanted to do it in real life quite as much as I do right now.

I have to scrabble around to get enough bondage material from Rex's flat. Two ties – one navy blue and one dark green – secure his wrists, twisted round the headboard with random and impromptu knots that Rex assures me feel secure. I use a belt to fix his ankles together – I'd prefer them spread, splaying him wide, but the single bed doesn't really have the room for that. I fix his bound ankles to the bed end with Rex's dressing gown cord. The final result isn't going to win any prizes for aesthetics, but when Rex twists and shifts and promises me that he really can't escape his predicament, I don't care about how amateur my bondage looks at all.

I start by straddling him, using my tongue to flick and lick his face as he turns his head, moaning, trying to capture my mouth with his. But I only stop for the most flighty of kisses before I'm sliding my lips down his alabaster chest.

I bite his nipples, feeling his cock harden underneath me and rocking down onto it – meeting his growing arousal with my own. I move slowly down his helpless body with my mouth. I lick and bite and caress his stomach, hips and thighs, hard and soft, over and over, before finally letting my mouth flicker onto his cock. He strains at the ties around his wrists, pulling hard enough to make the headboard creak, as he tries to lift his head up enough so that he can see my lips closing around his cock. I suck and tease and lick him until he stops struggling, until he has stopped straining and is lying back in his bondage, soft against the pillows, almost delirious. And then I stop.

He starts, his eyes snapping open, forced back to

reality by the sudden lack of warm pressure around his cock. But before he can say anything I'm scooting back up his body, repositioning myself so he can't say anything, so his world is suddenly full of nothing but me.

I lower myself onto his mouth, facing his feet so I can look at his long, confined body, and shift a little so I find a way to be comfortable, bracing myself against the wall behind me. I feel his tongue instantly, drifting softly across me and I gasp and tense my thighs. The pressure from his tongue grows almost immediately. And his hard cock is pointing right at me, jutting and luscious. I take hold of it and stroke him firmly, matching my rhythm to that of his tongue, as he rushes me up to a peak.

I cry out when I come, and fall down onto his chest, still clutching his cock, which spasms against my hand as I hear his now liberated mouth cry out, matching my calls, as we buck and writhe together on the tiny single bed.

A good first night, indeed.

The next morning brings several obstacles. First there is a slight awkwardness about whether or not we really meant for Rex to keep my money. I can't really afford it, but I sort of want him to. And I can tell that although he doesn't want to keep it – thinks it wouldn't be right – he sort of wants to too, because it's sexier that way. In the end we manage a sort of compromise of giving it to Oxfam and I stuff it back into my purse, meaning to stop off at the shop on my way back home.

(I don't actually – the money ends up knocking around in my purse for a while, and then stuffed in a conscience-pricking jar on my mantelpiece for the next six months.)

That negotiated, I then have to take my leave of Rex:

unpicking your way from a one-night stand is never easy.

Even though he has no net access, I leave him my new work email address – I haven't had an email address before and the novelty is quite exiting ('no, not "at" the word, the symbol at, the a in the little circle,') – and we also exchange numbers. It's a little awkward, a little clenchy, but its really nothing compared to the living nightmare that awaits me when I get back home.

My flat, though not actually trashed is in a pretty sorry state that will take all day to fix. And right in the middle of the chaos, just as I expected, an angry Pete is lying on my sofa, watching Sunday morning cartoons with an expression of deadly rage across his face.

My first attempt at explaining myself begins: 'Remember that reunion we went to, six months after we left University?'

But Pete is having none of my meandering explanations of why I just had to leave his fully conceptualised party and shag some Blast from the Past. He's not even looking at me, craning around my glittery, Girl-Power torso to see day-glo anthropomorphic animal things slap each other around. I'm losing badly. But then I remember my Joker and realise what a special card I'm holding in my hand.

'But I did it for you really,' I say. Pete still doesn't look up. 'Well, okay only partly, but it's a bloody good part. He's a copywriter, just graduated, wants to get into advertising. He needs a designer to buddy up with.'

And then Pete finally looks at me. 'Oh right,' he says, his voice so dripping it's practically a sarcasm bukkake. 'So you thought you'd go and sleep with him as a way of introducing us?'

'No, I did that because I wanted to. But it was my

birthday. And, look, I've got his number – do you want it or not?'

And Pete gives me the most grudging sort-of-smile I think I have ever seen. 'Okay,' he mutters, 'I 'spose.'

But it is sort of working. He is sort of thawing. A creative partner is the number one thing he wants on his wish list, well after a ten-inch penis and a hard-bodied man attached to another ten-inch penis. I smile that sort of placating smile that I've seen other people do but never really tried myself. I'm not convinced it will help.

And then, when Pete gets up from the sofa and gives me a hug, I'm so relieved I actually start to cry. Which I think Pete is secretly rather pleased about.

12

Six years later – in The Pink Elephant Cocktail Bar, Brighton

So yes, Pete is right: Rex = the hotness. But that was then. I can't help it if Mark Valentine is all new and sparkly, and confusing issues by having eaten my brain.

And, perhaps that's just it. Maybe the Mark Valentine obsession is happening because I just have an insatiable appetite for new and sparkly right now. And maybe one of these weird-ass paying-for-it options – the magazine boys, the lap dances – that both Rex and Pete (and Mark) seem so keen to press on me would fulfil that.

So, perhaps they're right. Perhaps I need to get this fantasy out of my system so I can settle down like a good girl and not always be looking over Rex's shoulder for what ever else might be coming along. That seems to be what everyone wants me to do. Hey, it might even solve my work crisis too! (Well, it won't actually make it any worse, which might be the best I can hope for.)

The problem with saying yes to what they're pushing is, of course, the extra factor. The Mark Valentine factor. The thing Rex and Pete don't know about. While they're pushing the make-your-dreams-come-true line, they don't realise my dreams have changed. My ultimate fantasy has mutated in the short time since I slurred it over the table at Oregano's. My ultimate fantasy isn't to have sex with a male prostitute any more, it's to have sex with Mark Valentine. I still have that same reservation – the one about whether this fantasy really ought to be acted out or not (even though I am the only person alive who seems to even consider the fact that this one should stay in my head), but Mark Valentine it must be. Which means Pete is so barking up the wrong tree right now. He's in a whole other forest.

'See, I have this idea. Maybe if we took Rex out of the equation.'

'Hmm?'

'Well, maybe that's the problem. Maybe you don't want to have a lap dance bought or call a guy from the classifieds if Rex is right there peeking over your shoulder. Maybe you need to put Rex over in one box, put this, shall we call it a "bizarre obsession", in another, deal with it and move on.'

'When did you become Raj Persaud Jnr?' I say, because it is all getting a bit daytime television now. I can see myself on *Trisha*. God, the caption could even be: *You want to pay men for sex – but what about Rex?*

'Soph, babe, I've got this friend . . .'

And this is where Pete plays his Joker. But timing was never his strong point and, unfortunately, he plays his about a week too late.

Pete's friend is called Wolfie. Or, to be accurate, he calls himself Wolfie. I could be generous and assume his given name was Wolfgang, but let's be realistic, it probably isn't. And, anyway, the real fact is, his name isn't Mark Valentine, now, is it?

We finish our cocktails quickly. Looks like I'm not going to get to relax over a drink once tonight. And then head off on a barely discussed, but tacitly agreed mission to meet Wolfie. Or not-Mark-Valentine, as I have renamed him.

He lives on the other side of Brighton. The dirty part. The part too far out from the sea to get washed clean by the squally breezes and the exfoliating salt air. The part where Pete and I once rented a very nasty house as students. Far enough from where we are now, in both space and time, that we definitely need some transport.

We scuttle through town to the taxi rank, nestled just off the main road on a wide street of sodium-lit cobbles.

There's a lot of people waiting – mostly very straight-looking young professionals – but there's also a long line of cabs, all looking toothpaste fresh in their minty turquoise and white Brighton livery. We join the end of the line and then shuffle forward as the taxis stop-start, loading their customers in strict order – even though there are clearly enough cabs for all of us, the system must be maintained.

I smile to myself when the allocation system delivers Pete and me the roomy splendour of a traditional Hackney Carriage – they always make me feel a bit special. Sprawling across the backseat in a slight haze caused by my speed drinking of one dolly daydream of an alcopop and one chokka-mudda-lots-of-vodka, I look up at Pete, relaxed next to me, and I smile at him.

Of course, like any girl anywhere with a gay best friend, I have taken the time to consider whether if Pete were, say, struck by freak-lightning and turned into a heterosexual, I would consider him marriage/boyfriend/shag material. And, I do have to say, it would probably be a no. Well, a no to the marriage and the boyfriend, although possibly not to the shag – just for curiosity's sake really. Although I'm not really sure what I'm curious about exactly. I probably know more about what Pete's like in bed than most of the people he has actually slept with, because Pete, bless his little cotton self-obsession, doesn't hold back with the details when he's got some.

So, yeah, pretty sure I don't fancy Pete – not enough to actually do anything (if he were available, obviously) – it's just sometimes, I don't know, he just has such a beautiful mouth.

I like mouths. I like everything to do with them. I like my own mouth a lot. It's my best feature – kind of pouty but not too pouty. Generous, but not so generous that it looks as if I've had pig's bums (or whatever it is they use) injected into it. I like my mouth. I like putting things in my mouth. I like eating, I like kissing, I like talking. I guess that's what would be called an oral fixation – well I'll put my hand up to that.

And I like men's mouths too. I like men who know how to use their mouths. Men who know how to kiss and how to lick. How to talk dirty and how to twist their tongues inside me. I like men with pretty mouths, who aren't afraid to soil their cupid's bows with dark words and dark places. Who show their teeth and tongue when they talk. Who lick their lips when they eat. Who let you know exactly what they will be like in bed just from the way they drink water from a sports cap bottle.

Dirty men with pretty mouths. So, although Pete is about four hundred per cent more geeky looking than Rex – with his limp blond hair and his Milky Bar Kid glasses – and even though I have given this issue time and thought and come to my decision, there are times when I look at Pete, especially from unusual angles like this, and I do think he's kind of sexy. Just because he has a great (and filthy) mouth.

So I smile up at him, as the taxi slides up the Steine away from the sea, away from Brighton's version of the bright lights and into a world where the seagulls are still allowed to scatter rubbish across the streets and the only bright lights around are the ones burning in the 24-hour convenience store.

The dirty door to Wolfie's flat is squeezed between an Indian restaurant and a crumbling betting shop. Pete leads me through it. The door isn't locked or anything, it just swings on its hinges at a push, revealing a dirty communal corridor, which is littered with old betting slips and unmentionable nastiness. The corridor is pitch dark, and I have to hold on to the back of Pete's puffy bomber jacket as we fumble our way into the unknown.

Another door, at the other end of the corridor, opens into a small courtyard, where not-very-clean-looking washing hangs dripping on a line, and clangy-bangy metal steps lead up to the flats that are over the betting shop. As settings for sexual fantasies go this is about as unglamorous as it gets – short of meeting my whore-to-be in an abattoir.

It isn't until Pete rings the bell that I even wonder about Wolfie's reaction to a couple of semi-strangers tipping up on his door step just after closing time, because they want to meet him. And I'm suddenly sober and biting my dry lips as my easy-come-easy-go alcoholic haze starts to fade, leaving me with a horribly what-the-fuck-am-I-doing reality check.

Oh dear. This really can't be going anywhere good. In fact, I'm about to make an excuse – pretend I feel ill or something, anything to get out of this situation. But I miss my chance because, before I speak, the door is opened by a delicious vision in navy blue towelling. And I suddenly reassess the situation.

In fact I have to put my hand over my mouth when I come face to face with the inhabitant of the towelling dressing gown, because this is very, very much more than I was expecting. Wolfie is beautiful. He's Venus as a Boy and then some. He's a perfect shimmering pearl, lurking here, unclaimed, in a sea of old betting slips and dirty washing and the smell of discarded takeaways. And all that, that miasma of everything that is wrong with the world, that seemed to be strewn around him just makes him all the more breathtaking. He's like the prince, waiting at the end of an adventure story, after all these trials by urban terror – well, OK, a bit of a nasty corridor – I have finally reached my reward.

He's a dreamboat.

Well, dreamboat might not be quite the right word. He's a kind of scuzzy kind of dreamboat. All dirty blond hair and dirty boy smile.

Actually, on second thoughts, dreamboat is so the right word for him.

'Hey,' he says, kind of vaguely, and then he points at Pete and says, 'uh, Pete, right?'

Pete grins. 'Hey, Wolfie, you remembered.'

Wolfie shrugs and ushers us through into his little kitchen, which is right inside his front door. We pick our way through this tiny crockery-cluttered space and then into a little lobby area, which has a flight of stairs off it, a nasty bathroom with a bright pink suite, and a sitting room, which is where we are headed. The sitting room is small, but not as small as the other rooms we have encountered so far. The furniture is horrible to look at – black leatherette with coloured cushions – but perfectly comfortable.

We relax into it, as directed by Wolfie, and, once we are sat down and mildly distracted by the portable telly in the corner muttering out one of those Channel Four Top One Hundred Something-Or-Other Shows, I actually feel rather at home.

Wolfie, despite his kindly gesturing for Pete and I to take our seats, is still standing in the middle of the browny-orangy patterned carpet. 'Well,' he says, brightly, 'would you mind waiting a while? I have a previous upstairs?'

I'm slightly shocked out of my skin by this statement. Paid-for-sex, my number one fantasy, is actually going on right here, right now. In this very flat. I can't speak.

Luckily Pete is less dazed. 'Right, yeah,' he says, taking his turn to play the vague person in the room as he half-heartedly watches the subliminally quiet television and gives Wolfie a blithe hand wave.

And then Wolfie is gone and Pete's giving me a look. A look that seems to be saying, 'Well?'

I shrug. 'He's gorgeous.'

'See. And he's nice. So what do you think?'

'What do you mean, what do I think?' I frown hard. 'You said you had this friend who sometimes did a bit of escort work on the side. You said you thought it would do me good to meet him. Well here I am meeting him. Uh, he's not quite what you said, is he? I mean, either it's a huge coincidence that we've arrived here while he's got someone upstairs, or this is rather more than a sideline for him.'

'Well, yeah, fair point. Actually, I don't really know him very well. Sorry about that.'

'Don't worry. He's very, well, he's very pretty. And, I

have to say, it's sort of interesting.' I feel my cheeks flush a little. I'm a bit embarrassed about how much I am turned on by the idea of Wolfie. Not the idea of actually doing something, not at this moment anyway, but just by the idea of him. The fact he exists.

And it isn't until that moment that I even ask myself the question. That I even begin to wonder how Pete met someone like Wolfie, and start to realise that there might be a sex story from Pete's life that I am yet to hear. And that it might be one that I am really, really going to like.

I look at Pete and he looks at me. He knows the look I'm giving him. He knows he has to tell me all.

13

'Do you remember my twenty-fifth birthday?' he says eventually.

'Yours, um.' I rack my brains for a minute, and I'm a bit ashamed to realise that I can't. 'No. I mean I remember mine. The party. Rex.'

'Mine was six months after that,' Pete says, 'and the reason you don't remember it is because . . .'

'Because it was around the time I'd just got together properly with Rex,' I say, interrupting partly because at least it sounds a little better if I say it myself.

Sad, but true. That was how it went. When Rex and I hotted up, Pete and I practically froze solid.

It didn't happen straight away. There was loads of pussy footing around after the party. Rex and I danced around each other for ages, playing games, loving every minute of being on, then off, then on again. But the thing that made this game playing really great was the fact that it didn't quite have that Do or Die desperation of most embryonic romantic relationships. It didn't have that cold-sweat edge that one clumsy fuck up could blow this forever because, about a month or so in, Rex and Pete were already working together as a creative team, their working lives already hopelessly entangled – practically married. So I always knew all roads would lead to Rex. We didn't have to have any clenchingly embarrassing conversations about next dates or anything like that, because we could ruthlessly use Pete as a sort of go-between. And then, after a few months, I didn't need Pete as chaperone any more and I dropped him like a stone.

By the time we were at the six-month mark (not that either of us was counting – oh, no), we were at the relentless shagging stage of a new relationship. And I hardly saw Pete at all around that time. Roles were reversed and I ended up just relying on Rex for the odd update on the world of Pete.

It didn't last long. It was well before we hit my twenty-sixth birthday that the gloss had worn off our relationship to the extent that I didn't need to shag Rex twice a day, and I had picked Pete back up again (albeit mainly so I could complain about Rex's shortcomings). But I never really acknowledged that brief little interlude of shoddy treatment. Or that little blind spot in my complete history of Pete.

'I was really quite lonely without you,' Pete says, twisting the guilt knife, although probably not really meaning to, and probably not really enjoying it. 'I'd never really had to negotiate Brighton on my own. I don't think I'd had to walk into a single nightclub alone before. And everything seemed so much seedier without you. On my own, I felt kind of desperate – like it was obvious I was desperate – like everyone could see. When it was the two of us, we just went out to places and smoked in a corner and bitched at the poseurs – or whoever we considered to be the poseurs – and then, when I was properly relaxed, well, I could pull without it feeling, I don't know, nasty. And sad. And desperate.'

Pete sounds so sad, so fragile; it's not like him at all. And I don't really know what to do. But what I do do is get up from my leatherette armchair and go over to the sofa. I squeak down next to Pete and put my arms around him. 'Why didn't you ever tell me this?'

Pete shrugs. 'It never came up,' he says, in a voice that sort of fades away. Then he looks over at the television for a minute before continuing. It's still that Top One Hundred Show. Someone I sort of recognise (if only from other shows like this) is prattling mutely about why something – probably something banal, or something just sort OK – is really rather great and astonishing. I hate these shows. I hate them most of all when they feature stuff I like. Because nothing takes the lustrous edge off a treasured memory like some moon-faced, self-styled pundit enthusing about it.

'One night, about a week after my birthday, when you were otherwise engaged,' Pete says, eventually, 'instead of going into the pub like I usually did, I went down onto the beach instead.' He pauses and stares at me for a sec. 'Have you ever noticed how the sea at night works to enhance any mood? It's a bit like gin – in that respect.'

I'm not sure whether he's being rhetorical or not, but I don't attempt an answer.

'Anyway, I stood on the beach. It was late at night – tennish, maybe. And it felt like the end of the world – but then that was probably because I was drunk, and twenty-five, and a drama queen. But the tide was right out, so there was quite a lot of beach. And I was right down there on the stones, a long way from the promenade. And that's when I saw it.'

Pete looks suddenly all distant and dreamy. Stuck in his moment. Miles, or rather years, away.

'What?' I say, keen to crack the glassy-eyed stare. 'What did you see?'

'I saw the sea, like ink, and Brighton was anchored into the mire. There it was rising up from the depths, fifty storeys high, like a Rococo Godzilla.'

'A Godzilla? Brighton?'

'I did say a Rococo Godzilla, but fair point. A Godzuki then. A Rococo Godzuki with a doily on his head.'

'And more like about five storeys high, rather than fifty storeys high, was it fifty?' I start trying to hum the theme tune to the telly show to try and remember how many storeys high Godzilla was supposed to be, but Pete stops me before I've finished the first bar, with a simple facial expression that tells me that Godzilla's vital stats are so not the point here.

'Yeah, okay, look forget the whole Godzilla comparison idea. It doesn't really work anyway. In fact I think – when I looked at Brighton that night – I thought of it more as a, well, I don't really know what they're called, but you know those diagrams you see in museums where they show, like, a cross-section of the earth and all the layers? Like dinosaurs are right down here, and then fish even lower down than that, and cavemen right up the top. One of those things. Have I lost you?'

'Uh, no, I think I get you,' I murmur, beginning to wonder how on earth this is ever going to connect to the story of Wolfie.

'Well, whatever, but the point is, I stood on the beach and Brighton looked like it was rising out of the sea in layers. Above the beach was King's Mount, you know, the gay cruising ground. That was like level one, the ground floor. And then above that was the trashy touristy stuff. The beach gear shops, the crazy golf and the little railway thingy. The world of the weekender. And above that was my Brighton, our Brighton – the tall skinny houses all split into more flats than they have rooms, and the nice civilised pubs and bars, the station – young professional land, commuter central. And on top of that the flea markets and antique shops and estate agents, and then grimy studentville with 24-hour convenience stores and rip-off rented houses going on and on, until it finally reached the tower blocks and the estates and the cut-price supermarkets, right on the outskirts. And then the ring road. And then finally the South Downs, hemming it all in.

'And I realised that I only lived in a tiny part of Brighton. I never moved outside my tiny little Brighton world. First, I was just about student life. And then, without even blinking it seemed like I'd moved into civilised responsibility and being too dog-fucking-tired from three hours spent on a train every damn day to ever venture outside my little box. And that's when I thought, fuck it, I'm going to explore the other side. Or at least one of them. I'm going to go over to the dark side for a bit. And so I chose the side that was the nearest to where I was standing. And the one that – quite by coincidence – involved me getting the most sex the most quickly.'

As I realise where this story is going, I'm actually quite surprised. Suddenly I realise that Pete is going to tell me a very seedy story. Not that I'm surprised Pete is telling me about his sex life. Pete is anything but discreet. But his stories are usually about relatively normal pick-ups, pubs and clubs. He's promiscuous sure, but he's not . . . well, he's never told me anything this seedy. He's not that kind of guy. Not a pick-ups in the bushes kind of guy. At least, I thought he wasn't.

'I headed back up the beach and into King's Mount. It's a maze that place, all concrete paths cut into the cliff and bushes, lots of bushes, lots of cover. You can see why it works as a cruising ground. I was really scared, though. And I felt silly that I was scared. Picking up a man in a cruising ground, well, that's kind of like a gay rite of passage isn't it? But I'd never done any-thing like it before. I didn't even have the first clue about the etiquette. I ended up just giving the eye to the very first person I saw – though it was pretty dark, I couldn't even really see what he looked like – but I guess he picked up on my signals, because he stopped, and he laughed.'

Pete pauses, but I don't say anything. I just nod and smile because I've got to hear this.

'It turned out that he was like some bloke from a charity, like a safe sex place. He was giving out free condoms. So I took one, because it seemed like a good idea, and managed to kind of laugh off the whole picking him up thing. And then, straight after I left him, I ran into this other bloke.

'And then it was strangely easy. We both knew what we were about. I guess I had been worrying about nothing. Everything we needed to say was said with a few meaningful looks, and then I was following him into the bushes and getting onto my knees.'

'And that was Wolfie?'

'Uh, no actually, I haven't quite got to Wolfie yet. Um, I don't know this guy's name, we didn't exactly exchange business cards. Although,' Pete stops then and laughs a bit, 'right then I was quite new in my first proper job. I was so proud of my bloody business cards I probably would have given the guy one if I'd got the chance. But I didn't get the chance, not for that or anything else, because just before it was turn around time, just before I was about to get my turn in fact, there was this noise. Someone was coming and I really don't know if it was teenagers, or the police or just someone walking the dog, but – I can't really explain – it didn't sound good. And he ran before I did. Well, I was still on the ground. So by the time I'd got to my feet he was gone.'

I crease my forehead with confusion, because I really can't see where this is going, perhaps Pete has forgotten what story he is meant to be telling me. 'Right. And Wolfie?'

'Well, you see, that's kind of how I ended up in the mood I was in that night. After I'd scarpered from the cruising ground, up to the main road and back into the gay village, I headed for the nearest pub and that's when I saw Wolfie. Now, you've seen him, right? And you've seen the men I usually go for. Now you've got to agree that I wouldn't normally try my luck with a guy like Wolfie. He's way too pretty for me. Out of my league. No point setting yourself up for a fall. But right then, well, I'd lost out on my action, I was chocka with adrenaline and all pent up, I wanted some risky business. And what better risk than to chat up the prettiest guy in the place.'

'And you pulled Wolfie,' I say, sort of stating the obvious, but I kind of wanted to say it. 'Did he, you know, did he charge you?'

Pete grins. 'Yep,' he says, triumphantly, 'that was what was so perfect about it. He made it clear as soon as we started talking what he was about. And I wanted something dirty and wrong. So, yeah, perfect.'

'I can't believe you never told me,' I say, because really, I can't. Pete has known about my fantasies for years, of course. I think he knew before Rex ever did.

Pete looks a bit odd. A whole flock of sheepish. There is a little pause, and then he says, 'I was a bit too embarrassed.'

'What! You never get embarrassed. You tell me everything.' Because it's true. Pete always tells me everything. And he never seems embarrassed. I get a bit embarrassed sometimes with his tales from the Queer As Folk Frontline, but I've never seen him so much as flush during his tales of rimming and felching and spit roasting. 'You told me about that guy with the massive dildo, and the two blokes at once and the really, really old guy. And besides, you know how I feel about this sort of thing.'

'Yeah, but it wasn't that.' Pete's face is suddenly so earnest and truthful. 'I didn't really want you to know about how I felt when you sort of dumped me for Rex. I suppose . . .' He pauses, looking at the floor. I've still got my arm around him, but I'm not really sure if I should do anything more comforting. I rub his shoulder a bit, but that feels half-hearted and lame. 'I suppose I didn't really think I wanted you to know how much I missed you.' And he has tears in his eyes.

'I don't know what to say.' I shake my head. 'I'm sorry.'

'Don't be silly. You came back as soon as you realised there was more to life than Rex-cock. And besides, everyone does it. It was just, well, I couldn't admit I needed you. Needed you in order to live my big gay life. I mean, I'm a gay man. A fun-loving shag-a-muffin. I can't need a fag hag, a breeder like you. You're supposed to be the one that needs me.' And then he laughs, only a bit, but enough. And I laugh. And then we're both laughing – teared up, but laughing.

And then I say, 'You silly sod.'

And Pete says, 'I know.'

And I say, 'Tell me then, tell me now.'

Pete laughs again then, and for a minute I wonder if he's actually going to, but as soon as he starts to talk I realise that there was no way he wouldn't.

'We went to my place. Not the flat I live in now, but my old one, the little mole hole.'

The flat Pete used to live in before he bought his current, too-lovely, almost-entirely-made-of-glass designery place, was a tiny, practically subterranean little box, with run down communal areas and barely any natural light. 'That was good because the bar we were in wasn't much more than a hop skip and jump away. I remember being a bit embarrassed though, because, you know that place was pretty squalid. Oh God, you know what I did? I started boasting about my new job – I didn't want him to judge me based on that place. And you know what he said?'

'I should charge you double?'

'Um, yeah actually. Well, he might have put it more like, "Ooh, Mr Big Time, maybe I should charge you double or something."'

I laugh.

'But that was like, the last time we were jokey. It was almost seconds after that, that I looked at him, and the real meaning behind that throw-away comment – the fact he was charging, I was paying – suddenly hit home. And then it was just...'

'Sheer lust?' I interrupt, because this whole set-up seems to be very familiar from – I don't know what, role-plays with Rex, fantasies about Mark, something like that. Probably both.

'Yeah. It was a real nought-to-sixty moment, straight from laughy-jokey to up against the wall, rough snogging, fingers tangled in hair, sheer hard need.'

I swallow.

'He was on his knees before I really knew it, undoing my trousers with his hands and tongue and teeth. His mouth was so warm and wet. And I was looking down at his beautiful face. It was dark in my kitchen. I don't know why, but I hadn't put the light on. I could only see him in the yellowy slice of illumination seeping in from the hall, but that was enough. That was enough for me to know that I had the most beautiful man I'd ever seen wrapping his lips around my cock. And ever since I started working properly my money had been burning a hole in my pocket. I'd been poor for so long I didn't know what to do with my new-found income. But right then, suddenly, I did. I could do whatever I wanted with Wolfie. Anything I liked.'

As Pete speaks I feel like a weight has been lifted from me. I really feel like at last I'm hearing someone else saying all the things I've always thought about paying for it. But the difference is, Pete has actually done it. This is real. And it really is like I've always thought it would be.

And a devious voice in the back of my head starts whispering, starts me wishing I had a phone in my hand right now so I could call Mark Valentine and get myself pencilled into his next vacant slot.

But then Pete says something that comes as a bit of a shock.

'You know, Sophie, um, just talking about this has made me really horny. I was wondering, would you be really pissed off if I asked Wolfie if he could fit me in tonight?'

'Uh?' I say, because I thought this visit was meant to be about me. Hey, a bit more of this sexy talk and a couple more drinks and I could even end up being the one handing over the notes to Wolfie. Maybe. Maybe I'd be the one saying, 'Sod just meeting Wolfie tonight and thinking about things, how about I just go for it?' But Pete has beaten me to it.

'Sorry, Sophie, I know this was meant to be about you meeting Wolfie, but now we're here, well, you can still meet him and then I can stay. What do you say?'

And what I say is, 'OK.' Because I guess that's only fair.

I've barely finished saying it, when there is some

noise outside the sitting room, then the rhythmic rattle and clang of someone leaving down the wobbly metal steps, and Wolfie is back in the room with us.

'Hi,' he says, grinning through the words with pin-up boy teeth.

'Hey, Wolfie, great to see you again,' Pete says, standing up and greeting his once-upon-a-shag with a light kiss. Then he turns to me. 'This is Sophie.'

'Hey, Sophie, charmed and all that, I'm sure,' he says, rather bizarrely.

'Hi,' I reply.

'So,' Wolfie is so suddenly brusque and business-like I feel sure he clapped his hands together just before he spoke, 'what can I do for you two? Three way?' And then he looks at Pete with a puzzled little expression. 'I thought you were one hundred per cent homo?'

'I am,' says Pete, 'and, nah, we don't want a three-some, we're more interested in, well, separate deals.'

Wolfie, of course, is thrilled by the prospect of two clients for the price of one – or rather for the price of two, which is the whole point. 'So,' he says, after a few seconds of what-do-we-do-now silence, 'who's first?' And then, as a sort of afterthought, 'Are you both after a session tonight?'

'Um, no,' Pete says, 'I am, but Sophie just wanted to check out the prospect.'

'Right. Well check away,' Wolfie says, all super sug-gestive. He gives me a pouty wink and follows that up with a dainty little twirl. 'Like what you see?'

I'm a bit startled and not quite sure what to say. I can hardly say no, but I don't want to commit right now, not with Mark Valentine burning a hole in my brain. 'I, er.'

'Oh, don't worry. You don't have to say right now. But, well, if you decide you want a bit more than a free sample, call me.' And he grabs a little card from a pile on the mantelpiece and passes it to me with a grin. I shove it into my pocket.

It must be less than five minutes later that I'm walking down a deserted late night street. I know how to take a hint and Pete was hinting hard that he really wanted me to leave him and Wolfie alone as soon as I could. Of course, they both wanted me to call a taxi before I left. But I turned them down. I had my phone. And, for some reason, I've never felt uncomfortable walking around Brighton at night.

Brighton's my city. I never feel scared on its streets.

So I'm walking, and I'm scanning the street for my promised cab, and then I see someone walking along the road ahead of me. It's a man. A tall man. And I don't really pay him any attention because I'm too busy trying to keep my feet in contact with the pavement while I fantasise about calling Mark Valentine. And then, it slowly dawns on me, that weirdly, unbelievably, I'm thinking about calling the very person that is currently walking about twenty yards in front of me.

I'm about to shout out to him, hesitating a bit in the hope of not sounding over-eager or just plain sad. But before I do, just before, while I'm actually inhaling in readiness, a beetle-sleek black car oozes past me and slides to a halt next to Mark.

Instinctively, I stop where I am on the street, and so does Mark.

Quick, slick and silent, the back door of the car opens and then it all gets confusing. It looks like two men dart out of the car and bundle Mark into the black car. In fact, it's alarmingly like the opening scene in my Mark-kidnap fantasy. But I can't really be sure what exactly happened. It's so fast and yet so slow – it's like a dream. And just scant seconds after I watched it happen, I'm not even certain there were two men, maybe there was just one, or maybe there were three, or maybe Mark just got into the car. I'm just not sure, but as the car whips away, in the empty street, I suddenly feel uncomfortable – like I just saw something bad. And all my feeling safe on the streets of Brighton bravado has vanished – whisked away, just like Mark in that big black car – just like that. Gone.

'You okay, love?'

It's the taxi driver, calling to me through the rolled down passenger window as he glides into the kerb beside me. My taxi is here. Out of the night. My mint-liveried cavalry.

I slide into the back seat fast and urgent and, not believing I'm hearing myself right, I say, 'Um, could you, uh, could you follow that car? If that's okay.'

14

Surprisingly the taxi driver doesn't question my sudden burst of Am-Dram sensibilities. And the big black Mark-napping car is still just visible, turning off the main road a few hundred yards away. So, the driver doesn't need to rev the engine like a maniac or hurtle round corners, tossing me from side to side, to keep up with it. He just follows a very normal car in a very normal way on a very normal journey.

First we roll back a little way through seething, still-wide-awake Brighton studentville, where the streets are alive with ridiculously dressed, ridiculously young people, and then we turn right, and head up, over the hill behind Sainsbury's, and across the barricades, out of garish, glarish Brighton– where everything is splattered on the surface – and trundle into Hove – where everything seethes underneath.

Hove: Brighton's lesser known, more gentrified, and much filthier, older sister – where it's all hidden under net curtains, and chintz and bedding plants. Whatever could my Mark Valentine be doing here?

And, it soon becomes clear, we're not just going to Hove, we're heading right into the depths of Hove's prettiest, nastiest suburbs.

Finally, we reach our mysterious destination and I get the driver to drop me off just around the corner, from where the car we are pursuing has pulled up, and then I scamper back, just in time to see two of the men – I think the ones who did the actual bundling of Mark into the car – saying goodbye at the door of a small house and then scooting off in a blue three-door hatchback.

I watch and wait. As a cover for my furtive-lurky activities, I make sure I'm loitering by the bus stop on the other side if the road. I stay there, watching precisely nothing happen over the road, for quite a while. I wait until a bus pulls up, which is a bit embarrassing, because it's completely empty and has stopped just for me. When I wave the driver on he warns me he's the last one tonight, but I shake my head and watch the brightly lit double decker rumble away. When it's out of sight, I cross the road.

I look around in the dark, wondering what to do next. The house I'm focused on is pretty ordinary looking. A neat little detached place with a well tended garden, the only sign of anything being awry is the way the beetle-black car is sitting slightly malevolently in the drive.

In my head, I try to hatch a plan, or, at least, I list some options. My first idea, my Number One is that I could call the police. This is, I imagine, what one is supposed to do when one has just witnessed a kidnapping, but something inside me is telling me that I shouldn't – that I need to be sure of what is going on first, because I know what Mark does for a living and this could be more of a kidnapping in the way I've been fantasising about it. A "Kidnapping" – only for effect.

Number Two: I could walk up to the front door and ring the doorbell. In a way, I like this option. After all, I could easily invent an innocent reason for being there – like looking for a lost cat, say (like one does, at past midnight on a school night). That might give me a better handle on the situation.

I file that second option away in my brain as a 'possible'.

My Number Three option is to just leave. Run away, because whatever is happening here is none of my business, whether it's some kind of actual kidnapping, or a game, or some disgruntled client or client's husband, or whatever (because in actual fact I fully expect it to be something that my fevered mind can't even conceive of) and it's really not any of my business. But, my business or not, Number Three is only there in my head for show, because leaving just isn't really an option.

And so, it seems like the doorbell ringing of Number Two is the only option that's viable. And I'm just about to walk up the drive, when I notice the gate.

This might be a stately detached house, but it's not actually set all that far from its neighbours. On both sides shortish lengths of high dark fencing keep the back garden secure. Except on the left side of the house there's a gate in the fence, and with it a possibility that I could get around the back of the house.

And if I wasn't meant to sneak around the back of the house and try and gauge the situation by peering in the back windows, the gate wouldn't be left unlocked would it? And that's exactly the affirmation I mutter to myself, as I slip through the gate – which swings wide at a tap – and around the side of the house.

I find myself in a well-kept back garden, spookily moon-shadowed, and rather ominous. But, I remind myself as I close the gate with a slight click, even the most innocent suburban back garden would be dark and creepy in the middle of the night.

And there is some light, enough, at least, that I can stumble around in the inky gloom without having to hang on to the pebble dash. A long gash of pale yellow illumination lies on the neat grass – the light escaping through a gap in some improperly drawn curtains over the French windows. And that light is exactly the chink of hope I was looking for. I can't see inside yet, I'm too far away on the other side of the garden, but it's all very promising.

I move across the grass with a vain attempt at stealth – idly wishing for a misspent youth of teenage cat burglary – until I'm only a deep breath and some steeled nerves away from peeking into the house and right into the beating heart of whatever is really going on here.

And when I do look, my immediate and very incongruous thought is about how sumptuous the interior décor is for a suburban boxy house just inside the ring road. The room is all reds and golds and velvet and brocade. It's the kind of room that even the worst kind of bah-humbug merchant would want to spend Christmas in. It even has a grand roaring fire.

But there aren't stockings hung over this festive hearth – roasting on this open fire is Mark Valentine. (Which is why it is so strange that I spent any time at all dwelling on the décor.) He's naked (which is even more why it's so strange that I spent time dwelling on the décor), and he's tied to the mantelpiece. (And I don't think I need to keep making that point about the décor now.)

He's facing the fireplace, so I can't see his face. But I've studied his website enough that I can easily recognise him from the back in a fraction of a second. His perfectly shaped arms are outstretched, splayed wide, and each wrist is fastened with a cuff and a hook to each end of the elegant, tar-black, marble mantelpiece. If I twist my head a little I can see a kind of oblique view of a bit of his chest, pulsing and dancing orange from the fire, the shadows and light accentuating each deliciously toned curve and bump. He's glistening with sweat. He must be so hot. I squirm in the dark garden, wishing I could see more of him.

I need to take a little care so he doesn't see me – even though there's clearly no danger of him turning around any time soon, there is a mirror above the mantelpiece, where he might just glimpse me. But I've managed to stay firmly in the shadows so far, so, as far as he knows, he's standing by the fire with nothing but his reflection for company. And the reflection-Mark stares out at him, with the flush of heat and sex in its cheeks and the hazy glaze of desire in its lidded eyes.

His legs are shaking a little, which I assume is because they – like his bound arms – are spread so wide, held tautly splayed by a long wooden rod with an ankle cuff at each end. He must be so uncomfortable, what with his restricted position and the belt he is holding in his mouth. The belt, which I suppose is there to function as a kind of voluntary gag, hangs down from the corners of his mouth, dragging them down and so twisting his expression into one of strange aroused sadness. I find the belt-gag extremely sexy – this tiny element of compliance, mixed in with all the delicious strict helplessness. I squirm a little, rocking my hips as I watch him.

I look back at the fire burning cheerily in the grate below the mirror. His belly and chest – as far as I can see them – are sweating and smarting in the vicious heat. The heartless blaze is stoked high, popping and cracking and laughing as it all but roasts him.

He can't even know how long he's been there – there's no clock on the mantel. All he can do is diligently stand there, holding the belt in his mouth, and wait, naked and exposed in the heat. Aching and burning and watching his reflection as his spittle runs down his chin.

And I wait with him.

Despite my perfect view of exactly what is going on, I still don't know what this actually is. I am guessing that it's a job. I mean, obviously, it's pretty weird, and the way he was taken off the street doesn't seem to make a whole lot of sense – but I just guess this is the kind of thing he gets paid to do. I mean, this has to be something sexual.

But before I get any further with this clever investigative line of thought, the door to the room opens and suddenly Mark isn't so lonely.

I'm looking at a tall, effete and rather scary-looking woman. She's kind of feral, kind of bat-like – black and slick. Predatory. She's sexy, kind of in the way vampires can be sexy; a bit kind of campy-villainesque – a little bit twirly moustache. But, you know, I can go with that.

Clearly, Mark has heard her come in, because he tries to turn his head. But as the woman gets close to Mark, she turns Mark's face back to the mirror coolly, with a curt, 'Eyes forward, please.' (I guess the French windows aren't double glazed or anything, because I can hear what is being said quite clearly through the glass.) The woman leans in close over Mark's shoulder and gently takes the belt out of his mouth.

'Having fun?' she says, looking straight ahead and speaking to mirror-Mark.

Mark squirms, his body betraying a blatant level of arousal as the woman presses close behind him. 'Yes?' he says, sounding a little unsure.

In the mirror I watch the woman as she smiles and wets a finger in Mark's mouth.

'Been thinking about me?' she breathes as she reaches down and her lubricated finger disappears somewhere in the area of Mark's crotch.

'I never think of anything else,' Mark chokes, shaking as he seems to try not to buck against the touch.

'Oh good answer.' I can guess from the way the woman's arm is moving that she is slowly pumping Mark's cock. 'Now, tell me how much you want this.'

Mark's hips buck, answering for themselves. 'I do, I, I do want it.' He sounds so raw and needy. So different from the confident swaggering Mark I have spoken to. It's so fucking sexy.

'Good.' One last excruciatingly slow stroke and the woman lets go. Then she slides into a crouch at Mark's bound feet. I watch as she pulls a long metal poker from the holder at the side of the hearth and gently stokes the fire until it roars, lighting the dark room a blazing, leaping orange.

I watch as the dancing glow that lights Mark's face from below grows brighter, flashing and glinting on the metal parts of his bondage, the hard lights in his hair and the sweat that now covers his face – thick and grubby.

The woman stands up again, smiles again, silently replaces the belt in Mark's mouth, and turns and walks away.

After we are left alone again: Mark – strapped to the mantelpiece – and me – crouched in the garden – I notice a sweet little touch of cruelty in the tableau I have been enjoying that I hadn't spotted earlier. On the mantelpiece, right in Mark's eyeline sits a tumbler, half full of water, sparkling like gold and rubies in the firelight. I can see now that Mark is staring at it – clearly wanting. He must be so thirsty, trapped, as he is, so close to that roasting fire. But with his wrists tied he can no more drink from it than he can fly.

So evil. What a delicious torture. I rub my legs together as I watch him stare helplessly at the taunting glass. Poor thing – in fact, he'd probably be better off if he stopped looking at it. That glass – left deliberately to torment him – making him think how easy it would be, if he weren't tied, to reach and take it and drink. Making him imagine the cool water running down his baked throat. Making him think it and think it until he can't feel the relentless fire roasting him any more, or the strain on his taut arms, only the desert in his mouth.

I could watch him tormented like this forever. It is such a beautiful, beautiful sight. But it can't and doesn't last forever. The woman reappears in the doorway long before I've had my forever of looking.

Then everything is fast. The woman darts around with swift sharp movements. She uses one hand to remove the belt/gag and another to snake around Mark's shoulder and cover his mouth to stop the begging/questioning/protestations that were, I suppose, inevitable as soon as his mouth was liberated. She passes a quick gulp of blissful water into Mark's mouth in a brief, but sexily wet and messy kiss. She presses a soft warm body against Mark's cold back and lips whispering silk against his ear.

'Shhh, you've been such a very good boy, and I'm here now.'

And suddenly it's clear that multifunctional leather strap Mark has been holding in his mouth all this time is actually no longer a gag, or even a belt, but now a device to whip him with – and Mark's ordeal has really only just begun.

Right before my wide, wide eyes, the woman takes a step back and uses the doubled up belt on Mark's extraordinary arse, which, I have to admit, looks even better a few moments later when it is criss-crossed with vicious red stripes. And it doesn't stop there. With a continuing thud-thud of soft leather against hard muscle, the woman keeps on going until Mark's arse, and later his back, are as warm and pink as his roasted belly must be, and he is limp in his bondage, soft and loose and writhing.

Then Mark moans out loud and the woman pauses, dropping the belt to run a cool finger down the hot red ridges on his back.

Their glazed eyes meet in the mirror then, and they smile.

'You know, I really think I'm going to have to fuck you now,' the woman breathes, so ear-strainingly quietly I have to partly lip read and partly use psychic powers to understand her.

Mark, quite visibly, melts.

Decision made, the woman reaches out and unclips clips and unsnaps snaps, freeing Mark in easy seconds. She's holding him at the same time, which is a good thing, because it seems certain that if she wasn't Mark would have just turned into a puddle on the floor without the support of his bondage.

Moving freely now, drifting like characters in a dream sequence before my stretched and eager eyes, they cross the room to the sofa. The woman pushes Mark down on the gold plush cushions and, with only the slightest pause to reveal a magnificent dildo harnessed between her legs and lather up with a generous handful of lubricant, she takes Mark, slips inside him and owns him.

In easy moments, Mark is beyond incoherent, he's just a helpless piece of boneless flesh. He's only got one word left in his vocabulary: 'More.'

I have never before, in my whole life, seen other people having sex. I haven't even watched a porn film. I haven't even watched myself in a mirror. And I don't quite know why it's so compulsive, whether it's the bizarre tender brutality of it, the fact it's happening only feet away from me, or the fact that one of the participants is Mark Valentine (okay – that might be the main reason).

It doesn't seem to take very long – but my comprehension of such things is not really very on the ball right now. The woman is very quickly gasping and bucking, losing all her super poised cool. And Mark is close too. I can't quite tell from the angle but I think the tall woman is reaching around underneath him, masturbating him to his own quick breathless peak. And up, and over it as they both come together.

And it's only then – far too late really – that I slide my own hand into my knickers to find that I am hopelessly wet and sticky, and really pretty keen to have an orgasm of my own.

Through the window the woman is delicately pulling away from Mark, who sprawls semi-comatose across the sofa. I turn away from the floorshow, lean up against the wall by the drainpipe and start moving my hand vigorously. And, God, I'm so close so fast. Images flash through my head tumbling in on each other, there's so much I can't decide what to focus on: Mark tied to the mantelpiece, the water, the belt-gag, the beating, Mark over the back of the sofa being fucked senseless. And over-arching all of this, like a great big golden rainbow of sheer knee-weakening horniness, is the fact that Mark was doing all this because he was paid to. Because he was a whore.

And when I come I have to jam my spare hand into my mouth, because it's so intense, so hard edged and sparky that I scream and slide down the wall into a crouch on the ground.

15

I stay where I am for quite a long time, not wanting to return to reality. This might have something to with the fact that my reality is currently crouching in a stranger's garden with my knickers round my ankles. It takes me until I remember properly about Mark, and the intrigue through the window, before I stand up, adjust my clothes and peek back through the window.

There's not much happening. Just the aftermath of the sex. Mark is pulling on some jeans, the woman is bustling. I keep watching though, knowing that the show is over, but pathetically hoping for some kind of encore.

And then, a little bit after that, when Mark is human again, dressed and drinking tea, I get the shock of my life. Or, at least I am hit between the eyes by a twist in the tale. The very last thing I was expecting.

The woman comes into the room and sits down next to Mark on the sofa. She's all smiles in a bathrobe and I'm thinking how lucky she is, having had such a wonderful and kinky time playing with Mark. I'm wondering how much she is going to pay for the privilege. When it happens – the shock-horror.

The woman doesn't give, she receives – Mark reaches inside his denim jacket, and hands over a thick wad of notes. Mark pays her! Mark is the client!

I'm so surprised by this transaction that I take a step back away from the window. And then another – which is one step beyond, because I collide with the bird bath behind me, which sends me and a great noisy wodge of B & Q's finest stonework clattering noisily across the patio. Fucksie-daisy!

I'm still arse over tit, in the soft bedding plants (typical Hove), when light floods the patio and Mark Valentine and the woman appear at the French doors. I stay where I am, wondering if being flat on my arse in the mud actually improves my situation any – and then figuring it hardly makes it any worse. And then Mark Valentine, my saviour, really does save the day and says, 'It's all right, she's with me.'

I make a point of not looking in the mirror over the mantelpiece as I am ushered in through the French windows – I just don't want to know how red my face is. The woman looks amused.

'Why didn't you tell me?' she says, laughing, 'I wouldn't have charged extra for her and she could have at least sat in the warm.'

Mark shrugs. 'Wouldn't have been the same, would it, Soph?'

And I reply, 'No, it wouldn't.' Because that is actually the truth.

As awkward, embarrassing conversations go, this isn't too bad. The woman, whose name is Wanda, makes some more tea, which is really welcome as I hadn't actually realised how cold I was in the garden amidst all the pumping adrenaline and pumped up horniness. But mostly the conversation seems to flow so well because Mark is just so good at this kind of social stuff. He laughs and sparkles and tells me what great fun Wanda is, and how the two of them go way back. And then he tells Wanda stuff about me that is mostly true but with the odd embellishment to cover up how I came to be spying on him through the French windows. It's all actually rather fun, and it seems very hard to believe that less than an hour ago Mark was tied to a mantelpiece being flogged with a belt and paying for the privilege. Nevertheless though, that little fact does keep wandering back to the front of my mind, and the more I turn it over and look at it from other angles, the more I realise that I really, really like the fact that is was Mark who was paying for this abuse. It just adds another level of delicious wrongness to the entire thing.

And my desire to make my Mark Valentine fantasies real seems to have moved up a notch or ten.

A little later Mark and I share a taxi back to Brighton, and civilisation. It's the first opportunity I've had to ask the question that has been burning me up inside ever since I witnessed the bird bath-lunge-inducing-spectacle of Mark paying Wanda, and had been exacerbated by Mark and Wanda's obvious camaraderie and the news that they go 'way back'.

'So, you're straight then?' I say, keeping my voice sort of low because I don't really want the driver earwigging.

Mark laughs. 'Does it matter?'

'Er, yeah, it does actually. I mean it doesn't, generally, not for me, but as regards you and I, then yes, it does.'

'Well, if you say so. But the answer's no, not exactly, but I'm straight enough that you really shouldn't be worrying about it. And if you want the full expanded Director's Cut version of the answer to that question: I'm possibly bi. I can certainly get it up for men, but then I wouldn't have lasted very long in this job if I couldn't. But, really, to tell the truth it all sort of becomes academic after a while. I'm lucky enough that

I can pick and choose clients a bit and limit myself to those that turn me on.' And he shrugs, then folds his arms tight over his gorgeous chest in a 'subject closed' sort of a way.

And so I move on to burning question number two, 'Why did you? Well why did you pay that woman to do that to you?'

'Because it was actually my birthday last week too, as well as yours, and I never got around to celebrating it properly.'

I feel my face crumple into a frown. 'But why did you pay for it? I mean, surely you realise you could get that stuff for free. Exactly what that woman did to you. Well, some people would even pay you to get to do ... um, I guess, you know that.' I tail off realising I am stating the unbelievably obvious to the completely converted.

'Maybe, yeah.' And Mark shifts a little on the seat so he is suddenly far too close to me. 'So these people you're thinking of, the ones that would pay to do all that kinky stuff to me, anyone particular in mind?' he says, artfully changing the subject.

'Um, me,' I say, far too quickly, and then mostly really wish I hadn't, but also I am kind of glad that I did.

Mark grins and makes a sort of 'heh' noise, but instead of pulling me up on what I've just admitted to wanting he says, 'Well, yeah, but you know, I wanted something very specific. And sometimes the best way to get exactly what you want is to pay for it. It's like, you know, going private in the hospital or something.'

I laugh. I kind of like that analogy, although the Socialist in me hates the association, it makes a lot of sense.

Something kind of breaks between us then. Like an invisible wall that I didn't even notice was there until it had gone. I feel myself breathe out and then it's my turn to close the gap. I slide a little closer to Mark across the taxi seat. 'Can I see your back?' I say, so bold I surprise myself.

Mark looks at bit confused for a minute. And then I see his face change, watching the enlightenment actually happen. 'Oh, you want to see the marks.'

'Yes.'

Mark shuffles around in his seat so he can pull off his denim jacket and then he lifts up the tight white vest he is wearing underneath. I swallow. Hard. There is something unbelievably sexy about the angry red weals that decorate that beautiful expanse of skin. And I really don't know what it is that makes my mouth suddenly so dry that I have to wet my lips – the fact he has these marks all over his back, or the fact that they are there because he wanted them. The fact that he paid to have them put there.

Braver, bolder every second, I touch his skin.

'Does that hurt?' I say, gingerly running a thumb over a particularly nasty weal.

'A little,' he says, gasping at my touch, 'but in a good way.'

I look at him for a long time. And then I say, 'Would you like to come home with me?'

He looks a little taken aback, adrift somewhere between the cocksure Mark I met on my birthday and the timid, submissive Mark I've been watching. He swallows, 'What? Now?'

'Yes. Not to do anything,' I add, quickly, realising that even though I am feeling closer to Mark than I ever have I'm still not quite ready to sleep with him. Not quite ready to turn my fantasy real just yet.

And, besides, after the night he's had, surely he's pretty sated.

Mark shrugs dumbly. He still seems a little dazed. 'Uh, OK,' he murmurs, almost like he'd agree to anything.

'I'd just like to talk to you for a while.'

'You don't have to be up for work?' Mark says, suddenly sort of lucid. I glance at my watch. It's three-thirty.

'Work-schmirk.'

16

At what point on this journey did I stop caring what the driver thought of our conversation? Sometime before the taxi pulls up outside my flat, anyway. I pay the driver quickly, not wanting to make too much eye contact, and notice that my wallet is now empty, I actually gulp as I mentally tot up how much money soon-to-be-jobless moi has spent this evening on taxis alone. Best not to think about it really (although, I do make a mental note to get Pete to reimburse me for his share of it, he is absolutely bloody loaded – well, relatively – after all).

I direct Mark through my cramped bedroom and into my sitting room, where he practically flows onto the battered junk shop chaise-longue that passes for a sofa (I'm so Brighton boho when I want to be). I can't help thinking how lucky I have been this evening with this exciting encounter, not least because it means that not only have I now got Mark Valentine right before my very eyes, but I have also got him here wearing a rather seedy and sexy outfit. It seems that just because Mark was naked for the actual funtime birthday sex game part of his evening's entertainment, doesn't mean he skimped on the full-on sluttiness of his wardrobe. He's wearing white jeans – actual genuine white jeans like something from the last millennium! They are ridiculously tight and look absolutely incredible against his honey-nut skin. Along with the white vest and denim jacket, (which he quickly discards) he looks like the lost third member of Wham!. (Which is no bad thing for an ex-Whamette like me.)

The outfit – especially without the jacket – is also completely unsuitable for the January chill, which, thanks to my flat's general inadequacy, is a concern indoors as well as out. But this does bring the slight bonus of Mark's very visibly erect nipples – neat and biteable as they strain against the white cotton.

Apologising flappily for the cold, I spark up the huge Calor gas heater thing and select the maximum, three-bar, setting. Then, after a good dither about where to sit, and ending up perched uncomfortably on an upright chair at the table in the window bay, I have a few moments of complete blankness. Having already established that this is not about sex, but about yet more talk, I can think of nothing – not one single thing – to talk about.

My life is now officially way too complicated. I need a change of pace. A breather. There is really only one thing to do. Find the leftovers from that bar of chocolate that Rex brought me last week and pop the kettle on.

I get up from the chair that I spent so long deciding to sit on and take my leave to the kitchen. My chocolate foraging is a success – I am delighted by the fact that I have over half a bar left – I have been good!

One kettle boil later and I'm back in the sitting room with two teas and the sweet spoils of my cupboard rummage, however I then discover that Mark doesn't actually eat chocolate – he's doing the GI diet. Naturally I've read the book, so we end up talking Glycaemic Indices for the next three-quarters of an hour.

I end up really liking the sound of GI. It makes sense and doesn't seem to involve eating quite so many bizarre and never-heard-of-before-in-my-food-seeking-life foods than that regime off the telly that I've been trying, wholly unsuccessfully, to stick to since my birthday blow out. But I still eat all the chocolate by myself as Mark explains that it is full of white sugar, which he considers to be practically poison. Still, will-power – not my strong point really. Witness the male escort in my flat at 4a.m.

But the poisonous white sugar seems to have done something useful to my system, because I suddenly remember something.

'You know your website?' I say, half through a mouthful of not-quite-swallowed tea.

'Yeah,' he says, clearly bemused at this sudden and logic-free change of tack.

But I ignore his bamboozlement. 'What do you think of it?' I ask.

'I don't think of it. Not really. I don't look at it much,' Marks says, shrugging. 'It's just, I don't know, it's just there.'

And this statement seems to trigger a formula script in me that I use at work to potential clients – although this is probably the most unconventional pitch I've ever made. I can actually feel my eyes light up as I say, slightly manically, 'Aha, well, that's where you're wrong. It's not "just there", it's your shop window, your website. It's what most of your customers look at. A good number of them, anyway. If you Google "Mark Valentine" or even "Male Escorts Brighton" up it pops. And how many potential customers get no further than your God-awful splash page? It's your most important selling tool and yet, because it's hidden, you're not even bothering to make sure it's selling you properly, let alone selling you well, which is such a shame, because you put so much effort into selling yourself face to face.'

Mark stares at me, boggling, clearly even more con-fused than he was before I started explaining. 'What?'

he says, slowly. 'What are you talking about? Is that some kind of sales pitch?'

'Um, well, OK, this is a bit like what I say at work, yeah. But it wasn't meant to be, not really. All I meant was, your website isn't doing you justice so I, er, I looked at it for you.' And now I'm admitting this particular truth I'm more worried about not sounding like some kind of psycho-stalker than a hard sell merchant, because critiquing a person's website is one thing, but redesigning it uninvited does seem kind of loopy. And more than a tad obsessed.

But it's far too late to backtrack now. Not now as I'm sitting in front of my computer and loading up my brand new version of Mark Valentine dot com into my browser.

'Ooh,' says Mark as the new and exciting, lightly designed splash page appears, with the graphics trailing a few seconds behind, 'it's grey.'

'Um, yeah, you needed to change. Black is, well, you do know that only porn sites are black these days.'

'No, I didn't know,' Mark says, sounding serious, although I can't shake the suspicion that he is laughing at me a little. 'Uh, is that a bad thing, then? Looking like a porn site, I mean. I thought people liked looking at porn sites. I hear they do rather well.' And then I know for sure that he is taking the piss out of me.

But I persevere because I know I am right. 'Well, yeah, but, yes. It is a bad thing. Kind of. I mean looking like a porn site is a good thing, obviously, if you are a porn site. Well, actually it isn't necessarily all that great even then, but if you're not a porn site, well, people are just going to get the wrong idea.'

'And we can't have that,' Mark practically breathes into my neck. But I don't rise to it, or even turn around. I give up with the verbal logic, letting my fingers do the talking instead. I flick the mouse like a safety line, and begin to guide Mark Valentine through his new, and really quite beautiful, web pages.

When he actually bothers to look he seems kind of taken with the new sepia-tinted graphic button things I've made for stylish site navigation. Even more so when I explain that they are actually slightly manipulated thumbnails from his filthiest images, and show him which bits of which photographs I've made each of them from.

'So,' he says, sounding excited, 'if you took all these buttons and put them together you'd have a really filthy picture of me.'

'Well, more like a filthy photofit-type collage, but yes. If a person were desperate for yet more Valentine porn they could do that. Although all the filthy pictures of you are still there. In the gallery. See?' I click the appropriate link and a row of images of demi-clothed, semi-clothed and really-not-at-all clothed pictures of Mark sprinkle themselves across the screen.

Now here's a weird thing. I've seen all these pictures before. In fact I've spent more hours of my life than I care to add up fiddling with the colour balance on each of them. And Mark knows I've seen them – not least because he practically invited me to have a look at them that night. And yet, when my computer monitor suddenly becomes wall to wall Mark-Valentine-porn-o-vision, I can feel us both colour and twitch a little.

But I'm sighing while I'm blushing because they're all still there; the bunch of six pictures that have been my masturbation fodder for the past five days since I first saw them. Mark sucking cock on his knees, Mark tied to the bed, Mark in leathers. The lot. But it's the Mark standing behind me that breaks the now very heavy silence.

'I only just noticed,' he says, breathless and breathlessly close, 'I don't have a single heterosexual picture on here.'

'No,' I say, because he doesn't. 'Actually I hadn't noticed that either.' Because I hadn't.

'I mean, most of the people who look at the site are going to be men – that's just the way it is – so I know I have to cater to them, but even so, I ought to have one. Just so people know I'm not just for the boys. I'm equal opportunities.' And he says that last bit like it's a really clever thing to say, which annoys me a bit, because it isn't, really.

And I annoy myself even more by laughing a little, before I say, 'Yeah, you really should.'

'What should it be then? What should I have on here as a picture that shows I can give ladies just as good a time as I can give men?'

My eyes go a bit poppy. I don't know how to answer that one. So I settle for letting my mouth flap like a windsock, while my suddenly pea-sized brain rattles around in my head. Until, finally, this lameness emerges, 'Um, well, you and a woman.'

Mark smiles a micro-expression of a smile before he replies with enduring patience, 'Well, yeah, maybe. What would you like to see?'

And then, thank God, an image flashes into my brain. So simple and so perfect that I can't not tell him. Even though it is kind of squirmy embarrassing to say out loud. 'You just need something feminine, I guess, in the picture with you. You don't need a whole woman, really, just something that would be enough to suggest that the other person – the person you were with – was a woman. I would say something like a woman's hand, you know, nice manicure, nail polish and all that, maybe touching your face, or with one of her fingers in your mouth. Um, that'd be cool.'

'Sophie,' Mark says, all sweet smile, 'you really are a design guru, aren't you? You ought to be running that company of yours.'

What is it with this guy? He keeps saying this kind of thing. Weirdy compliments, which I honestly can't tell if he means sincerely or not, which means he can get away with stuff like this. Stuff that I would dismiss as slightly creepy oiling up to me if it wasn't just tongue in cheek enough to pass. It's really annoying. And really addictive. Although, thinking about it pragmatically, with my lust-coloured spectacles taken off, he probably is laughing at me. Patronising me a teensy, teensy bit, but in such a charming and affable tone that I can't really take offence, or stop fancying the white-denim pants off him. I properly blush now, anyway. I've been borderline ever since we got the heavy male nudity up on my computer, but now I feel my heartbeat banging in my ears and my face is suddenly very hot and bothered.

Mark reaches over my shoulder and puts his cool dry hand on my hot cheek. He laughs slightly, averting his eyes and shaking his head. 'You're really so cute,' he mutters. And then he turns my head with his light fingers and our eyes meet, ending up locked together for far, far too long.

I feel a little uncomfortable, but at the same time I don't want this magical looking-into-each-other's-eyes time to end too quickly. So I sit there, licking my dry lips and swallowing a weird jumpy anxiety for what feels like hours until Mark takes charge.

'Why don't we go into the bedroom?' he says.

I gulp so hard it's probably audible and cement my sex appeal and intelligence by responding, 'Guh!'

'Come on. Trust me.'

17

In the bedroom Mark is so in charge it's a bit unnerving. I lie down on the bed at his instruction, and he flits about, creating subtle lighting effects and calming music. It's like he pulls a relaxing atmosphere out of nowhere – and it works, I sink helplessly into the duvet, exhaling all my troubles up towards the original Regency coving.

And somehow I manage not to tense up again when Mark slinks over to the bed and tumbles onto the eiderdown next to me.

'Now,' he says, in that familiar honey voice and should-be-too-oily-but-somehow-isn't manner, 'let's stop all this website talk and other silly nonsense and relax properly. Why don't you tell me your fantasy?'

It seems that now it's Mark's turn to pull a strange, and seemingly illogical subject matter change, but he seems to have done it with far less cog-crunching than I managed. I laugh. 'You know my fantasy.'

'Do I?'

'Yes, to pay a man for sex.'

'Oh that's not really a fantasy,' he says lightly into the shadowy ceiling above us, 'that's more of a facilitator for your fantasies. I mean, once you've got your man and paid your money, what do you want to do to him? Why do you want to pay a man? Is it that you want to do something so twisted that you think you'd need to pay the guy to make it OK?'

When he stops talking I find I am waiting for him to

say something else, but he doesn't. I feel so trippy. It's like I'm right here, right in this moment, but I know, I just know, I'm going to remember this conversation forever. This is one of the key scenes in my life, and normally you don't know that until after the event. But here I can watch myself breathing in and out in real time and know that this is my personal history in the making.

'Well,' I say, eventually, because I want to get this momentous conversation right and a 'well' gives me another syllable of thinking time. But it doesn't really work. In desperation I add a further, 'well, um...' but that's it. Extra syllables or not I still have nothing more to give.

Luckily, though, Mark knows just how to keep digging. 'Tell me what you do with your boyfriend. Rex, right?'

'What I do with Rex?'

'You said that you get him to pretend to be a whore. On your birthday. I was there, remember?'

And it's funny because up until that moment I had actually sort of forgotten that Mark was there. Forgotten how this all started, with my birthday and Kate's jaw-dropping date. 'Oh well,' I begin, for once actually opening my mouth and knowing where I'm going in this conversation. 'The last time we really did it properly was that afternoon – on my birthday – I picked him up in the bar of The Palace Hotel. Do you know it? On the seafront.'

'Of course.'

'He was wearing this sort of trashy outfit, playing the part of a whore that picks up well-to-do women in the bar of a posh hotel. But, well, I guess in reality a man who did that would dress up kind of smart and respectable, but I like the whore-clothes. They turn me on.'

And I laugh a gentle little laugh, partly because Mark is wearing such spectacularly whorish clothes himself at this moment, but mostly to try and hide the fact that just talking about this stuff, just thinking about it, is turning me on.

'What sort of clothes? Tell me.'

'Oh you know, you must know, too-tight trousers, ripped jeans, mesh tops, thin white T-shirts, all that really trashy stuff.' Which is kind of embarrassing to admit – to admit to being so clichéd – but also kind of not, because it's Mark, and I only have to look at him to know that he isn't averse to dressing like a walking advert for what he is. Plus I've seen the website. I know he's not afraid of going for the lowest common denominator.

'So,' Mark says, his voice gossamer light, 'when it comes to clothing, you have a fondness for the classics. But that's not what I really want to know. What I want to know is what you do with your whore once you have him. What did you do with Rex once you had taken him up to your hotel room?'

'Oh.'

'Because I might not have known you very long, Sophie, but I'd bet double the amount I paid Wanda for my little birthday treat tonight that you didn't just have a sweet bit of vanilla flavour sex and call it a night.'

I swallow, but I don't think because if I really think then I won't be able to answer. 'I tied him up.'

'Mmm,' Mark says, so soft I'm not even certain it was him and not me. 'I'm glad you said that. I like that.'

'You like that I tied him up?'

'Oh yeah.'

And Mark really does sound turned on. Of course, as ever with him, I find myself second guessing every sound he makes. He might just be pretending to be getting hot to get me hot, but guess what, if it is his eagerness to make a sale that's driving him, that turns me on even more.

'You know what I really like?' Mark says, sounding kind of thoughtful. 'I really like the idea that you would be paying me and then tying me down, and in a way that makes it seem like you're the powerful one, but really you're not, because you want this so much. It's like a complete power fuck. It turns me on.'

I'm listening. And I like what he's saying. I connect with what he's saying, but at the same time I have to check him on a point or two. 'Hang on, who said I was going to pay you and tie you up?'

And Mark just laughs. A proper laugh this time, not nervous or time filling, just a real laugh. And I laugh too. And the mutual laughing really seems to move us up a level.

'Power fuck,' I say slowly, after a little while or breathless silence. 'I like that.'

'Good. But that's not all. Remember what I asked at the beginning? What is it that you want to do with men that means you have to pay them? Tie them up, sure, but that can't be it. Nine guys in ten love being tied up, believe me, Sophie, I know. So just imagine, imagine you can do anything you want to me. So what are you going to do?'

This evening has been so surreal. From the strip night, to the Incredible Journey into Hove to meet up with Wolfie (I wonder how Pete is getting along?) to this – a whole other dimension of weird-assness. So there's no other place on earth I'd say this in real life. I've never really admitted these things to anyone. My über-dark side. But this isn't like real life. At least it's no kind of real life I've ever experienced before.

So I start to talk. I start to tell Mark about some of the really nasty things I've been day dreaming about doing to him lately. 'When I saw that car pull up and those guys drag you in, well, the real reason I followed it wasn't because I was worried about you. Not really. I followed because it was like a scene from one of my fantasies about you. The idea of hiring you so I could play out taking a man off the street. Just grabbing him, bundling him into the back of a car and spiriting him away to a secret location. That's kind of what I hoped was happening to you.'

'So you weren't strictly my little knight in shining armour then?'

'I'm afraid not. I wasn't only in it for the valiant rescue. Even if that was what I told myself. Most of me was just there because I reckoned I was going to come across something hot.'

'And did you?'

'Oh yes, but not exactly what I wanted to find. Not exactly what I was hoping for.'

I leave a pause for Mark to ask me what I was hoping for, but he doesn't. However he does make an encouraging hem-hem type noise, which will do.

'I was hoping they were going to drive you to some kind of dungeon, well maybe not a dungeon but a deserted warehouse at least and, um...' And my momentum gives out because, actually I was wrong, I do need more encouragement than the single hem-hem type noise to keep talking all the way through this.

Mark rolls onto his side, which brings his body close and hard up against mine. I feel myself tensing up, and I wish I was being more cool and laid back about this whole thing. For the first time in this whole surreal episode I find myself wondering about whether Rex would be OK with what I'm doing. I don't really think he would be, but then it's getting very hard to tell with him these days – I honestly don't really know where the boundaries are any more.

I can feel Mark's breath on the side of my face then, as he says, 'Tell me about the warehouse.'

I shiver a bit, although the room is quite warm – those Calor things really start to pump out the heat after a while. 'Dirty, well, dusty, at least. Dusty floor. Concrete, metal, greyness, pillars, that kind of stuff. Just somewhere that looks totally bleak and in the middle of nowhere. With no escape. And this group of guys, well, because of what I saw I thought it would be a group of guys in this case, and they'd have you tied up on the floor, and be taking turns on you, forcing themselves on you, into you, using you.' And now I really am shivering. I'm so turned on to be talking about this. Mark slides his arms around me.

'But in your real fantasy version, it isn't a group of men who kidnap me and take me to the warehouse. It's you isn't it?'

'Well yes, but it isn't you, at least it wasn't, until I met you.' Because, of course, since I met Mark, most of my sexual fantasies have been very much Mark-centric.

'Oh,' Mark says, his eyes glowing in the soft light and betraying just how much information he has just extracted from what I've just said. But I don't care. Talking about these ideas has got me buzzing with lusty adrenaline.

'But yes,' I say, conceding in a way and letting him have just what he wants from me. 'It would fulfil a fantasy to kidnap you somehow, take you to a deserted place, keep you prisoner, use you.'

'Well if that's what you want, well, you do know that you could have that don't you? You do know that I could make that happen for you. Just tell me what you want.'

I roll over onto my side so I'm facing him, our bodies pressing so close now I can feel the warmth coming off him, a kind of comfortable yet sexual heat. We're nose to nose, eye to eye, our pupils big as saucers in the dark-light. 'I don't know,' I say, playing it a little coy, 'I mean how could I kidnap you for a start? You're a big guy. It's not like I could bundle you into my car.' And I reach out, not knowing how I could be so brave, and put my hand on his bicep, which is typically perfect – every bit as big and defined as I would have wanted it to be, and no more.

'Oh that's simple. I mean I would have had the same problem with tonight's little game if I didn't do the obvious.'

'The what? What obvious?'

'Well I had some extra hands didn't I? The guys who pulled me into the car. I just called in a couple of favours. Or at least Wanda did. Just to make it work.'

'Oh.' And God, was that really just earlier this evening? It seems like a million billion years ago now.

'We could do that, or something a bit like it. How about we get a van? Then we'd need a driver and a couple of guys to be the muscle. The guys can grab me and pull me into the back of the van. You're there, in the back ready and waiting with your ropes or whatever you like. Easy peasy. I'm your prisoner.'

My heart races in the dark. Mark's words trickle over me, sparkling like droplets in one of Charlie Dimmock's finest water features. Everything he's describing does indeed sound so easy, so erotic, so perfect, I almost forget myself. I almost fire up the computer, connect to the net and check my bank balance. I almost declare myself a single girl with no responsibilities other than to my own selfish whims. But I don't. Not quite. Because across the room, all the time we've been talking, a little red light has been flashing. A little winking red light, which has been whispering quietly to me, over and over, wink, wink, wink. Red for danger. Stop, stop, stop.

I'm looking at the blinking red light all the time Mark is telling me how the van would transport us to a deserted warehouse, how I'd tie him up and parade and humiliate him. The amazing games we'd play. And, of course, how much he'd love it. How much we'd both love it.

At first, he's just painting too many arousing pictures for me to listen to the silent message from across the room. He's describing himself bound – he likes the idea of chains, real metal manacles, no escape, like I said. He's telling me how he'd squirm. How futile it would be. How he'd plead with me for release (if I even let him speak, of course). How I would see the desperation and then the desperate arousal light his eyes. And most important of all, how it would be OK to do all of this to him. How it would be fine, because I would have paid him.

But the light keeps on insisting; stop, stop, stop. Until eventually its urgent message manages to find a place in my brain that isn't closed to everything except Mark's filthy talk, and I listen. And I stop.

'Mark,' I say, interrupting his description of how the dirt from the warehouse floor would mix with his sweat and make grimy patterns on his naked body, 'hang on a minute.' And I get up, fumble my way over to the source of the insistent red winking and realise it's my answer phone.

I have one new message.

'Hey, babe,' says Rex's voice, 'it's me. Listen, I'm sorry. I'm not really sure what happened back there. Um. Look, why don't I come over in the morning? I'm working from home so we could do breakfast. You said you wanted to talk about that work thing. Is seven too early? Text me if it is.'

I listen to the message twice, swaying a little bit as reality comes hurtling back, way too fast. Oh yeah, Rex. As in, Rex: my boyfriend.

Mark is still lying on my bed, a strange and slightly stupid-looking smile dancing over his face. It's very obvious that he knows exactly who this message is from. In fact it's told him more than he could have possibly wished to know about the current status of my relationship with Rex.

'Seven,' he says eventually, 'isn't that kind of early?'

'Well,' I begin to reply, in the most bizarrely matter-of-fact voice – as if it is completely normal to be talking to a male escort about one's boyfriend, in one's bed-room, in the very tiniest hours of the morning – 'he knows I have work.'

'Oh right, work, how considerate.' And somehow, the way Mark says considerate here, manages to make being considerate – which is quite a nice thing to be really – sound all pathetic and lame. He has just, very effectively, castrated Rex simply by calling him considerate, which is very nasty, but also, in a totally evil way, very nice.

'You do realise,' Mark continues, 'that it is six-thirty now.'

'Huh?'

'Six-thirty, as in, the six-thirty that is half an hour before seven.'

My features fall inadvertently into an attractively fish-like gape. 'Oh. God.'

'Do you want me to leave?'

My mind says 'yes' at exactly the same time that my heart (along with various other parts of my anatomy) say 'no'. I wonder briefly if it's too late to head Rex off with a text. (It so is.)

I am rooted to the spot with dithering, unable really to move or speak because both of these would require far more decisiveness than I am capable of.

And while all this is going on inside me, Mark gets up off the bed with a text book athletic grace that gives me goose pimples. Everything he is wearing really is far too tight. He walks over to where I am standing by the phone and doesn't stop walking until he is standing far too close.

Is it me, or is it hot in here?

'I said,' he says, reaching out and touching me gently on the shoulder, 'do you want me to leave?'

And I say, 'Yes.'

But it doesn't really go as smoothly as all that, because by the time Mark has got his stuff together – I wasn't aware he had stuff, but somehow his phone and keys and wallet are strewn around my flat – and had a quick wee and a quick wash, and put his jacket on, and we're down at street level, it's too late, because the last person in the world I wanted to see at this moment is coming around the corner.

I open my mouth to say either 'Hi Rex,' or 'You're early,' I haven't decided which, but I don't get to decide, or to say either, because in the next second Rex stops walking and clocks Mark standing next to me. He stays where he is for a moment, looking at me, looking at him. We have a whole telepathic argument, which I lose. And then Rex turns on his heel and walks away.

Suddenly – finally – I'm all decisive. Leaving Mark on the pavement, with what isn't so much a good-bye as a sharp intake of breath, I run after Rex.

Round the corner, on the main road opposite the 24-hour Co-op, Rex is standing at the bus stop. Which means I don't have long; at this time of day the number seven bus runs every five minutes. As I approach him, he turns slowly away to look through a shop window, as if I, or anyone else who was passing, would be convinced he was really interested in what was going on in a betting shop.

'Hi,' I say. Putting my own personal stake on a breezy like-it-never-happened type demeanour, I set my face to who-is-Mark-Valentine-anyway? 'So, what about breakfast?'

Rex doesn't look at me, he keeps right on looking at the gleefully Magic Marker-scrawled odds on Somewhere-or-Other United beating Something-Else Town. And I can't help noting that if someone I've never heard of (but who I'm willing to guess has great legs, a terrible face, and is paid far too much for what is basically glorified PE) scores the first goal I could earn fifty quid for a two pound-fifty stake.

With Rex unwilling to even look at me I'm stuck, I just have to stay standing there and when Rex eventually does answer his voice sounds angrier and sadder than I have ever heard it. He still doesn't look at me. 'How about you stop taking the fucking piss out of me, eh, Sophie? How about you just do the decent thing and dump me like you really want to so I can carry on with my life?'

'What?' I say, or half say really, because Rex hasn't left any kind of a gap for me to say anything.

'What you've got to understand, Sophie, is that when a person loves another person as much as I love you, something that I know you don't really understand, but all the same, when somebody really loves another person they are willing to make a few sacrifices for that person.' His voice is so quiet now I can hardly hear it, which is understandable I guess, as there are now about five other people at the bus stop, but nonetheless, his quietness can't really be a good sign. 'That's why I was more than willing to help you hire a male hooker. I don't mind helping you fulfil your fantasies, after all you've fulfilled so many of mine. But to laugh in my face when I try and give you what you want and then go behind my back like this. Get that guy over without even telling me. Without any discussion. No, Sophie. That is not acceptable. No matter how much I love you.'

And I know I ought to say something back. I suppose it's time for the case for the defence. Time to hum a few bars of but-I-didn't-do-anything. But I can't quite find the will. After all, he's right. Everything he's just said is true. Case for the defence? What I've done is indefensible. Plus, while he's been talking, the bus has pulled up.

Even so, as Rex turns to get on it I do say, 'But I didn't do anything.'

But it's much too little, much too late.

And, anyway, the bus has already gone, leaving me on the pavement with nothing but a swirling mélange of old takeaway food wrappers and seagull screams for company.

18

Welcome to Hell. The weekend after relationship meltdown.

Which isn't to say that the Thursday and Friday after relationship meltdown weren't utterly horrible, because they were.

(Plus I now know I am officially old because it took me those two entire days of blearily swearing about the place to get over my up-all-nighter with Mark.) Oh, and that's without having Dave-Steve-Ed creeping around me, acting super weird and trying to ask me – without actually outright asking – if I've made a decision about their 'job offer'. (Or job ultimatum, as I prefer to think of it.) Normally we'd be all chummy about this break-up thing (Rex and I have had semi-serious break-ups before, although none of them have actually lasted past the 24-hour mark) and they'd hug me and even buy me cakes at lunchtime and generally be all fatherly and supportive. But the awkwardness caused by the job situation means that I don't even tell them about Rex and my depressive mood is no doubt put down to my looming big decision.

The one little sliver of silver lining is that even though they really wanted an answer on Friday, they agree (when they finally act like big brave men and find it within themselves to broach the subject) to give me until Monday morning to decide. Great.

So, yes, utterly horrid. Two sleep-deprived days at work might have been miserable for the newly single, but at least they had direction and, dare I say it, purpose, as opposed to the cold thud of horror that greets me on Saturday morning when I realise, before I have even left the embrace of the snuggly duvet, that I have two entire days of uninterrupted singledom to endure. Singledom and big echoey loneliness.

So, if ever there were a time when I needed my friends, this is it. My friends should have been dropping everything to rally round. It's in their contracts.

But if ever my friends were planning to let me down big style . . . well, let me explain.

Kate is at a conference. Apparently, it's been in her diary for months. She practically dropped the phone when I called her on Thursday night to tell her about me and Rex, and she couldn't apologise enough for her reneging on the whole set-in-stone friendship contract, but she was already booked and packed – practically in transit.

And as for Pete. Well for starters it took me two days to even get hold of him. Which isn't that unusual for Pete, he does have a tendency to go to ground. But this was a dire situation. I rang his mobile all through Thursday, knowing he was at work with Rex and getting far too much of the other side of the story. And then, when I did catch him on Friday I found out that Pete is, get this, Pete is visiting his parents. An event even rarer than a something in a blue moon – Pete visiting his parents is practically mythical. He, like Kate, was head over heels with the sympathies when I called him, but swore on his not-even-dead-yet grandmother's grave that he was on the brink of being disinherited if he didn't show his face this weekend – some kind of wedding anniversary or something. He didn't even stay on the phone long enough to tell me any salacious details about Wolfie. The selfish bastard.

Of course, by Saturday morning I've already pouted long and hard about what a crap bunch of friends I have, deserting me in my hour of need. And I'm actually over it, because really, really truly, there's only one person I want to see right now. Only one person I want to spend this weekend with. And that's Rex. And he isn't picking up his phone – landline or mobile.

I've left him precisely twenty-seven messages – each one sobbed into the heartless abyss of his top of the range digital answer phone. I've explained exactly – painfully exactly – what happened after he left the pub on Wednesday, from The Pink Elephant through to Mark Valentine ending up in my flat on my bed talking dirty to me. I have told the whole truth. Rex has not called back.

But I need Rex. Or, as I put it in message thirteen: I nee-ee-eed him. Because there are things only Rex can do like sex, entertainment, midnight runs to the 24-hour petrol station and, in this particular case, sort out my career stuff. Because Rex is the one who does career. Rex is the one out of us who does grown-up. Rex is the one who saves his money, understands mortgages, and probably even has shares and that kind of stuff. Damn him – Rex is the good one.

So here I am, without entertainment, without career guidance and without sex. And with nothing to fall back on but my own resourcefulness.

So I do the following things to try to alleviate my misery and stop myself remembering that it really is all totally self-induced. I buy a huge newspaper with lots of sections and read far more of it than probably anyone else in the country – even its editor – has ever done before. I turn on the television and find a lot of sport on most of the channels. I attempt to watch some of the sport, hoping to find it surprisingly engaging, but, in fact, finding it unsurprisingly not at all engaging. Reaching a point of desperation, I even pop upstairs and see my decrepit landlord to pay my next month's rent a whole week before it's due, and accept his offer of a cup of tea laced with brandy and a listen to some ancient classical records turned up to an eardrum endangering volume (honestly, what with that and the beep-beep type music that occasionally wafts from the top flat when the weird guy from up there is in residence, I'm surprised we don't have subsidence or something). I leave Rex a few more messages to get the number up to a nice round thirty – and then a few more to get it up to a nice octagonal thirty seven. And then I give up all pretence at distraction and call Mark Valentine.

Mark, almost as if he is conforming to the new craze for letting down Sophie that is sweeping the nation, answers the phone with a slightly shifty sounding tone and claims to be busy.

'Are you working?' I ask, not even because I want to know so much as because I quite like talking to another human being – well, one that can actually hear me at least.

'Yeah. Sorry, babe, I've really got to go. I'm already late.'

'Yeah, um, but . . .' I scrabble around, desperate for a handhold to keep the conversation going for a few more pathetic seconds.

And then Mark Valentine says, 'Hey, though, why don't you come down here?'

'What? Why? Come down where?'

'Well, the hotel, you could come and watch me work. See how easy it is to walk the walk.'

'Watch you . . .' Every part of me is boggling. 'Won't your customer mind?'

Mark laughs. My God he has a good laugh. 'Oh Sophie,' he says, his voice still dancing, 'not every part of my job is about sex you know.'

So I agree, mostly because the mood I'm in I would have said yes to any offer that got me out of my flat, let alone one as intriguing as this. Mark tells me where to meet him and I scrawl the name of one of Brighton's lesser known – but still rather swanky hotels – on the back of an envelope. And I can't even hear the voice in my head, the one that is reminding me about my current life crisis pile up and how this is really not going to help. Not one bit.

The name scrawled on the back of the envelope, which is now scrunched in my pocket, is The Anchor. The Anchor is kind of on Brighton seafront, but not. Where most of the seafront hotels – big and small – line up as neatly as teeth in a Californian smile, The Anchor sits at a jaunty angle, oblique to the sea, like a solitary snaggle, oblivious to the regimented neatness to its east and west.

I've only been inside it once, when one of my friends came down to visit and got a cheap internet deal to stay there. Rex and I spent the evening drinking, quipping and generally being young and happening in its very pretty, very high-ceilinged bar. But I try not to think about this as I return to the same bar and scan the room for Mark, because I'm trying not to think about Rex.

Mark clocks me first, catching my eye in a way that makes me certain he has been watching for me ever since our phone call ended. Alert and yet discreet. I am also certain that his companion is completely unaware of his vigilance, from his sly wink at me, and the way he subtly directs me to sit at a nearby table.

Within moments of my bottom hitting the uphol-
stery a fancy cocktail is elegantly plonked on my table,
brought by a slightly too-knowing bartender – who
also lets me know that the drink is courtesy of Mr
Mark Valentine.

So here I am in the world of "Mr Mark Valentine" –
a world where, if you can put up with the almost
inaudible murmurs of snide disapproval, magic and
sparkle are there for the taking. Magic and sparkle and
rather fancy cocktails.

I push aside a small flotilla of cocktail umbrellas and
take a deep swig of something that looks not unlike
pink bubble bath and tastes of pure sugar rush.

It's after a few long sips of this concoction, when I
relax and get a proper look at the woman Mark is with,
that I really get it. What he's doing, that is. Not the
male escort business end – although I get that too –
but what he's doing inviting me along here. In short,
it's not just the kindness of his heart going out to
lonely old me. Mark, as ever, is trying to close his sale.

The woman Mark is sitting opposite is very ordinary.
She's an averagely good-looking middle-aged woman,
with a slightly-puffy pinkish face and slightly-puffy
blondish hair. She has that slightly sad look of a
woman who turned heads in her day, but now that
day is long gone, leaving her just over-eager, over-
dressed and overweight. She's the sort of woman that I
wouldn't look twice at. The sort that certainly don't do
what I know she is doing.

And so Mark's message is louder and clearer than
The Radio Four Today Programme blasting through my
ceiling every morning. 'Look, Sophie, look. This woman
is older, wiser and far, far squarer than you. And look
what she's doing! She's paying for sex! Just like you
want to and are too scared to go through with. You

dithering loser. This fast-fading, True-Blue, *Daily Mail*-reading housewife is closer to the bleeding edge than you'll ever be!'

And, OK, so that might not be word for word what Mark is trying to say, but that's my version.

I watch them over my brimming glass of liquid candyfloss for long minutes. Minutes that add up and up, and soon slide past the hour mark. The bartender refreshes my drink with another knowing look. And Mark just keeps on turning it on.

Tonight he's given his usual super trashy whore-chic a miss. He's wearing a suit. I'm not a huge fan of suits. I see Rex in a suit nearly every evening when he gets home from work, so I don't have that 'Wow! Look-at-you-all-dressed-up!' thing about a man in a suit. But Mark's suit is pretty good – for a suit. It's tight – but tight in that well-cut, form-skimming way, rather than in an ill-fitting way. And it's about two shades of blue darker than his cornflower eyes. (I'm a designer, so I can be anally precise about these things – I could even make a decent stab at the Pantone number.) Underneath the suit is a perfectly matching shirt and a perfectly matching tie. He's just a sea of perfect blue, melting and flowing all over his dirty, whip-scarred body. Which all abbreviates to: it's *so* a good look, not just for impressing Mrs Lady, but also for hooking me right back in as a lifetime member of The Mark Valentine Appreciation Society.

So with that outfit, over a package which contains all the usual Mark Valentine perks and highlights, you have something that I could watch all evening. And that's without the performance. Of course I know all about Mark's flirting, Marks lip-licking, pouting, winking, blinking, fringe-tossing, finger-sucking roadshow. But it's all new and exciting to see it being performed for someone else, without all the pressure of being the subject of such eye-popping intensity.

But at around the hour and fifteen minute mark, just as I'm really getting into it – along with the slight buzz from my noxious drinks – it's suddenly over. Curtain down, lights up, as Mark and Mrs Lady suddenly make a dash for the wings.

But before I can even wonder how my fun can be over so fast, my bartender is back and, instead of another Flaming Flamingo, he has an envelope, which I take.

Naturally the envelope contains a message for me, naturally the message is from Mark. I could lick the handwriting.

Hi Sophie-babe

Glad you could come – boring old work will be much more fun with an appreciative audience like you. Now, if you are reading this that means I've gone upstairs with Claudia and you're sitting there wondering why all the fun had to stop. Well it doesn't. Take this letter along to the security guards' room – go through the Staff Only door off the foyer and you'll find it. Ask for Artie and tell him you're interested in room 311. He should be expecting you, but show him this if he doesn't treat you perfectly.

Love Mark

And he's signed it with five kisses.

19

I'm so eager for the next act that I don't stop to think much. I want more fun right now. I simply burrow in my purse for a tip for my bartender and then make haste to the foyer.

It feels decidedly wrong to slip through a door marked Staff Only. I do a quick three-sixty round the echoey marbled reception, but no one is paying me the slightest bit of attention, let alone getting ready to pounce if I cross the sacred boundary that divides staff and punter. In fact the foyer is practically empty apart from a huge maple reception desk, behind which a blazer-clad babe is checking in a fat businessman.

Once I am certain neither of them care about what I'm doing, I ease open the door and step over the threshold into a forbidden kingdom, or at least, into a grubby corridor – what is it about my lifestyle choices these days and grubby corridors?

But I am undeterred by yuk and filth and I begin my quest for Artie. I scamper past hampers of clean towels and hampers of dirty towels, mops and buckets and little carts laden with miniature toiletries. I pass several closed doors and, after a few hundred yards, begin to wonder if I am heading in the right direction. I follow the corridor as it turns to the right and then, as I am seriously thinking about going back, I see a small flight of about five steps to my left and at the bottom a set of double doors marked 'Security'.

Through the glass panels set into the doors I can see

rows and rows of black and white television monitors. Well, well, well.

As I clip down the steps I can seen right into the security guard's room through the glass in the doors. It's a smallish room, not much more than a desk with two swivelly chairs set at it, and a bank of monitors which loom oppressively over the desk, reaching right up to the ceiling. Looking from one to another I can see – in full on grainy-black-and-white-o-vision, the bar, the foyer, something which looks like a very meanly appointed gym, and mile after mile of carpeted corridor. The Anchor is a strange sort of place really – not exactly posh, but not exactly shabby either. Flattened out into two dimensions on so many monitors like this it is clear just how schizo it is, with its gorgeously baroque, turquoise and grey, marbly-mapley foyer and soaring-ceilinged bar, sharing nothing but proximity with its run down-looking corridors and rather crumbly façade.

There's only one person in the room and I don't waste any time in making my presence known in the testosterone-heavy atmosphere. 'Hi, are you Artie?'

The man I'm addressing swings round on his chair to look at me and I purse my lips as I am on the receiving end of yet another knowing smile and an unmistakable quick once over.

'Oh, you're Mark's friend then?' He's a friendly looking man. His face has that sort of blank, open quality to it – just slightly gormless – but he's also big-framed and chunky. The bigness of him would be intimidating without the village idiot face, and the face would be snigger-worthy without the bulk. But it works; even though I shouldn't, I feel quite welcome. And after my heart-racing trespass down the corridor to get here, I start to feel myself relax.

I smile at Artie. 'Uh-huh,' I say, with a nod.

'Okay, well don't worry, it's all set up. 311, right? I've put the feed through to the viewing room.'

I smile and try not to let on that I'm not really sure what he's on about.

Artie nods over his left shoulder, directing me to a small door, which I could swear wasn't there a minute ago.

And it's only then that I really, finally, realise just what sort of entertainment Mark has set up for me this evening. And I just can't quite believe it. 'I can watch what's happening in the room?' I say in disbelief, my mouth and eyes both going just a little too wide.

'Well, we're not meant to of course, but if a nice guy like your Mr Valentine asks me to set this kind of thing up, well, anything is possible.'

'But why are there cameras in the rooms at all? You don't watch the guests in these rooms yourself do you? I mean, without them knowing.'

'Well, like I say, we're not meant to.'

And I make a mental note never to stay in a hotel ever again, as I follow Artie into the viewing room.

The viewing room makes the security guard's room look like a spacious palace. It is a cupboard. And that's not artful description – that's basic fact. A cupboard into which has been wedged a tiny swivel chair and a card table supporting a creaky monitor. The title 'viewing room' really has quite a few more syllables than this tiny space deserves.

But actually, I'm far too excited about the 'viewing' side of this place to complain too much about how it falls down on the 'room' aspects. So much so that I almost squeak with delight, as I cram myself into the hard, wobbly chair and look up at Artie expectantly.

Artie grins, flicks a switch and the monitor comes alive.

I instantly forget how to breathe. Mrs Lady – Claudia – is on the bed; a generous double, out of proportion, in a meanly sized little room. She's lost most of her clothes since I last saw her and is only just covered in a lacy negligée, which is brief enough that creamy curvy flesh spills out around the plunging neckline. Her voluptuous legs and manicured toes ruffle the duvet, while her tarantula-lashed eyes are closed over flushed cheeks, making her face a picture of bliss. On top of her, hiding the rest of her body, hovers Mark's broad, glistening back and bubble-wrap bum.

Sadly, I can only see the faintest traces of the marks that Mark showed me covering his back on Wednesday night. But that doesn't stop me enjoying the way he's thrusting elegantly – almost teasingly – and the way her mouth is moving in response, but I can't tell if she's making sounds of compliant bliss or urging for more.

In the viewing room I start to breathe again, if only so I can live to carry on looking at this image for longer. Behind me Artie is like a statue. And I can't help wondering if he's just enjoying the free sex show or if his willingness to do anything for 'Mr Valentine' is about more than just the Secret Brotherhood of the Service Industry.

Although I know that Mark knows we are watching him, although I know he facilitated the whole thing, it's still sort of shocking when he looks over his muscular shoulder and winks right at us – reminding us that he's putting on this little display full in the knowledge that he's being watched. I squeeze my legs together and hear my breathing get a little deeper.

Mark starts to move a little faster, at the same time taking hold of one of Claudia's wrists in each big hand and pinning her down on the bed, trapping her with his weight so she can't move. I can see the excitement build on her face when he does this. In complete contrast to the last time I saw Mark naked, now he's the one in control and Claudia is completely at his mercy.

He slows his rhythm again, teasing her further. I can see her squirming, trying to buck her hips up harder, but he has her so well pinned down she can barely move. Submissively, her head goes back against the pillows, and Mark presses his lips into the well of her pale throat. Her eyes snap open. And then he starts to move faster again. And then she starts to come.

It's like watching some perfect choreography – the way they seem so smooth, so polished, so in tune with each other. It's like someone is directing them.

But the best part – for me anyway – comes right at the end. After I've watched Mark step up his rhythm and Claudia melt in response. After I've seen Claudia twist and buck beneath Mark. After I've seen Mark tense and tighten – holding on and holding back until the last possible moment. After all that, my moment comes when Mark is sitting on the bed, in just his trousers, and Claudia is dressed and has one hand on the door, I get my (very literal) money shot.

She opens her handbag and pulls out a little pile of cash, then offers it to him with a coy expression on her face that makes me think that she is enjoying this part as much as I am. And with no special ceremony Mark gets up, walks over to her and takes the money.

To most people I guess this part would be nothing. Artie isn't even watching any more – but to me it's everything. It's the whole point. And I so wish I was taping this.

It's hard to explain. I don't usually even try. But Mark looks so sexy as he takes the money. It's not because it demeans him, although actually it does, a little bit. But it's way more complicated than that. There's just something about a man selling himself – it's so dirty and secret and wrong. Men just aren't supposed to do stuff like that. But this one does. I think that's what it is.

And so, after Claudia has left, when Mark turns to the camera and beckons me with a crooked finger, I barely even pause to thank Artie before I hurtle back to the foyer and up the stairs two at a time – not even thinking to take the lift.

20

When I get up to Mark's room, a bit out of breath, things start to go a bit wrong, or maybe go a bit right, depending on which side of the moral compass I look at this whole situation from.

Mark is all stretchy relaxed, like an athlete post-race. He's still topless when he answers the door and doesn't show any sign of getting any more dressed any time soon, as he perches on the edge of the bed and glows at me.

'God, Sophie, this might sound weird, but thanks for that. Having you up in the gods really enhanced my performance for some reason.'

'Really?' I'm kind of flattered, but Mark's so hyped – he almost seems like he's on drugs or something – it's hard to really take what he's saying straight. OK, that often seems to be the case with Mark, but this time it's different – and not in a good way.

He's babbling, 'Oh yeah. Claudia's a regular, but she's such hard work sometimes. She says she books me because she "wants to feel beautiful", she says that all the time, "Make me feel beautiful, Mark," but that's bloody hard work sometimes, because, you know, she isn't beautiful and sometimes I really don't feel like play-acting for her.'

'Yeah.' And I can feel myself stepping back suddenly, sounding as vague as I feel, because I don't want to hear this. The last thing I want is to hear Mark talk about a client in less than glowing terms.

'Silly cow. Anyway, did you like what you saw?'

'Yes.' Why lie?

'So come on, Sophie, when are you going to book me? I won't lie to you, I don't go to this much trouble for most potentials, but with you, I don't know, I can't seem to let it go.'

And, God, talk about scales falling from my eyes, I feel like I've just seen the real Mark. And I don't like it.

The words just fall out of my mouth. 'Maybe you should let go actually, maybe you really should stop trying to charm the pants off me.' And I do feel kind of guilty suddenly, sort of like I should be grateful after all the effort Mark has put in for me this evening. But I don't. After all, I've never seen *this* Mark before – as cocky as ever, but without any of the charm.

Mark's looking at me all confused. 'Oh, Sophie, don't do this. It's not that bloody Rex again is it? You really ought to let him go you know, he's no good for you.'

And that makes me think of Rex, and I suddenly realise I'd forgotten all about the horribleness of being dumped. Ever since I walked into this hotel I've been in a sort of bubble. A fantasy bubble where the outside world wasn't even a memory. That bubble burst when Mark started slagging off poor old Claudia. I don't just remember that Rex has dumped me though – I remember why. 'I have,' I say. 'Or at least he's let me go.'

'Well, same difference. So what's the problem?'

'I just, well, I just don't think you're a very nice person.'

And I can't even bear to hear Mark's response to that, so I turn around, not listening, and pull open the door of room 311. I practically sprint up the shabby corridor.

But I don't get more than a few feet. Mark's in the

hallway too, calling after me, barefoot and bare-chested. 'Shit, Sophie, sorry. Hang on, Sophie.'

He catches up with me just in front of the lifts, his eyes looking softer. 'Sophie, I'm sorry. I know I was a bit, well, a bit off back there. It's just, well, Claudia likes me to be, you know, dominant, and sometimes I can't quite turn it off that quickly. Sorry. I forgot that wasn't your sort of thing.'

'What isn't my sort of thing?'

'Oh, you know, the manly man stuff. Alpha male. Grrr.' And he grins at me.

And he's really already halfway to winning me back. 'OK,' I say.

'I just thought you'd like to see it though, see me do something different. See I'm not just a one trick pony. You did like it didn't you?'

'Yes,' I say, very tentatively.

Mark's face gets even brighter. 'I knew you would. You are such a pervert, Sophie. Now listen, here's the thing, the thing I really want you to understand, Claudia's never had to tell me to do that stuff. I just know, and she loves that she doesn't have to ask. I just do my research, read people a bit and give them just what they want. Just like I knew you'd like to watch Claudia. Just like I knew you'd like to watch me and Wanda.'

And then, when he says that, just when I was about to give it all up to him, it's like the whole world – which currently consists of The Anchor Hotel third floor lobby – comes crashing down.

'What?'

Mark doesn't say anything. His face is frozen mid-babble. He knows what he's just done and he can't believe it.

So I keep talking. 'What do you mean, you knew I'd

like to watch you and Wanda? Did you set that up like you set this up? Did you set me up?'

'Uh,' Mark says, then seems to regain a bit of composure. 'Well,' he says, sounding more defiant, 'you liked it didn't you?'

'Yes,' I say, livid suddenly, almost foaming at the mouth, 'I liked it so much it nearly got me. I nearly slept with you that night. I would have done, if it hadn't been for Rex on the answerphone. Fuck you Mark. You were there at my birthday. Didn't you hear me say that sex with someone like you was my fantasy? It was never meant to be something I was actually going to do.'

And I run then. I run down the stairs by the lifts all the way to the ground floor. I don't even notice if Mark is following, but he isn't there in the street outside The Anchor, which is when I stop and catch my breath.

It's twinkly-cold outside. There are no clouds and the stars over the sea are bright enough to jostle with the neon and sodium to provide illumination. Even at this time of year Saturday night means there are weekender-clubbers clogging the streets in search of sweaty Nirvana. I have to swim against the tide more than once as swathes of gelled hair and handbags swarm past me towards the nightclubs that throb in the seafront arches underneath the promenade.

I feel strange amongst these people. Strange and alien, even though I live here and they are the invaders, cutting down anything and everything in their way as they rampage from the railway station towards their first plastic pint glass of Stella. I think I feel like the interloper because they're meant to be here. What they're doing makes sense – in a drunken, shouty, lairy sort of a way. But me. What I'm doing. This bizarre path I've taken, what kind of sense does that make? At what point did I reach a fork in the road and decide to take the branch marked WTF?

Because What-The-Fuck is, without a doubt, where I have ended up. I seem to have decided to choose Mark Valentine over Rex. Which is a decision that no one in their right minds would make if they thought about it for more than a second. Yeah, actually, thinking – I knew there was something I ought to have done.

Rex! Part of me wants to run down to the water's edge – where the foamy white waves are slapping against the wet stones – and shout his name out to the night horizon. (But I won't because it's cold, and the tide's out, and it'd be a miserable scramble back up to street level.)

So instead of screaming out my torment to Neptune, I fish out my mobile and dial Kate.

'I can't believe he dumped me.' I squawk, before she's even finished greeting me, sniffing hard at the end of the sentence as my throat tightens and I have to force myself not to cry.

'I know, babe,' Kate commiserates. It's noisy wherever she is. Probably in the bar of wherever this conference is happening. 'I mean, I just always assumed you had him for keeps. You've always treated him like such shit, Sophie. Who'd've thought you'd finally find his limit.'

I stop walking, freezing on the promenade. This is a bit of a shock, frankly. I suppose Kate has been a bit vocal before how I really ought to be nicer to Rex. But I always put that down to her being a bit jealous about me having a boyfriend, when she has been making it clear for a while now that she thinks it is high time Mr Right showed up.

'Um, Kate . . .' I say slowly, still rather snivelly.

'Hang on, Sophie,' Kate interrupts, in full-on business-like mode, 'Look, I can't really talk now. But I'll call you tomorrow, because I do need to talk to you about Rex. There are a few things you need to know.'

And that's it. She hangs up. Not even a proper goodbye. And I'm standing there, amidst the stars and the 24-hour Party People and the ever-present bloody seagulls, wondering how on earth Kate could be such a bitch.

Half an hour or so later, I arrive home as cold as I am pissed off, and as pissed off as I am cold. I'm so in the mood for sugar, I'd probably inject myself with golden syrup if that were actually possible and I wasn't needle-phobic. Unfortunately though, either a horde of locusts has just ripped through my kitchen or I really need to go shopping, because the cupboards are bare. I have to settle for crunching on a handful of sugar-coated breakfast cereal, which is not very satisfactory and does nothing for my mood. So much for agreeing with Mark that sugar is tantamount to poison. And when I think about that I remember that that conversation was before Rex dumped me.

And then I do start to cry.

By the time I stumble into the bedroom I'm a snotty bleary mess. But I perk up pretty quick because the red light on my answer machine is winking and that can surely only mean one thing: Rex!

Ever heard the phrase 'Be careful what you wish for'?

Because Rex sounds weird – possibly drunk – and his message is punctuated by all these strange little exhalations that I realise, with a strange sense of betrayal, means he is bloody smoking. In fact, not only is he back on the fags, he is actually smoking one while he leaves me an answerphone message. 'Hi Sophie, listen, I'm still not ready to talk to you really, but Kate just called me and she wants to tell you something. I kind of said OK. But she's going to tell you it – not me. So please call her tomorrow night like she asked. But don't call me. I'm not picking up anyway.'

And that's it. Click. Whirr. No new messages.

To avoid going to sleep alone in my big cold bed I do the saddest of the sad. I sit down at my computer and pull up my folder of digital photos. I've only had a digital camera for a couple of years so all the pictures are pretty recent and, in typical photograph style, are mostly of birthdays, holidays and Christmases.

Like some future archaeologist I dig around in the mass of anonymous number-identified files until I find what I'm looking for. Perfect images of the happy life I used to have and totally failed to appreciate. Rex, beaming, standing with my parents in a sea of discarded wrapping paper, wearing the 'festive' jumper I'd bought him the year before. Rex, rolling around on my parents' kitchen floor with their dog – play fighting him into a frenzy. Rex, down on the seafront, grinning, all bad sunglasses and peeling pink nose. He always complains so much when the sun shines – covering himself in SPF several million and claiming red-heads should get sun block free on the NHS. I find more and more and fix them up as a slide show on my flickering monitor. As I watch Rex morph from one self into another, over and over, over and back, I get all teary again and finally I pick up the phone one last time.

I dial a number I know by heart and hiss to the over-familiar voicemail message, 'I really need you to come over. I know it's difficult right now. But, please.'

21

My desperate cry for help is answered at an eye-poppingly early hour the following morning. I open the door of my flat to Pete. He's driven through the night and is still in his special occasion suit – a generously-lapelled, powder-blue, gloriously retro number. He's also sporting a suitcase and a suitably sympathetic expression.

He flings his arms and mouth wide open and draws me in. 'Inheritance-schminheritance, I'm here for you, babe. What do I need a third share of a bungalow in Prestatyn for anyway?'

And in reply, I skip the greetings and the gratitude and cut straight to the tears.

Not much later, we sit in my kitchen. Something I hardly ever do because the room is so bloody cold. My half-arsed Brighton conversion of a flat and its lack of proper central heating. (And the fact I keep overlooking this and its other failings because of its lovely oblique sea views and real open fireplace in the sitting room.)

But I want to sit in the kitchen right now, because the mood I'm in, it seems right to be sat here, at 7a.m. on a Sunday morning in January, while it's still dark and I'm giddy from lack of sleep, trying to keep warm using nothing but repeated boils of the kettle and a fan heater that roars like an aeroplane taking off.

I drink camomile – I need something to bring the calm – and Pete drinks Café Direct. We crunch some horrible bourbons that the twenty-four hour petrol station up the road has provided and eventually, after much prodding from Pete, I explain what's on my mind.

'I think I've really blown it with Rex forever.'

Pete's reaction is like a volcanic eruption – he narrowly avoids spraying me with fair trade coffee and bourbon crumbs. 'What! Don't be so stupid.'

'I'm not being stupid. This is serious.'

'No, I think you'll find it is stupid. You are being stupid. Very. In fact, you're practically wearing a straitjacket and bouncing off the walls of your luxuriously padded cell.' Pete looks at me. And his face looks weird.

Talking about Rex with Pete is always a bit weird, these days. It's not like it was when Rex and I first got together and Pete would fill me in on every breath Rex had drawn about me (and Rex probably knew full well he would too). These days Pete tries to remain impartial as far as he can, almost acting as if he doesn't have the inside track on disputes from Rex. But he usually gives away what he knows sooner rather than later.

'Are you sure?'

'Of course I am,' Pete hoots, 'I spend every bloody day with Rex. I spend more time with him than I do with you. He tells me stuff. He tells me all about you. He was going on about you and this pathetic break-up – that no one except you and him believe in – for all of the end of last week. He loves you. Haven't you bloody noticed that? I mean, at all?' Rex rolls his eyes.

I feel a lump forming in the back of my throat. 'Don't be mean to me, Pete, I can't stand it.'

Pete smiles. 'I'm sorry, sweetie, but you are so damn stupid.' He reaches out and touches my hair, gently, nicely.

'So what is it that Kate needs to talk to me about?'

'What! You think Rex is sending Kate to dump you? Do I need to shake you? At a guess, I think she probably wants to smack some sense into you. Now, really, is that all?'

And I say, 'No.'

And I tell all.

Mostly, I talk about Mark Valentine. 'Remember the guy that Kate brought to my birthday meal?'

'Remember him? He's practically seared onto my retinas.'

And I explain everything in detail. Retelling the stuff he already knows and filling in the gaps: how Mark propositioned me in the ladies' loo; how I ended up calling him, etc, etc.

'Oh, and you know that night you took me to meet Wolfie?'

'Yeah?' Pete prompts breathlessly. He's so wide-eyed now he could get an evening job as an owl impersonator.

'Well after I'd left you I kind of ran into Mark,' I continue. 'In fact I was planning to call him anyway, that's why I didn't taxi it straight from there.'

'Oh, and that'd be the night that Rex found Mr Valentine leaving your flat in the morning.'

'Yes. And the two things are connected, but not by the straight line you've just drawn.'

And so I tell Pete about the little scene I came upon, amongst the net curtains, and chintz and bedding plants, in the seething depths of one of Hove's prettiest suburbs. And because it's Pete I tell the full widescreen Technicolor version of the story, complete with a part where I stand up and act out various positions. And then I tell him about The Anchor, and Mark's confession that it was a set up to hook me in. I even take a quick detour there to mention my phone call to Kate, and how cross she was with me. After this Pete's eye-stretching owl transformation is practically complete. He practically flies up to roost on top of the kitchen door.

And then I tell him my side of a story I'm sure he knows well from Rex: how Rex ran into Mark on my doorstep; how I hadn't done anything – although maybe I would have; how Rex dumped me at the bus stop, telling me I was taking the piss.

'I mean, in some ways I just don't get it,' I conclude, 'Rex seemed fine about the whole fantasy thing. That particular evening started out with The Cum Boys and him offering to buy me a lap dance. But then when he runs into Mark, it's all wrong.'

Pete looks at me, and he actually looks quite sympathetic. 'Well, actually, Sophie, I'm not all that surprised you are confused. I mean, I thought Rex felt the same way as me, that you should just get this stupid fantasy out of your system. Live the dream, and all that.'

'And he doesn't,' I leap in, sort of interrupting, 'but what about the magazines, the lap dances, the, all the everything.'

'Hang on, hang on.' Pete waves his hands to shush me. 'Let me explain. Like I said, I thought he was doing all of that to help you get over your thing and that's why I brought Wolfie, um, to the table. But it isn't quite as simple as that. Wolfie would have been quite, quite wrong, just like Mark Valentine was. See, at first, when Rex told me what had happened I couldn't understand why he wasn't pleased. But, well, I guess there's a big difference between a boyfriend and a gay best friend, and it isn't just the lack of knicker action.'

And this is where the fact that Pete has the inside

track on Rex's psyche pays dividends yet again, because Pete, it seems, has all the answers.

'Firstly,' says Pete, making his point with a single digit held in the air. 'He likes that you are turned on by this stuff. It's practically what brought the two of you together, after all. It's your song. It's what Simon Bates would play for you instead of *Everything I Do I Do it for You*. When you two get married it's what you'll both get up and dance to at the reception. But, secondly, it's only OK if it's about you two together and Rex is involved. If it's just you going off on your own and indulging in whatever sexual deviance you like, well, that's where Rex feels you are taking the piss. That's the line. And you crossed it, which just confirms all Rex's worst fears.'

'What fears?'

'That he is just a casual fuck. Okay, a casual fuck that you have been casually fucking for about six years, but, God, Sophie, look at it from his perspective: you won't marry him, you won't move in with him ... Did you know that when you finally gave him a key to this place he actually took me out for a lunchtime drink to celebrate?'

'Oh God.' And Pete is right. Rex did sort of explain this to me. I just don't think I could really admit it before. So it seems that while Rex plus me plus lap dance fun is OK, me appearing to have a Mark Valentine expense account is so far off the OK scale its practically in orbit. 'How am I ever going to make it up to him?'

22

And Pete's certainly right about the casual fuck thing. I certainly do seem to have Rex and our relationship misfiled for something that's been going strong for six years. But it's not my fault, the relationship just sort of worked out that way.

When Rex and I got together – after my birthday party – the whole relationship just had a weird kind of semi-permanence. I never really saw Rex as a genuine prospect. In fact I had him down as a one-night stand – never really meant to see him again. Because a dirty kinky night like that is the stuff that memories are made of. The kind of memories that one looks back on fondly, when one is happily married to someone else. I never really thought I should settle down in blissful long-term with the person who I shared so much of my depravity with – we'd never get anything done. Rex was filed under kinky bastards I have known – not a huge file I'm quite glad to say – and he would have stayed that way if fate hadn't muscled in.

My twenty-fifth birthday party, and the fun that followed it, swiftly became a memory, and my sparkly new job took the top slot in my personal things-I-am-excited-about chart rundown.

Just four weeks' notice later, I was sitting at my new desk in my new job and still smirking about the *Three Men and a Baby* poster that adorned the space next to my workstation, when I got an email from Pete – in fact that email was a small landmark, my first ever personal email received at work, the beginning of the end for proper productivity.

I fumbled slightly with the unfamiliar knobs and buttons of Outlook, and finally managed to unravel the message.

It turned out to be good news, Pete had gone for a coffee with Rex – the guy I'd 'met' at my birthday party – and apparently discovered that they were made for each other, advertising-creative-teamwork-wise. Plus, Rex had asked after me, which might have been out of politeness, but was still nice to hear. So, although I wasn't really planning on seeing Rex again, as Rex and Pete were now a match made in advertising heaven, it looked like I would be seeing Rex again, somewhere along the line. And that was kind of why my one-night stand with Rex just kept getting repeated over and over again.

Well, it was partly that, partly cruel fate, and partly my own pathetic lack of willpower, because once I knew Rex and I shared this kink, and Rex was suddenly on tap as my best friend's new-best-friend, I was stuck. I couldn't say no. And so the age of Rex-as-fuck-buddy began. And it never really ended – not properly – it just sort of drifted into something else, but sometimes I forget that things have changed. Especially as I have stood resolutely in the way of anything that might mark the dawning of a new era (i.e. moving in together).

But once Rex had re-entered my life, albeit in a subtle and sideways manner, via Pete's jubilant email, our relationship was taken for granted. At first it was just me going to meet Pete from work in the pub over the road from the station, and Rex being there too, and then ending up in Rex's bed, enacting more fantasies from the red hot to the risible. One night he'd be tied to the bed again and I'd be holding a cheque just out of reach of his snapping teeth and another he'd be dancing on his table in the ubiquitous golden shorts, with me tucking fivers into the waistband until we both couldn't stop laughing.

And my new job suffered in the early days as I spent far too much time fantasising about my out-of-office hours shag-a-thon.

I started dwelling on him, far more than was really appropriate in between nine and five. So, although, from the outside I looked as if I was just fiddling around with the settings of my brand spanking new email account, on my ridiculously huge monitor, really I was suddenly enjoying fantasies about Rex so lurid I was surprised the air around my brain hadn't turned luminous purple. I dreamed of a half naked Rex parading across a stage in his amazing gold shorts, with a buffed bronzed chest (hey – it was a fantasy, after all), and he was wearing manacles and a metal collar. It was like some kind of fantastical version of ancient Rome. And while I dreamed my little dream I squirmed in my swivel chair and let the phone ring far longer than I really should.

And it's this stuff, these early days that I recount to Pete over a meat-free breakfast fry-up in the vegan café round the corner from my flat, as I try and explain exactly what 'my fucking problem' is as part of Pete's unique getting-to-the-bottom-of-things therapy .

'So it's all your fault,' I conclude, a lentil sausage waggling at a precarious angle from my fork. 'I probably wouldn't even have seen Rex again if you hadn't started working with him. We were meant to be ships that pass in the night sort of thing.'

'So, you're saying what? Rex is king of *Groundhog*

Day? A one-night stand you keep having over and over again? No wonder he's pissed off.'

'Yeah. Kind of.'

'Well the only problem with your little pet theory, babe, is that most evenings you and Rex don't even come close to shagging. He just drags himself down from the railway station to your place – which, by the way, is an entire bus ride away, when his own place is an easy walk – in order to eat a microwaved baked potato and fall asleep in front of the ITV 2 repeat of *Coronation Street*.'

Which just goes to prove that Rex really does tell Pete everything. Sadly, I look down at the space on my plate where my fried egg would be if the strict vegan doctrine of this café allowed such abominations.

'Look, Sophie, you and Rex are made for each other. It's obvious. I've known it for ages, and would have done even if I hadn't had bloody Rex telling me so twice a day for most of the last year or ten. Kate knows it too. That's probably why she's being so arsey with you.'

'You think?'

'My God, Sophie!' Pete shrieks, even though he'd swear on not-even-dead-yet grandmother's grave that he never shrieks, he does this time – it's enough to endanger the windows. 'What is this – *The Strange Case of the Sophie Taylor in the Night Time?* Have you had some kind of empathy bypass? Try looking at things from someone else's point of view some time. Maybe from Kate's! You have exactly what she wants – a lovely guy who wants to settle down with you. And as Kate is basically a nice person, she is actually peeved to see you blow it. So sort it out. For all our sakes.'

'Hang on a minute. I get what you're saying, but

isn't this a bit of a U-turn? Wasn't it you who's been encouraging me all along to fulfil my fantasies – to go for it?'

And at this point Pete at least has the decency to hang his head a bit. 'Yes. But I know now that I had got it all wrong – that was before Rex explained the way this worked, after that *High Noon* showdown thing when Rex and Fuck-Me Valentine crossed paths outside your place, and it all went a bit shit-shaped. I'm sorry I complicated things, but I thought Rex was OK with this stuff and we could just have a laugh. It was like old school Pete and Sophie, from the pre-Tyrannosaurus Rex era. Hanging out in The Pink Elephant. Taking that mad taxi ride to Wolfie's. Bonding in that seventies sitting room. I stopped as soon as it all started going a bit wobbly didn't I?'

'Well, yeah.'

Of course that isn't exactly what Pete did – what Pete did, I can see quite clearly now is found out about the Mark–Rex interface from Rex on Thursday morning, and how bloody wrong he'd read the whole situation, and then hid from me for a day or so by not returning my calls, conveniently dashing off up north for whatever it was he was obliged to attend yesterday. I'm pretty sure, looking at him right now, that he hid because he thought he might be to blame. Which he is a little bit. I'm also pretty sure that he drove through the night last night because he feels horribly guilty about the whole thing.

'Look, Sophie, never mind anything I might have said or done or anything. I might be living La Vita Loca, myself, but, honestly if I had a guy like Rex chasing me to ground I would so roll over and let him catch me. What do you think you're going to do? Do better? You think the streets out there are paved with Mark Valentine look-a-likes all panting to commit to a weird-ass flakey pervert like you?'

'Okay then, Mr-I-Know-Him-So-Well, what do I do?'

'Heh,' Pete grins, 'you just need to take your Uncle Pete's advice.'

Somehow this seems like an ominous prospect. 'And what's that exactly?'

'Simple, babe. You call up Rex and you ask him to marry you.'

Simple.

'Oh yeah,' Pete adds, 'and while you're at it make sure he knows that you didn't actually fuck Valentine, because I don't think you've actually told him that have you? It is quite an important detail.'

And Pete's right. I hadn't. In all my manic answer phone messages to Rex I'd, in fact, forgotten about that. I'd come so close, so many times, I'd actually forgotten I hadn't quite hit a home run. Which might be just the break I need.

I spend the afternoon lying on my bed, watching the dust floating in the air and listening to an, only slightly muffled, Radio Four play which is throbbing down through the ceiling from my landlord's flat above. Pete – having clubbed me into submission with his drawn-out monologues and the sheer force of his being right – has long since left me, leaving nothing but a Pete-shaped dent in my duvet and the last of the Bourbons.

When it starts to get dark, I sit up to turn on the bedside light. As the sudden illumination snaps around the room, in and out of dark far away corners, I see the wardrobe, one door half open, peekabooing Rex's bright white shirts hanging there in the blackness. Rex has made no attempt to retrieve his stuff – which is surely a good sign, particularly as he seems to keep more than half his life in my flat. But I don't muse on the wardrobe contents for long, because I'm easily distracted. And next to the wardrobe is the telephone table.

I sit and look at the phone for ages, cramming the last of the bourbons into my mouth, without even noticing. Without Pete here to buoy me up, his plan to phone Rex and tell him I didn't sleep with Mark and then ask him to marry me seems pretty dumb. After all – shirts still hanging in my wardrobe or not – doesn't Rex ever so slightly hate me at the moment? Surely people don't welcome marriage proposals from people they hate. And there's still a little voice deep down inside me that keeps insisting that I'm supposed to be the one who is against all that sort of thing?

But all those objections can just take their places in the backseats of my mind because somehow, now, as I think about the idea of Rex coming back – of me and him living together somewhere – somewhere nice, perhaps even somewhere with central heating. Of him telling me what I should say to Dave-Steve-Ed tomorrow. Of him and his gold *Fame*-reject shorts. I think I finally get it. It might have been as impenetrable as an IKEA shortcut – but I think I've found my way back to the right path. Well, nearly.

I walk across the room, and in the same tiny second that I reach for the phone it rings. Well almost. It gives a little spluttery ping, just the embryonic start of a ring, but easily enough that when I pick it up there's someone already there on the other end. Someone I'd sort of forgotten about. But someone who changes my plans completely.

'Hi Sophie, it's Kate here. I really need to talk to you.'

23

Whatever Kate has to tell me it isn't something that can be done on the telephone (apparently). In fact it has to be done over breakfast, at 8.30 on a Monday morning, in Brighton's most pretentious new wi-fi-tastic breakfast venue.

I'm sitting in what I suppose is an atrium, essentially a foyer, but one that has been designed to within an inch of its life. Is that what turns a foyer into an atrium? Rex would know.

I can't yet be ushered through into the inner sanctum – and the venue for my breakfast summit with Kate – because it's members only. So I'm stuck here on the tan leatherette, leafing through one of Brighton's content-free listings papers, while I wait the predictable fifteen minutes until Kate turns up.

Beyond the swing doors, through which I am not sanctioned to pass, I can see a bit of an Elle-Deco-worthy concoction of glistening chrome and impossible-to-clean matt white. But I can't really see the whole room, because the rest of my view is restricted by a veritable Mount Everest of fruit sitting on the matt white bar. Which means I can predict, without the aid of any kind of crystal appendage, that the menu is going to be positively heaving with a near-infinite variety of juice blends and ubiquitous smoothies. Not proper food at all – but at least it means I'll get a good start on my five portions of fruit and veg for the day.

I check my watch repeatedly as the ticks eventually

tock their way to 8.45, and then before I can say 'whoever heard of a café that you had to be a member of', the answer appears. Kate, right on cue, and looking embarrassingly immaculate.

After a quick burst of air kissing and pleasantries, I follow her through the swinging doors from nonentity-land into the glass-domed realm of the special people.

I can't help staring at Kate's hair as she walks in front of me. Kate has always had the most amazing hair. But it seems more noticeable at breakfast time – somehow. It must really take some work. God knows what time she has to get up to make her hair look like that by 8.45 in the morning.

It's kind of like straw, but in a good way. It's a beautiful sunny-honey yellow and it sort of shines in the way that normally only happens in shampoo adverts. It also manages to flop into various artful shapes when she shakes it out, or runs her hand through it, or cascades prettily into her seat like so much taupe cashmere and caramel suede and choc-olate-brown leather. I don't know how she does it – but it may be somehow linked to the fact that she is always fifteen minutes late. I guess she is what's called a high maintenance person (whereas I am so low mainten-ance that I'm surprised the disparity doesn't cause her styling products to leech towards me via tablecloth osmosis).

Don't get me wrong, I love Kate, I just wouldn't want to be her on a weekday morning.

When Kate doesn't launch straight into the thing she is here to tell me, I can't quite bring myself to demand it. Despite Pete's proclamations and eye rolling yesterday morning I've still managed to convince myself that whatever Kate has to tell me is bound to be the worst possible news. I've half sold myself on the idea that she is here to tell me that there is no future for Rex and me, or even that he is getting engaged to someone else, someone nicer and more responsible, perhaps he is even getting engaged to Kate, even though I know full well that the totally glossed-up look really isn't for him.

And if any of my worst case scenarios are, in fact, what Kate has to tell me – and possibly even if it isn't – I just don't want to know, yet. I'm grateful for the five or ten extra minutes of blissful ignorance.

Either way, I know Kate is pissed off with me about the whole Rex situation. I know the very best I can expect here is a strict telling off from the shiny-haired, smoothie-drinking lady executive in the immaculately layered neutrals.

Which is probably why I steer the conversation round to small talk, well, medium-sized talk, medi-umish. My job. Or the soon to be lack of it.

When I give Kate the lowdown on the whole Dave/ Steve/Ed situation, she sucks her teeth a little, though far more elegantly than that description sounds, and pouts. 'Well, honey,' she says, her lip liner enhancing the pretty shapes her mouth is making, 'you know what I reckon you should do?'

'No,' I reply and even though I know this is just conversational politeness, it irritates me, because, of course, I don't bloody know.

'You should tell them to stick it. Or at least, take the redundancy package. I mean, why join their crummy, little, obviously-failing outfit, when you could set up on your own? Go freelance and take your address book with you.'

'My address book?'

'Your client list, whoever you deal with.'

'Oh right.' So far, so typically hard-nosed Kate. And

although this is a good idea in theory it's also a bloody terrifying one. So terrifying in fact that I'm desperate enough to avoid further discussion by saying, 'So, Rex said you had something to tell me.'

Kate suddenly seems to come alive in front of me. Not that she seemed un-alive before, but suddenly she snaps into hyper-real mode, leaning forward to fill my frame and strangely seeming to be in ultrasharp focus.

And everything gets even sharper suddenly when she says, 'Yes, yes I do, Sophie. It's about Mark Valentine.'

And a whole lost drawer full of memories suddenly come crashing back. In fact, I got a glimpse on Saturday night, when Mark reminded me he'd been at my birthday party, but I was so busy gawking at how weird that was, that I forgot the really astonishing thing at the root of all this. Mark was at my birthday party because Kate brought him. Kate, who was sitting there when I told my fantasy about paying for it, was with a man she had hired herself. Okay, so she turned down his offer of after hours playtime pretty firmly, but even so. It was Kate who first introduced me to Mark. He came to my birthday dinner as Kate's date.

I lean forward, over eager. 'What about him?'

'It's about why I brought him to your birthday thing. I guess, now you know what he is, you've been wondering why.'

And, although I hadn't, I can see why Kate thought I might have been. I certainly ought to have been. After all it doesn't make a lot of sense – a woman who's desperate to find Mr Right and settle down comes to a birthday do with a Mr So-Very-Wrong in tow.

'Well,' Kate continues, talking over my train of thought, 'the thing is I didn't. Well, I did, but I did it because Rex asked me to.'

Somewhere across the achingly sophisticated bright-white room someone drops some plates. The crash stops everything, freezes time, as I stare at Kate open-mouthed and try and translate what she has just said into a language I understand.

Long after the sarcastic applause for the dropped plates has died down I'm still staring at Kate, and she is still waiting for me to say something first.

'Why?' I squeak, like the world's most confused mouse.

Kate swallows so hard I can see it in her crease-free neck. 'Because he wanted to see what you would do.'

The value on my shocked-o-meter cranks up even further at this. As soon as Rex's name was mentioned the contingency planning part of my brain started rattling out the idea that maybe Mark was supposed to be my birthday present. Maybe that was why Rex had had him brought along – and something had gone wrong. But it seems like this wasn't the case at all. It seems like . . .

'He was testing me,' I say, each word a struggle.

'Yes. He wanted to see if you would really go through with it. The "for real" thing, if it were right there in front of you for the taking. I really thought you wouldn't. In fact I told him so. I told him it was stupid. And then when you started saying at the table that it was always meant to stay just a fantasy I really thought I was going to be proved right . . .' And she tails off into a shrug.

'But you were right,' I insist, almost knocking over our banana and papaya concoctions with my desperation to get my point across.

Kate frowns.

'I never slept with him,' I say, this time with even more desperate insistence. So much, in fact, that Kate picks up our drinks and holds them safely out of the way of my flailing gestures. And I go on. I tell her exactly what happened that night. Well, in truth I tell her a slightly expurgated version, because Kate is no Pete and there's no point giving her details she really wouldn't appreciate.

'So,' I finish up, 'all I need to do is tell Rex the truth.'

'Kind of,' says Kate.

'What do you mean, "kind of"?'

'Well.' Kate makes a face. 'He might not believe you. I don't want to be a total pessimist, but, seriously, you can't just expect Rex to trust you now. After all, put yourself in his place, what he saw was pretty incriminating.'

'But he has to believe me. I'm telling the truth. You believe me, Kate, don't you?' I'm on my feet now, although I don't remember standing up.

'Yes,' says Kate, not really sounding that much like she does. 'But that's not the point. The place Rex is in right now, well, just don't expect him to fall for the Sophie charms and be a pushover like usual.'

That last remark feels a bit below the belt. I feel sort of sick. This seems so unfair. I'm willing to put my hands up and say I've been treating Rex badly lately. I'd even own up to not being a model girlfriend for most of our relationship. But to be let off all of that and then dumped for something I didn't even do, well, that's just not right.

'Kate,' I say earnestly, leaning right over the table, 'I need to make him believe me. How can I make him believe me?'

'In all honesty, Sophie, I'm not even sure you can, like I said, the mood he's in at the moment, you'd practically need a signed confession from Mark Valentine himself.'

Which is all I need to know.

'Right,' I say, straightening up, 'well if that's what he needs, that's what I'll get him.'

And I'm on a mission now, turning around, heading for the doors, passing the matt-white bar and the matt-white waiters. I'm through the swing doors, through the foyer, out onto the street. I'm pressing my mobile to my ear. And, what thirty minutes ago would have seemed like the most retrograde step possible, is now the only way forward.

'Mark, it's Sophie. I need to see you. Give me your address.'

24

The weird thing about where Mark lives is that it is so ordinary. A first-floor flat in a converted Regency house just round the corner from Waitrose.

Which is disappointing, sort of. Even though I know I should be totally over Mark Valentine now and therefore scoff at the idea that he ought to live in some kind of decadent dungeon strewn with sex toys and exotically perfumed lubricant, I'm not quite there yet. So I'm still a little bit too hooked on the whole fantasy package Mark sold me not to feel a pang or two when I discover his address.

I cross town quickly, apprehension making me walk at a kind of scout's pace – alternating between fast walking and outright running. It's a relief when I hear Mark's voice on the intercom, and he buzzes me in without question.

I trot up to first floor and find the door on the latch.

Mark's flat is small, or, at least, smaller than my place, but perfectly OK for one person, and pretty much what is to be expected this close to the centre of town. The décor is unappealing and peeling, and the furnishings are so eccentric and mismatched that they must have come as part of the place.

But really, no one who entered this flat would really be looking at the décor, or the lack of cat swinging opportunities, because in the middle of this sea of almost depressing tawdriness is the beautiful paradise island of Mark Valentine, far too pretty to exist in this universe. He's perched on the sofa eating toast, in his underpants.

'Hi,' I say, trying not to let the underpants – or rather the lack of anything but underpants – throw me too much.

Mark doesn't look at me. 'I need the money upfront this time,' he says.

I gape for a moment, wondering if I've got the wrong address and this is in fact the flat of Mark's eviller (and much more business-like) twin. 'Mark?'

'Just put it on the table.' He turns towards me then and his beautiful face is flat and grey. 'Sorry, but I've had a lot of trouble with time wasters lately.'

'Mark, I don't want to . . .'

'No, Sophie, that's enough. You have officially run out your free sample meter. I don't care what you actually want right now. Fuck alone knows, as far as I'm concerned. I don't care if you want to tie me to the rafters or discuss your bus route here, my time is your money and it's about time you started paying.'

I swallow. His face tells me everything I need to know about the futility of arguing this one.

'How much?'

Mark rolls his eyes. 'How much have you got on you?'

And, although usually I'm pretty crap at having cash on me – being a fully paid up member the plastic generation – I have got a twenty pound note, which I brought with me in case I needed it for breakfast. The breakfast which, I now realise, I left Kate to shell out for.

When I say, 'Twenty pounds,' I'm pretty sure that won't be anything like enough. Funnily enough, in all this, I never got as far as asking Mark what he actually charged.

'Have you got a credit card?'

'A what?'

'A credit card, you know, little plastic thing, you get a bill every month.'

'Oh.' I fumble about in my wallet, which I already have in my hand, and pull out my single credit card. While I'm doing this Mark stands up and walks across the room. From the small table sitting in front of the flat's pretty bowed window, he retrieves something. At first I think I have never seen anything like it, but then I realise it is one of those old-fashioned credit card machines, the ones with the carbon paper and the thing that slides across to take the imprint of the card. He walks back to me, takes my card out of my hand and puts it in the machine. But he doesn't actually clunk the metal thing over it; he just sets the whole lot down next to him, on the arm of the sofa.

And then he smiles. 'Right then, Sophie, what can I do for you?'

'It's about Rex.'

'Would that be Rex, as in the Latin word for king?'

'No, Rex my boyfriend.'

'Oh, is that who it is?'

And that's when Mark's bitch act finally gets too much for me. 'Stop it.'

'Stop what?'

'Please, stop it. I know you were only nice to me before because you thought I was going to be a client, but you don't have to be like this. Can't you just be normal? Nice, even, now that I am paying.'

And Mark actually looks a little hurt. 'I'll be whatever you want me to be, Sophie, you know that. It's just with you, I'm starting to feel like I've tried everything and I still haven't got a fucking clue what you want. You've beaten me, Sophie. I really thought I was good at reading people. But with you, I give up.'

'What, and this is the real you?'

'Maybe.'

I don't know what to do next. My goal of getting Mark to write me a note saying he never slept with me seems to be somewhere in the middle distance and drifting further and further beyond my reach every time one of us speaks.

I lean back against the wall next to the door and then slide down it, coming to rest with my back pressed against the welcomingly warm radiator. And then, with the soothing heat seeping into my cold body, comes a kind of epiphany.

'Okay,' I say slowly, softly, 'I'll tell you what I think. I don't think this is the real you, I think I hurt your feelings on Saturday, your professional pride, maybe. And if I did I'm sorry, because I have been acting like an absolute cow. And, well, I suppose it's not right to mess someone about like I have done with you. After all, paying for sex might be a hot fantasy to me, but, well, it is your livelihood.' I shoot him a shy smile. 'I've only just realised that, actually.'

Because looking around Mark's flat I realise that although I'd been imagining Mark as an impossibly glamorous figure, he isn't really. He is gorgeous, of course, I was right about that, but he still lives in a normal flat and eats normal toast and has a normal – if currently muted – television in the corner, which is trying to sell him normal cleaning products.

'Oh,' says Mark, 'well, I guess, if that's the case then, I'm sorry too. Sorry I pushed you so hard. It was partly because I thought you wanted me to, but also because I just needed the money really. This time of year is so dead.' He twitches his shoulder in an almost subliminal shrug. 'And I'm really sorry you were so upset when you found out that deal with Wanda was a bit of a set-up. I didn't mean that.'

'I, I still don't really understand that,' I say, hesitantly. 'I mean, how did you set it up? How could you? How could you know I'd be walking down that street? How did you know I'd follow you and spy on you? And more to the point, why? Why did you do that just to get me to sign up as a client? I don't really see how I could have been worth it.'

And Mark smiles, he seems a little embarrassed, and he says, 'Well, there are one or two things you don't know about that night, Sophie, and the first one is the fact that I have this friend called Wolfie.'

It had never occurred to me that Mark and Wolfie might know each other. But I suppose it isn't that surprising, they do do the same job, after all, and Mark had already shown me, with Wanda, that he knows other people in the same line of business. And once that fact is out in the open it does seem something of a coincidence that my stumbling over red hot Mark Valentine action happened just minutes after I left Wolfie's flat.

'Wolfie tipped you off?' I say, proud of my deductive powers.

'Well, yeah. Except not. Not exactly. What happened was, I was round at Wolfie's place one evening last week. I'd set up this kidnap thing with Wanda, as a birthday present to myself, which you know about, and I just had to call her to activate it. Anyway, I was a bit nervous because even though I had chosen the whole scenario right down to the cushion covers, it was still a heavy duty scene for me. I was pushing the envelope, you know. So I went to Wolfie's for a bit of moral support, because he's cute and very understanding.

And, anyway we were sat there watching this Top One Hundred thing on Channel Four, and I was telling him about you. Female clients, or even potential clients, although they aren't rare, exactly, are still notable enough that we talk about them. So I'm talking about you to Wolfie, and then we hear a taxi outside, and I wouldn't normally have bothered looking but I happened to be standing right by the window, and I almost dropped my drink when you got out with that guy from your birthday do.'

'Pete.'

'Yes, well Wolfie recognised Pete too. And he reckoned the two of you must be here to see him. And I was well pissed off to think you might have blown me off, but still be up for it with bloody Wolfie. I mean Wolfie's cute and everything, but, well, I don't want to brag, but I am so much cuter.'

I laugh. Mark is really getting into this story.

'But anyway,' he continues, 'Wolfie and I don't have time for any discussion about you and Pete, we don't hatch a big plan. I just scoot upstairs. And when the two of you are safely tucked up in his living room, Wolfie comes upstairs and tells me he reckons Pete's up for it, but you're still wavering. And that's when I hatch my plan. I just reckoned a bit of, well, a bit of a taste of what you could get from me might be just the thing to stop your dithering. I called Wanda and, well, set the whole thing up from there.'

'Oh.'

'I know, it was a bit not on. But it was just circumstances really. And I thought it was what you wanted.'

I look at him. He looks so earnest (and so cute). 'Well it was, sort of. The trouble is, Mark, seeing you like that nearly made me do something really stupid. You know I have a boyfriend.'

'I know. I know I should have let you go. Can I make it up to you?' And Mark picks up the credit card machine from the sofa arm, takes my card out and holds it out to me. 'No charge, by the way, that was just me being pissy – I couldn't keep it up, not when you said you were actually sorry. I don't think you really have anything to be sorry about. I mean, after all, your saintly boyfriend hired me in the first place.'

'You knew all about that then?'

'Well yeah. Of course I did.'

And, although it's not the thing he has in mind, there is something Mark can do to make it up to me. In fact, with a bit of luck, he can make everything all right.

With a smile I walk over to the table where he got the credit card machine from. It's littered with a variety of admin paraphernalia – it looks rather like he's doing his tax return. (Well it is nearly the end of January.) As I reach out to grab a piece of blank paper and a pen from the table, I wonder briefly whether I should ask Mark about the pros and cons of running one's own small business, but I decide that's for another place and another time. There's something more pressing I need to sort out right now.

'I need you to write something for me,' I say as I cross the room, 'sort of like a confession.'

And, as a rather bemused Mark takes the paper from me and spreads it out on his knees, using a *TV Guide* as a surface to rest on, I explain what I need him to do.

'OK, OK, how's this?' Mark says, once he gets what I'm after. He leans over the paper and starts to write, speaking each word aloud as he goes in a very flat sounding voice.

'I, Mark Valentine, have not had sex with Sophie Taylor. Not at all. Not in any kind of genital to mucus membrane contact sense. And not for want of trying on my part. If she really does have this male hooker fetish, then she has fucking rock solid willpower. You're a lucky guy. Bye-bye. Signed Mark Valentine. Male Whore.' And then he straightens up and looks at me.

I take the paper. 'Thanks.'

'You're welcome. See, I am a nice person.'

And I remember one of the things I said running out on him at The Anchor. 'Yeah, I guess you are. Sorry.'

'That's okay, Sophie. Although I don't really know why you suddenly decided I was a Dirty Rotten Scoundrel. I thought you kind of liked me. I mean actually liked me as well as the fancying me part.'

'I did. It's just, well, at first I thought it was because you let on that you'd set me up, but actually what really upset me was you slagging off Claudia, more than anything. She seemed quite sweet really, and lonely . . .'

I tail off for a minute, but when Mark doesn't say anything, I continue. 'I guess it made me see how shallow it all is compared to, well, I hate to say this, but compared to a proper relationship. You don't care about Claudia. And why would you? You don't know her. And you don't know me.'

Mark shrugs. 'Isn't that the point?'

'Not any more.'

Back in the street, I'm on a high. I start to pound the pavement again, heading back through town and up the hill to the station. But all my resolution starts to fade away as I realise that, despite my wonderful trophy – the precious piece of paper in my hand – I'm still such a long way from getting Rex back. For example, Rex currently isn't talking to me, isn't picking up when I call. How do I let him know about my, newly proven, innocence?

In the town centre, I flop down on a vacant bench.

At this time on a Monday morning in January vacant benches aren't that hard to come by on the High Street. Just out of curiosity I call Rex, dialling his number from memory rather than using my address book, and listen to his voicemail for a few seconds before hanging up without leaving a message. I picture his phone, sat on his desk. (His phone is an ultraswanky, paper-thin, flippy thing that does emails and the web and probably house work too.) I imagine him looking at the little square screen as it sparks into life, heartlessly betraying the fact that I am the caller so he can dump me straight into voicemail. I imagine the silent missed call message I have just generated, which he also ignores.

And somewhere in the middle of all this mindless musing I look up, and there, right in front of me – sandwiched between a huge Marks and Spencer's and an almost as huge Starbucks, like something from a bygone age – is a little newsagent. It's so tiny it almost appears to be being crushed by the sheer corporate weight of the shops on either side. And in the window of this newsagent is the answer to my prayers. My salvation is a tatty sheet of paper, which proclaims in blocky caps, 'YOU CAN FAX FROM HERE'.

A little later I sit upstairs in the M and S café, finally having a breakfast that I can chew. Every so often I have to blow the croissant shards off my mobile, which sits expectantly on the table next to me.

I'm about a third of the way through my pastry when my phone rings. I snatch it up and punch the little green telephone key without even looking at the blue-light screen. I'm so sure it is Rex that I almost fall off my chair when my excited greeting is met with a solemn, almost stern, 'Sophie?'

Oh, please God, not now! Work. The job I had almost

forgotten about. It's past ten on a Monday morning and I'm sitting here like a lady of leisure, in the middle of town, gazing out over my breakfast towards rails and rails of universal underwear, and I hadn't even thought to call in sick.

'Hi,' I say. I can't decide whether it's too late to feign a bit of an ill-sounding creaky voice or not, so I opt for a sort of half way house, which means I just sound a bit like I need a good cough.

'Um, Sophie,' Dave-Steve-Ed continues, 'we were just wondering if you were OK.'

'I, I'm fine. I just need to take this morning off. Sorry. I know I should have called.'

'That's OK . . .' he begins

But I jump back in before he can get any further, because I suddenly have a stroke of absolute blinding genius. 'I've got a meeting with my accountant.'

And even though I can't quite believe that Dave-Steve-Ed (along with the entire upper floor of Marks and Spencer's) doesn't scream with laughter at me for claiming to have an accountant, this is met with a simple, 'Fine.' It's almost like being an honorary adult for the day.

I wonder if Rex counts as my accountant. He once showed me how to balance a chequebook properly.

My croissant is just lonely crumbs, when my phone finally jangles again. I jump so violently I send it flying off the table. As I chase it under coffee-laden tables and amongst the coffee-coloured legs of the café's middle-aged patrons, I realise that if this call is from anyone but Rex I will have to hunt them down and kill them.

Luckily I reach the phone just before it clicks over to voicemail. And even more luckily I don't find myself having to turn all Charles Bronson.

'Hello, Rex,' I say breathlessly and I wait for my connection to be finally re-established.

'Hi, Sophie,' he says, sounding rather resigned and soft – not like him at all. It seems no one is themselves today.

'So?'

'Yeah. Um, we need to talk. Shall I come over tonight?'

'No, Rex, I need you now. You have to get on the train and come back here right now, because . . .'

'Sophie . . .'

And then we're falling in on top of each other. Each trying to interrupt the other, to hold the conversation. But I start to talk fast, leaving him nothing to grab hold of. 'No, look, Rex, you've made a mistake. I didn't do it. I didn't do it! Even though what you did to try and make me do it was practically entrapment. You've made a big mistake and you need to come back here right now and be nice to me.'

'Yeah, OK, Sophie. I get that, but I have to work. And don't you have to work?'

'I might not have any work if you don't get back here quick. Please, Rex, pull a sickie, Pete'll cover for you. I need you. I need you right now.'

25

The dreary grey morning's nearly gone now, and it's actually kind of sunny, Brighton-brightness cutting through the freezing cold. As I climb the last hill, in the sun-sparkle, the railway station looks really ghetto-fabulous. They renovated it a couple of years ago, and now its glorious (and slightly pigeon-shit splattered) vaulted roof arcs over what is really – in this city of Carmaggedon – the only decent entrance to Brighton.

And this is where I loiter, waiting for Rex, amongst tardy commuters, early-bird students and maybe even other wrongly accused girlfriends. I'm waiting for my man.

I've flicked through every magazine in the tiny newsagent-cum-shed that sits on the concourse, sampled the pastries and the coffee from both the snack outlets – and I don't even really like coffee – and spent far too much time reading the backs of the sandwich packets in the Marks and Spencer's Food Shop (not to be confused with the full-fat Marks and Spencer's I was wasting time in earlier), and I'm doing mental gymnastics in my head, trying to work out how long it will take Rex to get from his office to Victoria, what the average waiting time for a train is likely to be at this time of day, and guessing whether or not he'd get one of the high speed ones. I try and try to work out how much time I'm going to have to kill and end up concluding that it could be anything from one to about five hours, depending on various factors.

I'm just thinking, for about the fifty millionth time, that we really should have organised something better than this for our reconciliation meeting, like why didn't I tell Rex to come to my flat and so I could have spent the last 90 minutes watching daytime telly, when I finally see him. Or at least I see his hair.

Another train has just pulled in. I haven't managed, during my long exile on the concourse, to figure out the arrivals board, so every train that arrives could possibly be his. Each time I see a new engine hulk into the terminus, or become aware of a fresh swarm of people negotiating their way through the bottle neck of the automated ticket gates, I go totally Pavlovian and stare hopefully into the mass.

And this time I get lucky (finally). I see an unmistakable crop of carroty goodness riding above the expressionless heads of the other passengers. Rex isn't the kind of guy it is possible to miss in a crowd situation; his height plus his brightness make him as easy to spot in a swarm of commuters as Ronald McDonald.

As he gets nearer I can see that he looks sort of businesslike, all suity-booty-commutey. And, although he kind of looks like that first thing in the morning, or last thing at night, this is slightly different. Not so sleepy, not so crumpled. He actually does look like he means business, with a hard glint in his eye and a smartness to his stride. I've never seen precisely this before. It's sort of hot – and also cool. God, I've missed him so much. It's been a bloody long nearly-a-week.

In the last few seconds before contact, I realise it would be so nice to go for subtle. To be the kind of person who could meet Rex at the gates, hug him coolly, maybe peck him on the cheek and then slowly and demurely walk hand in hand out of the station and board a number seven bus, back to Kemptown, and my place, and my bed.

I am so not that kind of person though, which is why, in a few snappy seconds, I'm clinging to Rex with all the charm of a piece of discarded chewing gum, and smearing snotty tears down his collar.

We don't talk straight away. I don't think either of us wants to be the one to start. We buy more coffee – I am now in a position to recommend the best in the vicinity – and settle down at a cold metal table in the draughty cathedral-like vastness of Brighton station.

Rex looks at me, smirks very slightly, and pulls a piece of paper from his pocket. It's the exact twin of the one I have in my pocket, except his has a smudgy black line down one side of the paper – obliterating some of the words.

'Your fax machine needs a clean,' I say, pointing out the blemish. And I know about these things, being the person in my office who deals with dirty fax machines. Not that anyone really uses our fax machine these days.

'It's not my fax machine, Sophie,' Rex says, slowly, with heavy emphasis on the word 'my' and a tone to his voice that could be annoyingly playful of playfully annoyed, 'it's the department's fax machine. And you know that don't you?'

'I guess. I didn't really think about it,' I reply, a bit confused by the provision-of-fax-machines turn this conversation is now taking. Not what I was expecting.

'So you couldn't have called me to say you were faxing me something?'

'You wouldn't have picked up.'

'Or texted me, or called Pete, or something.' Rex's

voice is getting ever so slightly louder. One or two people look at us. I'm trying not to laugh, and I think Rex is too. He stretches his eyes. 'Do you know how many people saw this before it made it onto my desk?'

'Er, five?' I say, smirking.

'Well, yes, probably about five,' he says, through spluttery chuckles. 'Five so far, though. Who knows whether photocopies have been made. It's probably being scanned and emailed far and wide by no –' And he stops because he's laughing too much. And I am too.

After we've stopped laughing, and calmed down a bit, and drunk a bit of our coffee (maybe I am starting to learn to like coffee), Rex says, 'Look, Sophie, I know we could go over this and over this, and I am sure you think I did lots of things I shouldn't have . . .'

'No, just the one thing really,' I interrupt.

'Well, yes, and you did lots of wrong things too. But not really, really wrong, like I thought. So could we maybe just forget it? You know, in a kind of faults on both sides sort of a way?'

'Well, yeah, I suppose,' I say slowly, feeling like this is quite a good deal; feeling, in some ways, rather like I am getting off lightly. 'There are still a few things I don't understand though.'

'What things?'

'Well I know about Mark Valentine, now, Kate told me, and I think that was a bit of a low down thing to do, but I take your point about faults on both sides . . .'

'Yeah,' Rex interrupts, 'I know I shouldn't really have done that. I know it was stupid, but it seemed like such a good idea at the time.'

'But what was the idea? I don't think even Kate was clear about that.'

'Um, the idea? Well I kind of thought I'd book Mark, and he'd come with Kate – as Kate's date – and at some point in the evening he'd let it slip to you what he was and then I'd see what you'd do.'

'So that was your idea, when he asked me in the ladies'.'

'Um, no, not exactly.' Rex looks a bit bashful. 'Well it was, but after you started talking about it at the table and saying it was all just a fantasy, well, I sort of meant to tell him to forget it. But then I ended up following you to the loo instead and then, well, I got distracted. And, actually, when I heard him trying it on with Kate I even thought he must have figured that out himself, but then, after Kate told me she'd seen the two of you, well, then I knew different. And, oh God, Sophie, as clever plans go it was a bit of a bloody mess really. Never mix cunning and drink. Cunning and drink and sex. Bad combination.'

And my mouth is open now, because the truth is dawning on me and I can't quite believe that this whole stupid mess is mostly due to Rex getting distracted by our toilet cubicle shenanigans and if he had just managed to get his act together Mark would never have propositioned me at all.

'Anyway,' Rex continues, 'so after that I rang Mark from work the next day and he said you'd said no. Or as good as.'

'Right.'

'But I didn't reckon on ...'

'You didn't reckon on him giving me his card and me phoning him a few days later and changing my mind a bit.'

'Yeah. I don't really think he should have done that – given you his card.'

'No, he shouldn't,' I agree, 'but I think he'd got the idea that you weren't really a very nice boyfriend.'

Rex looks a bit game-up when I say this. 'I'm sorry.

Like I say, stupid idea, shouldn't have done it. But it was when we were planning that afternoon at The Palace Hotel, you seemed, you just seemed so into it. I started to wonder if you'd really prefer it if it were real and not me.'

'Well, at least that's one thing that has worked out reasonably OK from your plan, because I used to ask myself the same question, but now I think I know the answer.'

'Really?'

'Yeah, I think so. I mean, you're not perfect – but I think I finally learned that perfection, that living on fantasy island, well, it isn't all it's cracked up to be. And some things are best kept as fantasy, maybe. It's like Pete says, you need to have something to fantasise about.'

Rex smiles then. 'So, it sounds like my stupid idea was actually rather clever.'

'I wouldn't go that far,' I say, my mouth half full of coffee. 'But what about all that other stuff? The things after Mark Valentine. Was that part of the test too? The escorts in the magazines and the strippers? I'm kind of confused about that, because at first, when I spoke to Kate, I thought it was just the Mark thing. But then later I thought maybe, well, all the other stuff . . .'

Rex sighs as I tail off, because I'm losing my thread and not really sure what I want to say. 'I'm sorry, Sophie,' he begins, 'it's all a bit confused really, but the Mark Valentine thing, that was a bit stupid, but I just had to know how serious you really were about me. The other stuff, the stuff after your birthday was nothing to do with that. In fact, I was just happy because, well, it seemed like you hadn't been interested in Mark at all. I was, kind of trying to reward you. But then it all went a bit wrong when you didn't like the magazines, or the strippers and then, just after that, I saw Mark leaving your place.' Rex pauses to draw breath, the memory is obviously still tender and swollen, before he goes on. 'So, well I thought I'd got you all wrong, and then it seemed like I had got you right after all, but now, well, I guess I was wrong after all, I think.'

'Maybe, maybe you were somewhere in the middle,' I say quietly and then quickly add, 'but more wrong than right.' And then I have to check myself because this conversation is getting rather confusing. 'You being wrong is me not sleeping with Mark, right?'

'I think so.'

And we both kind of laugh again, not as much as before – it's almost a melancholic sort of laughter – but it's enough to feel that stuff is OK.

'Well then,' says Rex, once the air feels clear, 'what do you want to do with our bonus day off?'

'Oh.' And I suddenly the memory of work comes flooding back to me with a wave of nausea. 'Oh, God, Rex, I haven't got the day off. I have to go into work. Remember that little, um, problem I told you about?'

Rex looks thoughtfully at me. 'Maybe you better remind me about what's going on. I know you did tell me something, but I've had a lot on my mind since then.'

So I do just that. I re-acquaint Rex with my Number Two most pressing life problem, which has now, since this morning's resolutions, suddenly been promoted to my Number One most pressing life problem.

After a very truncated version – I'm getting a bit sick of explaining stuff – Rex agrees firmly with Kate. I should go freelance, grab the cash and leave Dave-Steve-Ed with nothing but an empty desk and a Sophie-shaped hole in their lives.

But I'm not so sure. 'I can't, what about paying the rent? I'd need a good few months' living expenses in reserve to do anything like that. I mean the redundancy package they're offering me is OK, but it's nothing like enough for me to feel safe.'

'Well haven't you got savings?'

That question is so dumb that the only respose I can make is a sort of razzing noise.

Rex tuts at me. 'Well, haven't you?'

'Only about seven hundred quid.'

Rex frowns. 'Maybe you could get a loan.'

'Oh God, no, that would involve writing a business plan, going to a bank, all that. I can't face it.' And I bang my fist lightly on the wobbly metal table. 'Why can't things just stay as they are?'

And there's a long, long pause and then Rex says, 'Maybe you don't need a bank. Maybe you could get a loan from me.'

And then we just look at each other because, as commitment goes, this really does feel huge. And I don't say anything.

But I don't need to say anything. Neither of us do. Rex stands up and offers me his hand, as if to shake hands, so I stand up too and take it.

In that moment, I finally stop making excuses.

Rex stares at me, he can't believe I'm agreeing to do this any more than I can.

My breath dries in my mouth. We keep our hands linked together as Rex turns and starts to lead me away from our cooling coffees and out of the station. I don't know where we're going. I don't even think as Rex leads me out of the noise and bustle of the concourse, and into the (relatively) quiet streets.

26

We head downhill towards the sea, walk-running. First we pass estate agents and employment agencies. Then we start to move faster, the momentum of the hill catching us. We pass the clock tower and the buildings around us become a whizzy blur of generic shops and chain pubs – this is probably the one part of Brighton which could actually be anywhere in the country. No quirks and eccentricity here. No dark corners and whispers of deviance. Nothing out of the ordinary, apart from the seagull calls and the shuddering mass of the sea; the water itself seeming to race to meet us as we run now, hand in hand, towards it.

The concrete under our feet gives way to pebbles, which clatter and slide away from us as we skid to a halt, trying to bowl us on, headlong towards the endless horizon.

The tide's out right now and the sea itself is in the far distance. The beach goes on forever and the pier stands right beside us. It's rusty and seaweed-swirled, with legs stripped bare by the tide – the gap beneath it too inviting.

We dive underneath, scuttling like recently evicted hermit crabs – vulnerable and furtive. Our mission would be clear to any onlooker from our flushed rush and locked eye line.

It's horrible under the pier – seaweed slimy and barnacle briny – not exactly one for the tourist guides. But its quiet in the sun-streaked daylight and the twenty minutes it would take us to get to my flat simply wouldn't be possible with our mutually enflamed loins (at least that's the line I'm preparing in case we get our collars felt – not that either of us will have collars in a few short moments).

It really is too cold for this, too cold and ouchy with pebbles. My *From Pier to Eternity* moment really oughtn't have been scripted for a frozen January morning on a stony British beach with roaring traffic from the roundabout at the end of the Steine (something of a major hub) floating in the air. Rusty water is dripping from the huge structure above us, and I shiver as a big droplet splishes on my forehead. But all that discomfort vanishes when Rex touches me. He's like liquid warmth, like a ginormous microwavable heat-pack. His hands relax my muscles, unwinding me until the pebbles in my kidneys feel like foam rubber. And he sprinkles his sparky breath on my neck like a magic spell.

His right hand slides between my legs, fumbling with the clothes I'm still half wearing, teasing me through cotton layers as his fingers puzzle their way to the heart of me.

It seems so fast – too fast – but, as he strokes me with one finger, I'm already rising up off my stony bed, shooting towards the rusty underbelly of the pier, pushing into his embrace. His teeth are out now, the flat blades of his incisors pinching at the skin in the angles between my neck and my shoulders. I feel like a musical instrument. Like he's playing me with his mouth and fingers as I squirm and twist beneath him – glad of his body weight holding me down, when my own personal gravity field seems to be seriously malfunctioning.

I give a squealing breathless gasp when Rex takes

his fingers away, but he has his trousers and under-wear down now and he doesn't leave me hanging for too long. The last sharp stabs of the cold pebbles dissapear as wave after wave of impossible warmth flood through me and a connection is made. Made and re-made.

I reach around and find Rex's bare (and barely there) little Sugar Puff arse. It's working overtime, up and down, above the place where our hips are soldered together. And I return his earlier favour, fumbling my own way to his centre and sliding inside him with one tentative finger.

As I push inside him – gentle and firm – while he's inside me I feel like I'm completely some kind of magic circle. I'm inside and out. As I glide and slide, he gasps and pants harder suddenly, telling me I've hit the right spot inside. And I find myself doing likewise, because, my God, he so has too.

Under the damp pier, on top of the damp stones. In, out and around Rex, I feel myself coming up to meet him as he finds a rhythm, fast, slick and hot. The friction is getting more and more intense and Rex's face, his eyes closed and his lips parted, is turning me on more than any of the billion and one sensations washing over me like the waves only feet away on the shore.

And in the midst of all this everything, Rex's lips find my ear. He presses them close, warm and dry, where everything else – even the air – is cool and damp.

And Rex slows the movements of his hips to a tease and says, 'Why don't you move in with me?'

I roll my eyes, solely for the benefit of the crusta-ceans stuck to the underside of the pier. 'Rex, don't start.'

'OK, let me put that another way,' he breathes – half his words getting lost in our mutual so-close-it-hurts arousal – 'why don't you pay me to be your permanent, naked, live in sex-slave for life?'

I gulp. 'I don't know that I could afford that.'

'Oh, I reckon you could.'

'How much?'

'About seven hundred quid.'

Later, and still under the pier, I find I have one last question. 'Rex,' I say, snuggling deeper into him, out of the cold, 'have you started smoking again?'

'Um,' Rex says, which, when accompanied by the sheepish look he is now sporting, so means 'yes'.

'You little fucker,' I say, quite pleased to have grabbed a plum spot on the moral high ground. 'How long?'

'Ah, well,' Rex says, pulling a familiar square gold box out of his pocket, taking a cigarette from it and lighting it expertly with a green plastic lighter, 'that's the thing, Sophie, I never actually gave up.'

And it's this, more than any of the revelations I have heard recently that really shocks me. 'What?'

'I just stopped smoking when I was around you.' He shrugs. 'Um, sorry about that.'

'So you still smoke when I'm not there?'

'Yeah, in the pub, at the station, at work.'

'So Pete knows?'

'Oh yeah, Pete knows, Pete smokes most of my fags.'

Bastards!

27

Almost a year later

It's almost a year to the day since Rex and I nearly
imploded for good, and I know this for sure because
I'm celebrating another birthday. This year we aren't
so razzle-dazzle though. This year, it's kind of low-key,
but I like that. Thirty-two – it's a low-key sort of age.

And everything about the day so far has tied in with
the low-key theme. In the low-key, cash-strapped
month of January, we bowl down to the windy,
deserted and very low-key beach. The part of Brighton
beach that you hit when you walk out of our front door
and head due south for a few hundred yards happens
to be the nudist beach. But this isn't the weather for
nudity and even this little nook of (mostly) all year
round hedonism is silent and still.

We sit side by side under the grey-blue sky on the
grey-brown beach and stare out at the grey-green sea.

And, out of absolutely nowhere, Rex says, 'So, Mark
Valentine? Do you still think about him?'

I breathe in. The lie I could tell right now is sparkling
in the air in front of me, so near I could touch it, but I
also know my fingers would ghost right through it.

So I say, 'Yes, sometimes. Not so much lately. But,
yes.'

'In bed?'

'In bed with you or in bed on my own?' I stall.

'Both. Either.'

'Both.'

'Do you ever wish things had gone differently? That you had slept with him, paid him, all that?'

I turn in Rex's arms so I can look right into his eyes. They're glistening a bottomless green, more infinite than the distant horizon.

'No,' I say slowly, walking on a tightrope between true and false. 'I don't, because if I had you might not have taken me back ...'

Rex interrupts me with a sort of part cough, part scoff. I guess he means, of course he would. But it's easy to say that. Or, at least, it's easy to scoff/cough that.

I forge on, anticipating his question and answering it, 'But if you're asking whether I wish I had done it and I could have it as a freebie, no consequences, then the answer is yes. Yes, I do wish that. Because he was delicious. I can't help that. Actually that's your own fault. You chose him.'

'And would you now? Would you sleep with him if there were no consequences?'

Shit, but this conversation is heading onto dangerous territory. I open and close my mouth twice, and seriously consider citing the not talking about this kind of thing on my birthday clause, because, not least of all, we're having a curry tonight and I don't want Rex and me to split up now and have that spoil my enjoyment of a delicious and diet-busting Sag Paneer. But bottling out of the discussion would as good as answer the question, and I'm a terrible liar, so I turn away, look back out at the Deep Grey Yonder and say. 'Yes. I guess.'

Rex reaches out and pushes his long fingers into the well of my fist, twining and lining our hands together on the cold stones. 'Good,' he says, gently, 'come on home. It's time for your present.'

And while we walk up the hill, keeping up the pace to keep out the cold, Rex explains exactly what I'm getting this year. Thankfully, it's not another deep probe into my moral values. Well, not so much, anyway.

We only moved into our new flat a couple of months ago. It didn't take Rex long to convince me that a responsible double income couple like us really ought to have a mortgage, rather than continue to slum it in my breathtaking but stupidly laid out and bloody-cold-in-winter flat. Rex seems to be able to convince me of such things much more easily these days. I guess I've mellowed. Plus, we needed an extra bedroom, once my work picked up, so I could have a proper office.

And then, when I saw the estate agent's details for this place, well, it just sounded so lovely: a maisonette in a little cobbled mews, and I've just always wanted to live in a maisonette.

On all those house selling programmes they always go on about not having décor that is too OTT, because it will put buyers off. Well, the previous owner of our place must – through some miracle – have managed to never see any of those ubiquitous programmes. Because, inside, this flat was more than slightly outré. It was practically gold-plated. Obviously not literally – because that would be something of a unique selling point and a half – but in a 'Look what I can do with half a barrel of cheap gold paint', kind of a way. Everything was gold, from skirting boards to coving, everything except the walls themselves, which were various shades of magenta, scarlet and other selections from the day-glo rainbow. It was beautiful, in the worst possible way, and in the worst possible taste. And that was before we saw the mural.

The mural was in the bedroom, glorious on the chimney breast above the headboard. It wasn't visible from the bedroom doorway, so we both trooped in after the estate agent oblivious, expecting nothing more shocking than the now standard, bling-bling woodwork and fluorescent walls. But as we rounded the bed, we saw a strange expression cross the agent's face, squirmy yet resolute. And then we realised why. The mural.

It stretched up to the ceiling and was rather like a sub-standard version of Michaelangelo (something he might have done in his spare time though, really not something the Vatican would have commissioned). It was more than six feet of naked writhing male flesh, all in exquisite detail.

'Um, yes,' said the agent, awkwardly. 'Of course this could very easily be painted over. Interesting that's actually the vendor himself, right there.' And he leaned forward and pointed to a reasonably fit-looking middle-aged bloke, sitting square in the middle of the debauchery, with his legs splayed and a delicate looking blonde head nestled in his crotch.

I looked at Rex. Rex looked at me. I simply couldn't resist. I gave the mural one more long look and said, 'I think we'd like to make an offer.'

We did paint over the mural though. Part of me didn't want to, and I even went so far as claiming we should keep it because it was part of the history of the house. But Rex pointed out that if I wanted the mural room for my office – and I did, as it was the bigger of the two bedrooms – then it was going to have to double as a guest room too. And then I had to agree with him that neither of our parents were the types who would enjoy sleeping under a huge piece of porn on plasterwork. So we slapped paint over it, along with quite a lot of the rest of the house's unique décor.

But it was while I was obliterating the last of the golden showers and double fisting with a tin of pale blue emulsion, I noticed what I would swear was Mark Valentine, tucked away in the top right corner, naked and grinning right at me.

I never told Rex about it.

Back from the freezing beach we wrestle free from our bundles of winter clothing and set ourselves up with over-sized mugs of hot chocolate. I'm trying hard to keep from bouncing up and down.

'When do I get this present then?'

'Whenever you like.'

'Um, now?'

How can I wait?

I think from what he's told me, Rex got in touch with Mark first. He still had all the details from when he tracked him down for Kate. He'd explained his plan of getting something Mark Valentine-shaped for my birthday and it was the ever perceptive, 'I'm-so-good-at-reading-people' Mark, who knew exactly what I'd like.

'Now it is then, birthday girl,' Rex says, the elegant quietness of his voice sounding very strange compared with the bounce, bounce, bounce of my excitement inside. And then, while I sit and watch him, he picks up the phone and makes a couple of quick calls.

I'm still internally bouncing when we leave the flat. Rex has a hire van parked in the cobbled square mews outside our front door. It's a neat little van, cute and boxy. I know I'm going to need Rex to help me in the back, so we need to wait for the driver before we can get going, which is torture!

So I'm expecting someone, which is why I'm not surprised when a tallish man in a big anorak appears round the corner, as I sort myself out in the back of the van.

But I am rather surprised to find that the man is Pete.

'It's alright, babe, take that horrified look off your face, I'm not staying,' he says as makes for the driver's door, 'because, you know, it would be too weird.'

'Yeah,' I agree, 'it would be too weird.' Because even in this world of weird there is still a too-weird.

And then Rex climbs up into the back of the van and closes the door. He gives me a little isn't-this-exciting? dig in the ribs, and I have to dig him back, because it is.

When the van starts to move it takes me by surprise and I stumble a little into Rex. As he holds me to stop me from tumbling, sparks seem to rush through me, shooting from the places where his hands are on my body. I cannot believe we are doing this!

I start to kiss Rex, both of us swaying back and forth, stumbling and catching ourselves as Pete's driving seems to make every corner feel like a hairpin bend. We end up rattling around in the clanging back of the van, clinging to each other as we roll over and over, doing things that almost certainly aren't in the Highway Code. And I almost forget what I'm here for, forget why I'm in the back of a van with Rex, hurtling around Brighton.

I'm sliding both my hands down the back of Rex's brown cords, as he bites the top of one of my ears and grazes his fingernails over the back of my neck, which is more than enough to make me take leave of my senses. But then the van rattles to a halt, and Rex pulls himself away from me and sits up. Bang. Back to reality. We're on.

Rex flings the door open and leaps out, with me right on his heels. We're on a quiet residential street, there's no one around. No one, that is, apart from our quarry.

Rex grabs hold of Mark, and I do the same only a split second later. Together we pull him into the van. Neither Rex nor I are very strong, but somehow we seems to be winning the fight against a struggling kicking Mark. Before anyone really has time to think, before I really have time to make sure I'm concentrating and committing this to memory, we're all in the back. The door is slammed and Pete's making the engine roar as we tear back across Brighton.

I look down at Mark. He's lying on the floor of the van, still for a moment, his face a pasty white with fear – although just as pretty as it was a year ago – and then I look at Rex, who's holding a roll of thick silver tape in his hand.

I do the taping. I wanted tape. Even though I have various cuffs and ropes from the games I like to play with Rex, I wanted tape for this, because it feels right. And, of course, the beauty of Mark is there's no need to worry about the tape hurting him or being too uncomfortable, because I know that Rex told him on the phone it was going to be tape and he said, 'sure,' and that was that.

I plan to wrap tape around Mark's kicking legs while Rex takes charge of the upper body. I almost don't concentrate on what I'm doing, because the sight of Rex, sweating as he uses his whole body to pin Mark's struggling torso to the floor of the van is intoxicating.

But I do manage to tear myself away from the sight

long enough to indulge in the equally diverting job of tying up Mark Valentine.

First, I wrap long lengths of tape around Mark's ankles and knees, cinching the dark blue denim and reducing his manic struggles to jerky spasms.

Next, and with Rex's help, I tug off Mark's denim jacket, leaving his torso in just a tight white T-shirt, and apply more tape around his chest and upper arms, fixing his arms in place. He tries to say something, shout for help maybe, but Rex jams a hand over his mouth just in time, and I finish taping his wrists together behind his back and then stick a short length of tape over his mouth, shutting him up.

Job done, I spend the last few minutes of the journey back to our flat just looking at Mark. Rex is still sweating and panting and so am I, as he crawls across the floor of the van to me and puts his arms around my waist. Mark is thrashing around on the floor, trying hopelessly to loosen the tape and get free. His eyes are flashing, full of evil navy blues as he looks at me. I'm so excited, almost burning with it. I so want to move things on to the next level. But I know I need to wait until we get him into the flat.

So I just take one little piece of pleasure from him – my victim – I pull my long grey skirt up past my knees so I can straddle him and then sit gently down on his squirming chest – which is squirming a lot less once I am pinning it in place. Then I lean down stop-frame-slowly and press my lips onto the tape sticking Mark's mouth shut. I can feel the heat behind it as the ghosts of his lips move under the seal. I kiss him slowly, my body frozen on top of him as he stills beneath me. We're like statues, but for our eager mouths which are working overtime to compensate for the barrier of tape between them.

I'm starting to drown in it, and then the van takes a right and then starts to judder as it slides into our parking space in the cobbled courtyard. I scramble to my feet and then, when all is still, Rex flings the doors open again. The courtyard is empty. Perfect.

We hastily send Pete on his way and then cut the tape from Mark's legs and rush-bundle him into our place and up the stairs into our bedroom, which is specially dressed for the occasion.

It's nothing spectacular really. Certainly not the warehouse/dungeon of my fantasies. But Rex has moved all the furniture out, blacked out the window with a thick blanket, oh, and set up a borrowed video camera in the corner of the room – which is a stroke of genius, because I'm thirty-two now, my memory just isn't what it used to be.

I spend a little time pacing, wondering what I want. I look at Mark, lying still now on the not-very-dungeon-like, retro-deep, shag pile. And I look at Rex leaning up against the closed door. He must have taken away the lampshade when he styled the room, because the centre light is now just a bare bulb, swinging slightly from all the hubbub, making strange shadows dance and loom on the walls.

Then Rex says, slowly, 'What do you want, Sophie?'

And I smile, because I know, and neither of the boys has any idea. 'Stay where you are,' I tell Rex, firmly. And then I walk over to Mark, bend at the waist, and pull the tape nastily from his mouth. He flinches and turns his head, cringing away from me like I might hit him. It's very good.

'Get up,' I say to Mark, pulling him up to his knees and then dragging him by the hair so he has to shuffle and semi-crawl after me. Just before we get to where Rex is standing I stop and look up at my boyfriend's bemused but excited face. 'Take your trousers down,' I snap at Rex, and he does it with a quick smile.

My next order doesn't need articulating. It's implicit in the way I position Mark, kneeling in front of Rex's naked cock. Rex is hard and jutting, the pretty pink tip of his cock only a breath away from the pretty pink tip of Mark's tongue. I find myself licking my own lips as Mark leans forward and takes Rex into his mouth.

Rex nearly takes off. His head tips back and his hips tip forward. He gasps and scrabbles at the wall behind him with both hands. I can see his rosy nipples hardening through the thin white cotton of his shirt. I can see his two top teeth biting deep grooves in his bottom lip. I can't see his cock, or the place where Mark's mouth is opening wider and wider to take it all the way down his well practised throat, but I don't need to. I can tell just from the way Rex's eyelids are fluttering that this is the best blow job of his life. I might even be a little jealous if I wasn't too busy sliding down the wall opposite them, with my hand buried between my legs, and finding myself juddering and coming into my hand far sooner than I wanted.

And it isn't long after that that I spot the little twitches and tells that mean Rex is about to come too. I watch and enjoy for a few seconds, but as soon as I see his cheeks flush a certain shade of red in a certain place, I know it's time to move.

Just as Rex starts to come, I'm standing behind Mark. I press close behind him, taking his head away from Rex's cock just as he thrusts his last thrust. I turn Mark's face to mine and press my lips against his, kissing him hard, licking and biting and tasting Rex. Tasting Rex on Mark Valentine's mouth.

Next, I pull Mark – still with his arms bound behind him – down onto me, nestling into the luxurious carpet. When I've finished kissing Mark on the lips, I move his head around, directing it to each place I want him to kiss me next, from neck to collar bone to hip to thigh. Rex watches me as I manipulate Mark over my body. He's leaning against the wall, super-spent and still panting.

Mark's licking my stomach. Little kitten flicks, trailing down and down. Heading south. Rex's eyes are only open the tiniest sliver, but he keeps them locked on mine. Watching, watching as Mark's tongue finds its way down, between my legs, and on, dancing around a little, teasing, but not too much, until finally, finally he's there. Right where I want him to be. And that first soft slow lick brings me springing into vivid, thrusting, keening life. I'm not really coherent enough to be able to tell what he's doing to me, and the sensations are all mixed up and tumbling over each other, but I'm sure at one point I felt almost imperceptibly soft teeth on me somewhere, and at another a tongue hard enough to find its way right inside me.

I turn my head to look at Rex, somehow knowing just where he is, even though I don't know which way is up. As our eyes lock together, Rex mouths, 'I love you,' and then, even though I have been teetering on the edge for ages, I really know I'm only a breath away.

It's almost too much, too quick, because even though in some ways it feels like Mark's mouth has only been where it should be for scant seconds, I'm bucking up and coming, seeing nothing except the inverted image of a bare swinging light bulb on my squeezed-shut eyelids.

I open my eyes while I can still feel aftershocks rippling through me. Mark is sat back on his heels between my legs. I note, a little distractedly, that he's still in his T-shirt and jeans, which is strange because I sort of thought I'd want him more naked more quickly. But then I didn't exactly plan this part out, I kind of wanted it to go with the flow.

And I'm going with the flow when I reach out to Rex, who is right where I left him, leaning against the wall beside the door with his trousers round his ankles and his neat white shirt tenting over his cock – he's either still erect or he regained his erection while he was watching me and Mark.

Rex drops into my arms, squirming into my embrace and shucking off his trousers in one graceless but practical move. He kisses me and I can feel his new improved erection hot against my thigh. I reach down.

In some ways it's easy because I'm so wet and slidey, but in other ways it's hard because I'm still so sensitive post-orgasm, but I manage to slide him inside me. Once he's there and moving, my prickly sensitivity fades fast. It's easier this time. Different. Less frantic. We're both holding on now. Taking it a little slower. Once we reach a kind of plateau where we're both panting and staring at each other glassy-eyed, we freeze-frame where we are for what seems like forever. I can feel rushy sparks zinging up and down my legs as Rex keeps moving, but ever so gently.

I feel something next to me and it's Mark. He's lying next to me on the carpet, pressing his lips close to my ear.

'Wouldn't it be hot, though,' he whispers, 'to imagine you're paying both of us. Not just me. You know you're paying to use me like this, tie me up and do whatever you please. But wouldn't it be a sexy idea to hire two of us. Have this threesome with added boy on boy performance with two whores – double the fun. I've done it before, and I'd really love to do it for you.'

And I close my eyes. Rex feels delicious, his warm familiar body sliding back and forth over mine with each delicate, expertly judged thrust. And then there's Mark. Not touching me, still bound in fact, nothing more than a dirty, evil, downright wrong voice in my ear, painting perverted pictures in my mind. It's like Rex is my beautiful cherub, a perfect red-headed angel, fucking me into blissful oblivion, while Mark is just a dirty devil, a filthy fucking whore. I feel like one of those cartoon characters that have a good-self and an evil-self on each of their shoulders.

Then Rex finds a slight change of angle and a perfect pace and at the exact same time Mark says, 'I'd love to do that for you. To whore for you again.' And I'm there, coming right between both of them, I couldn't even say which of them pushed me over the edge, but stars are exploding in my head and I'm screaming out so loud that I'm really glad I don't live above Irene any more.

28

We take the shower in shifts. Even though the suggestion is made that we share it in any one of a number of possible combinations, I want the break. I call ladies and birthday girls first and take the first go and the best of the hot water.

After I've towel-dried my hair in the bedroom – which makes me look a bit mad, but I'm not really in the mood to care about that right now – I go into the kitchen and make a cup of tea.

Before the kettle's even boiled, Mark, who bagsied second shower, appears in the doorway. His hair is wet and his T-shirt is slightly stuck to his damp chest.

'You OK?' he says.

'Yeah. You want tea?'

'No, not right now.' Mark's voice is too serious. I thought he would be all business-as-usual after the action, but he seems rather intense.

'You know,' he says softly, as he crosses the kitchen and finds a space to lean up against the work surface, 'I thought you'd be far harder on me than that.'

'Did you?'

'Well, yes. I mean that night at Wanda's you practically saw me roasted alive, then whipped, then fucked and all for my own personal pleasure. I thought you'd want something more extreme than a bit of roughing up and some forced oral sex.'

I shrug. 'Disappointed?'

Mark's face replies for him.

'Oh my God! You are! You're disappointed I wasn't more of a mad sadist.'

Mark looks a bit bashful. 'Yeah, OK, I guess I got you a bit wrong. But I remember talking to you one night and I thought that the reason you wanted to pay for it was because you wanted to do something really twisted. But you didn't. Well, not all that twisted.'

'I guess not. I mean, I didn't plan or anything, but in the end all I really wanted was a little bit of power play. Nothing more than what I usually do with Rex. But then, I guess you were wrong with your theory, because for me it really is all about this.' And I pat a squat little pile of twenty pound notes that is sitting on a shelf up about the kettle.

Mark's face cracks into an almost-but-not-quite laugh. And then he shakes his head to himself. 'OK, fine, but you never even got my clothes off.'

'True. That was something of an oversight.'

'Which means you never got my birthday present.'

'Your present?' I frown. 'You got me a present?'

'Course I did,' Marks says, with a little pout, 'be rude not to.'

And I can't not ask. 'What did you get me?'

Mark drops his gaze to the floor. 'I thought you'd like if when you stripped me I was already ... already marked. So I saw Wanda last night ...' And he stops talking and just flips up the bottom edge of his T-shirt, turning a little so I get an oblique view of his back. The mouth-watering little triangle he reveals is zigzagged with vivid red marks. My mouth goes dry.

I can't speak.

'You like them?' Mark asks, dropping his T-shirt and looking at me again. It's a pretty stupid question and I'm sure he knows it.

'Show me the rest,' I hear myself say, my voice sounding hard and distant.

'Uh-uh,' Mark says with a shake of the head, 'too late.'

'Really,' I say, catching the embryonic smirk forming on the edges of his lips and catching my own mouth starting to twitch with one in return. 'Well how much then? How much for you to strip for me right now?'

Mark makes a faux 'calculation' face. 'For you, here, now, say, another twenty.'

I take the stack of notes down from the shelf and place them on the kitchen counter, about halfway between Mark and myself. Then I take my purse, which lives on the same ever useful shelf, pull out two ten pound notes and add them to the top of the pile. When I put the extra money there sparks fizz through me and I have to lick my bottom lip.

Mark doesn't say anything else. He just looks at me, then glances at the money, then back at me. Then he takes his jeans off.

His long legs are smooth, elegantly shaped and brown. He pulls his T-shirt over his head next, but I don't get to see the marks on his back. Not until he turns around.

When he does, I feel myself grab hold of the lip of the counter behind me. His back is ravaged. Striped all over with redness, each one raised a little, softly swollen. It takes my breath away to think that he got them for me.

And then I see something that is possibly even better. Just at the edge of his white underpants, where his long thighs begin, I can see a couple of red stripes peeping out. A promise of some added value yet to come.

When he pulls down his underpants, only moments later, I am rewarded with yet more delicious red stripes marking out his arse like so much old-fashioned candy. I lick my lips again. And then Mark turns back to face me. And I love the fact that he's erect when he does so.

I stare a minute. Too long.

'How much to kiss you?' I say, my low voice betraying the fact that I am sure this is wrong. Wrong, wrong, wrong.

'How much have you got in your purse?'

'Tenner.'

Mark shrugs. 'For you, I'll do it for a tenner.' My mind is racing. Mark's voice is grating, gravely with arousal.

I nod, my hand going dumbly for the money.

And that's when I look at the doorway. And I see Rex standing there. And Rex looks at me, smiles and shakes his head, softly. And then he nods, 'OK.'

Mark crosses the kitchen and kisses me. I can feel his nakedness burning me through my clothes. Sparkly sensations shoot from my lips right through my body like tiny orgasms.

And before it's done, I half open one eye and look at the pile of money on the counter and the shelf above it. The shelf which is stacked with two family-sized bars of chocolate and two cartons of Marlboro Lights – testament to the fact that nobody who lives here has any willpower.

And then I look at Rex, still watching in the doorway, clothed in just a small towel round his waist. And I think to myself, this is so much better than my last birthday.

Visit the Black Lace website at
www.blacklace-books.co.uk

LOOK OUT FOR THE ALL-NEW BLACK LACE BOOKS – AVAILABLE NOW!

All books priced £7.99 in the UK. Please note publication dates apply to the UK only. For other territories, please contact your retailer.

CRUEL ENCHANTMENT
Janine Ashbless
ISBN 0 352 33483 5

Winged demonesses, otherworldly lovers and a dragon with an enormous sexual appetite collide with spoilt princesses, spell-weavers and wicked ancestors in Janine Ashbless's fantastic tales of lust and magic. *Cruel Enchantment* is a stunning collection of unique and breathtakingly beautiful erotic fairy tales. Seductive, dazzling and strange, with each story a journey into the marvellous realms of a fertile imagination.

Coming in January

BOUND IN BLUE
Monica Belle
ISBN 0 352 34012 6

When university lecturer Hazel Jones takes the most popular of her female students as a lodger, she expects a procession of attractive men to follow. What she doesn't expect is Tiggy's diary to be left out every day. Sharing her house with this shameless young woman encourages Hazel to realise what's missing in her own, rather dull, academic life. Knowing what Tiggy gets up to, she is unable to resist reading it. It's not quite what she expects, but the revelations in the diary quickly lead her down a path she never expected to take.

THE STRANGER
Portia Da Costa
ISBN 0 352 33211 5

When a mysterious young man stumbles into the life of the recently widowed Claudia, he reignites her sleeping sexuality. But is the handsome and angelic Paul really a combination of innocent and voluptuary, amnesiac and genius? Claudia's friends become involved in trying to decide whether or not he is to be trusted. As an erotic obsession flowers between Paul and Claudia, and all taboos are obliterated, his true identity no longer seems to matter.

Coming in February

BARBARIAN PRIZE
Deanna Ashford
ISBN 0 352 34017 7

After a failed uprising in Brittania, Sirona, a princess of the Iceni, and her lover, Taranis, are taken to Pompeii. Taranis is sold as a slave to a rich Roman lady and Sirona is taken to the home of a lecherous senator, but he is only charged with her care until his stepson, General Lucius Flavius, returns home. Flavius takes her to his villa outside the city where she succumbs to his charms. Sirona must escape from the clutches of the followers of the erotic cult of the Dionysis, while Taranis must fight for his life as a gladiator in the arena. Meanwhile, beneath Mount Vesuvius, there are forces gathering that even the power of the Romans cannot control.

MAN HUNT
Cathleen Ross
ISBN 0 352 33583 1

Fearless and charismatic Angie Masters is on a man hunt. While training at a prestigious hotel training academy, the attractive and dominant director of the institute, James Steele, catches her eye. Steele has a predatory sexuality and a penchant for erotic punishment. By seducing a fellow student, Angie is able to torment Steele. But she has a rival – the luscious Italian Isabella who is prepared to do anything to please him. A battle of sexual wills ensues, featuring catfights, orgies and triumph for either Angie or Isabella.

Black Lace Booklist

Information is correct at time of printing. To avoid disappointment
check availability before ordering. Go to www.blacklace-books.co.uk.
All books are priced £6.99 unless another price is given.

BLACK LACE BOOKS WITH A CONTEMPORARY SETTING

BLACK LACE BOOKS WITH AN HISTORICAL SETTING

BLACK LACE ANTHOLOGIES

To find out the latest information about Black Lace titles, check out the
website: www.blacklace-books.co.uk or send for a booklist with
complete synopses by writing to:

> Black Lace Booklist, Virgin Books Ltd
> Thames Wharf Studios
> Rainville Road
> London W6 9HA

Please include an SAE of decent size. Please note only British stamps
are valid.

Our privacy policy
We will not disclose information you supply us to any other parties.
We will not disclose any information which identifies you personally to
any person without your express consent.

From time to time we may send out information about Black Lace
books and special offers. Please tick here if you do <u>not</u> wish to
receive Black Lace information.   ☐

Please send me the books I have ticked above.

Name ....

Address ....

....

....

....

Post Code ....

Send to: Virgin Books Cash Sales, Thames Wharf Studios, Rainville Road, London W6 9HA.

US customers: for prices and details of how to order books for delivery by mail, call 1-800-343-4499.

Please enclose a cheque or postal order, made payable to Virgin Books Ltd, to the value of the books you have ordered plus postage and packing costs as follows:

UK and BFPO – £1.00 for the first book, 50p for each subsequent book.

Overseas (including Republic of Ireland) – £2.00 for the first book, £1.00 for each subsequent book.

If you would prefer to pay by VISA, ACCESS/MASTERCARD, DINERS CLUB, AMEX or SWITCH, please write your card number and expiry date here:

....

Signature ....

Please allow up to 28 days for delivery.